THE CLEARING

Other Books by Tom Deady

Coleridge

Haven

Weekend Getaway

Eternal Darkness

Backwater

THE CLEARING

BRAM STOKER AWARD-WINNING AUTHOR
TOM DEADY

The Clearing

Cover Credit: Gabriel De Leon
gssdeleon.com

ISBN: 978-1-64548-071-6

VESUVIAN BOOKS

Published by Vesuvian Books
www.vesuvianbooks.com

Printed in the United States

10 9 8 7 6 5 4 3 2 1

For Shannon, Alyssa, and Spike the Crime Dog (aka Maggie)

CHAPTER ONE

"**S**cout! Come on out of there, Scout!" Hannah waited for the jingle of her dog's collar but was greeted with silence. She peered into the scrub pines that bordered the trail and into the deeper woods beyond. A breeze whispered through the trees, carrying the scents of pine and honeysuckle. Birds chattered in the distance and heat bugs buzzed overhead, but no jangle of dog tags. No Scout.

She swatted at the cloud of gnats that swarmed around her, pushed a few unruly strands of her long brown hair aside, and stepped off the trail into the brush.

Don't leave the path, Hannah, the forest goes practically to Canada.

Her father's warning echoed in her head, but she needed to find Scout. The woods around her had grown quiet.

Maybe he's gone, Hannah, just like your mom.

The thought made her stomach clench, and she ran. She crashed through the bushes and tangles, oblivious to the scrapes

1

and scratches, calling Scout's name.

A glint of sunlight on metal caught her eye and she darted to a break in the trees.

Scout was in a small clearing, rubbing his head and neck on a pile of leaves.

"Scout!" Hannah ran to him, shooting her hand to cover her mouth and nose as the smell assaulted her. The pile of leaves was actually the carcass of some long-dead animal, probably a squirrel. Its body had decomposed to an oily mess with matted gray fur, barely recognizable. Choking back rising bile, she grabbed Scout's collar, dry heaving at the slimy goo that seeped between her fingers.

She managed to drag him away, leading him back toward the trail as she willed her stomach to not eject its contents. *Are there maggots on my hand?*

"Scout, stay," she commanded. She tore leaves from a nearby maple tree and wiped the miry mess from her hands. Not satisfied, she plunged the offending hand into the moist earth by the trunk of an old pine and squeezed the dirt in her fist. *Better dirt than squirrel guts,* she thought, bringing a fresh round of gags.

"Scout, you know what this means, right? Bath time when we get home."

Scout cocked his head and Hannah smiled.

"You won't be giving me that look when you're all wet and soapy. And you'd better not shake all over the bathroom." She sighed and got to her feet, resigned to the chore ahead of her. "Let's go, boy," she called, and turned toward home.

Hannah walked slowly along the trail, keeping an eye on Scout. She anticipated a lecture from Dad when she got home—*I told*

you to keep him on the leash, Hannah—and was in no hurry to get there. She crested a rocky rise and sat on a large boulder. It was a favorite vantage point of hers, with just enough breaks in the trees to offer a beautiful view of the woods. *Autumn isn't that far off,* she thought, catching hints of yellow on some of the leaves in the distance. She pulled out her cell phone and glared at the two words at the top of the screen:

NO SIGNAL.

"Life in the sticks," she mumbled, and stood. She would have to wait until she got home to call Ashley and make plans for later. "Let's go, Scout."

She kicked small stones as she walked, enjoying the day but wishing it didn't feel so fall-like already.

Something crashed through the bushes to her left.

"Scout, get back here!" *Why didn't I put the leash on him?* She pushed through the scrub pines, intent on catching Scout before he found something else gross to roll around on. She heard his tags off to her right and spotted a flash of tan fur. Then he was gone.

She slowed her pace and followed.

"Scout, come on, boy!"

The shadows deepened as she moved farther into the trees. Above her, the branches joined, conspiring to keep the sunlight from reaching her. She stopped to listen, unnerved by the quiet. The cicadas and early crickets had gone silent. Her own harsh breathing and the occasional sibilant whisper of the breeze through the trees were the only sounds she heard.

"Scout?" she called, softer, not wanting anyone else to hear.

A distant jingle caused her to let out the breath she didn't know she was holding. She moved toward the sound, careful not to make a noise, cocking her head for another warning that Scout was near. She stopped again, listening. A different sound reached her, not Scout's collar but a rustling. No, that wasn't right—it was more frenzied somehow. Then the dog tags were all she heard, growing louder.

"Good boy, Scout," she called, a relieved smile on her face.

Scout darted out of the trees with something hanging from his mouth. Hannah shuddered, thinking it was some poor animal. When he bounded closer, she laughed. It was just an old, pink Converse high-top. "Good boy, Scout, you didn't kill anything today."

Scout dropped his prize at her feet and sat on his haunches, looking up at her.

"Sorry, boy, I didn't bring treats." She bent to pick up the tattered sneaker and leaped backward with a squeal. She swallowed hard, her throat gone dry, and leaned in closer to the sneaker. "Oh, God …"

Scout's ears dropped, and he whimpered. Hannah bit her lip and crouched next to the shoe. Using a nearby stick, she pushed away legions of squirming maggots. The color washed out of the day. The normal sounds of the forest became oddly threatening. Then the smell hit her, and she gagged, falling backward onto her butt. She rolled to the side and threw up, spewing her breakfast onto the mossy ground. Scout barked frantically. Hannah stared at the pool of puke, watching it run down the slope. A string of saliva connected it to her mouth, and she reached up to wipe it away. The slimy texture reminded her of the maggots, and she dry-heaved until her head ached. Closing her eyes didn't help; all she saw were wriggling white things. Scrambling to her hands and knees, careful to avoid her recycled breakfast, she tried to stand. The ground tilted and she closed her eyes again, ignoring the sickly pallid shapes that moved there. *Would she ever not see them?* Using a low-hanging branch for balance, she tested her legs to make sure they'd hold her before letting go.

"Where did you find this, Scout?" Hannah's voice came out gravelly, her throat sore from vomiting. She stared off into the shadows of the trees where Scout had come from, remembering the frantic noises she'd heard before he'd reappeared.

Digging.

She looked around as if someone might be watching, or even sneaking up on her. She shook off the thoughts and decided it was the old sneaker freaking her out.

Well, not the sneaker itself, but the partially decomposed foot sticking out of it.

CHAPTER TWO

Hannah yanked Scout away from the sneaker. The smell seemed to follow her. She imagined it hovering in a noxious cloud of death under her nose. The image of the foot—the putrid, rotten strips of flesh hanging from the too-white bone—wouldn't leave her. She wondered if it ever would. She tried hard not to think about the squirming maggots.

Hannah walked fast, nervous-fast, calling Scout back to her side whenever he began to wander. Her thoughts jumbled with the implications of the sneaker, and she wanted to get home and have Dad call the police. She would be able to find the spot to show them, and then the problem would be theirs. Most likely, the sneaker, and the foot, belonged to some runaway kid who had gotten lost in the woods and died. Over the years, the animals had gotten at the body, end of story.

What if the kid was kidnapped? Murdered?

Hannah walked faster.

The closer she got to the relative safety of her house, the

more intrigued she became with the severed appendage. What if it *did* belong to a kid that disappeared under suspicious circumstances? And what if she solved the mystery? Wouldn't that break up the monotony of living in the middle of nowhere? Hannah began jogging, eager to get home, but not to call the police. To call Ashley.

She ran up the back steps just as Dad was stepping out onto the porch. He wore his "working around the house" clothes—a ragged pair of jeans and an old Harley T-shirt. Hannah couldn't help but notice how the outfit hung on his frame. He had lost weight since Mom left. She looked up at him and saw for the first time that Mom's absence was taking its toll on his face as well.

Dad's once-handsome features looked haggard in the unforgiving sunlight. His face was thin and creased with worry wrinkles. His hair, once the same chestnut as her own, was unkempt and streaked with gray. His two-day growth of beard was coming in all gray. Hannah's concern for him momentarily overshadowed the rush to talk to Ashley.

"What are you working on, Pops?"

Dad smiled and shrugged. "Just fussing around in the shed. I was building some window boxes ..." His voice trailed off.

Hannah winced. Mom had always wanted window boxes, had nagged him about them for years. His distant expression, like he was hearing her ask, was too much for Hannah. She almost blurted out what she, or rather Scout had found, but kept silent about it.

"Dad, can Ashley come over for dinner? Maybe stay the night if her parents say it's okay?"

Her dad looked at her as if she'd spoken in Latin, then he shrugged again. "Sure, honey." He walked past her toward the shed.

Hannah bit her lip, blinking back tears. It was lonely enough without Mom, but if Dad didn't get over his grief, she didn't know what she would do. His pain became hers. *I'll enlist Ashley's help to bring Dad back as well as solving the sneaker mystery.* She went inside with Scout at her heels. Having to use the landline phone to call people made her feel like a character in an old black-and-white television show. All she needed was a rotary dial to complete the picture. The perils of living in the middle of nowhere. She called Ash.

Ashley arrived in time to help her prepare dinner. They cooked chicken and summer squash on the grill and set the picnic table on the back deck. It was too nice a night to eat inside. That was one of Mom's sayings, Hannah realized, wondering when she'd picked it up. When the meal was ready, she went to fetch Dad from the shed. While she'd been manning the grill, she'd heard occasional sounds of building—a power drill, some sawing, but now it was quiet.

The shed was always Dad's place. Memories of when Hannah was younger and he used to let her "work" with him—building birdhouses or little wooden toys—made her smile. She'd always loved the smells of sawdust and paint that lingered there.

Dad was hunched over his workbench, cradling a window box in his arms, weeping. He'd been distant and quiet since Mom left, but always kept displays of emotion to himself. The sight broke Hannah's heart all over again.

Ashley called from the deck and Dad looked up, making eye contact for a split second before turning away to place the window box on the workbench. Hannah rushed to his side and hugged him.

He tensed at her touch, then his arms were around her and his face on her shoulder. His body shook with sobs and Hannah teared up.

"I'm so lost, Hannah. I don't know what to do." His voice was despair personified.

"I know, Dad. I miss her too, but I'm still here, and so are you."

After a moment, he pulled loose and placed his hands on my shoulders. His face was wet with tears, but he was smiling.

"You know something? You're right. I *know* you're right, but sometimes …" He trailed off and looked away, as if trying to form the right words. "I know I haven't been a very good father lately."

His words cut her. The last thing she wanted was for him to feel worse. "Dad …"

He pulled her in for a desperate hug. "I'm going to try." He looked at the window box, his smile turning sad. "Let's go eat some dinner."

She couldn't stop her own tears from flowing. Hers were tears of hope. "I love you, Dad."

They walked hand-in-hand out of the shed.

Hannah opened her bedroom window, shivering at the crisp night air. She had waited for the sounds of Dad moving about the house to cease. Since Mom had left, he would wander from room to room, sometimes opening the door as if waiting for her to come home.

She shook Ash, anxious to share her discovery. "Come on, lazy, we have an adventure waiting."

Ashley groaned and rolled over, her face hidden beneath a curtain of curly black hair. She pulled her pillow over her head.

They'd been awake the whole time but, of course, now Ashley was playing the drama card. Hannah knew she was just annoyed that she wouldn't tell her why they were sneaking out.

Hannah ripped the sheet from her and snatched the pillow. "Let's go, Ash."

Ashley sat up, blinking and looking around.

"Dad finally went to bed," Hannah whispered. "Get your sneakers and sweatshirt."

Ashley complied, moving like a drunken robot. "Can't we just go in the morning?"

Hannah sighed. "Dad insists on taking me back-to-school shopping. Come on."

Ashley pulled her sweatshirt over her head, leaving the hood on. A smile crept across her face. "I'm ready."

Hannah smiled back at her before they slipped out the window into the night. The sound of crickets and peepers echoed all around them. Here and there, a firefly winked. There were countless stars overhead, but tonight, they looked cold. Hannah had heard somewhere that some of them were already dead, but their light took so long to reach earth that they were still visible. She pushed the morbid thoughts of death away.

As they walked, Hannah reflected on the evening they'd spent together. After dinner, Ashley, Dad, and Hannah had played three-handed Whist, a card game Mom had taught both her and Dad to play. Then they'd settled in front of the TV to watch old sitcom reruns. Hannah couldn't remember a better night. Dad had been chatty and animated, with only brief interruptions by his sullen, withdrawn self. It mostly happened during the TV shows, and she'd assumed something in the plot had hit a nerve.

As if reading her mind, Ashley said, "Your dad was really funny tonight. Kind of like ... before."

Hannah smiled in the darkness as they walked up the hill toward the woods. "Yeah, it was really cool to see him like that. I think he might be, you know, coming out of it."

Ashley was quiet for a few minutes and Hannah knew a hard question was coming. As close as Ash and she were, in the eighteen months since Mom had left, they'd seldom spoken about where she might be.

"What do you really think happened to her, Hannah?" Ashley's voice was low, hesitant.

Mosquitoes buzzed by Hannah's head and she absently swatted them away. It was something she thought about endlessly. *But did she have a real answer?* "Before Mom left, she was acting pretty weird." she finally said.

"Yeah, even I could see that," Ashley agreed.

"Sometimes, I think maybe she was on drugs. Other times, I think it's like everybody says." Hannah spoke softly but firmly. She knew exactly what most people thought. Small towns weren't known for discretion, and kids weren't known for their sensitivity. She had heard it all, both in whispers and in taunts: *Her mom was a tramp that ran away with another guy.*

"I'm sorry I brought it up, it's just ... I never believed the stories. Your mom wouldn't do that to you or your dad. She was cool," Ashley said.

Hannah's eyes stung. Talking about her mom in the past

tense made it sound so final, like she'd died. "I know what you mean, and thanks for saying so. She really wasn't herself, Ash. She was so disconnected, distant. You remember how she would want to hug me every time I left the house and every time I came home?"

Hannah cleared her throat to cover the sound of a choked sob.

"She just stopped one day, and it was like she didn't even know I was there, or when I was coming or going. Same with Dad—she always used to kiss him hello and goodbye, but towards the end she was … different."

Hannah couldn't contain the tears any longer and let out a weak moan. Ashley put an arm around her shoulder and pulled her close.

"I know what you mean. I mean, sometimes I wanted to tell them to get a room. But I noticed it when it stopped, too."

Hannah buried her face in Ashley's sweatshirt, letting the months of anguish flow out of her. They stood together at the edge of the forest, oblivious to the night chill and the bugs. She'd always known Ashley would be her best friend forever, that the fleeting transformations and aspirations over the years wouldn't change it, but that moment cemented it.

"I love you, Ash, thanks." Hannah sniffed and rubbed her eyes, pulling away from her.

"I love you, too, Hannah. But don't get all weird on me, okay?" Ashley said in her old, wise-ass voice. The moment was over.

Hannah laughed and cried a little more. "Sorry, you're not my type." She pulled out her iPhone and brought up the flashlight app. "Wanna see something gross?"

"Holy crap. What the beep is that?" Ashley blurted.

Hannah wanted to giggle at Ashley's creativity in her near-swears, but it didn't seem as funny out in the woods at night with a rotting human body part nearby. "It's exactly what it looks like." Hannah was a little surprised another animal hadn't come and taken it for a prize.

"Where did it come from?" Ashley grabbed a stick and poked at the sneaker.

"Scout dragged it out of the trees up ahead a little." Hannah pointed, but Ashley was too busy examining the thing.

Ashley made a gagging noise.

Hannah ignored it. "I was thinking," she said in her best mysterious voice, "what if it's a kid that got lost in the woods and was never found? Or ..." She paused for drama. "Maybe a kid that was kidnapped, or *murdered*."

An owl hooted close by, followed by the whooshing of wings.

"Come on, Hannah, stop screwing around. Is this a joke?" Ashley's confidence had slipped—Hannah heard it in her tone.

A pang of guilt for being so mysterious about the whole thing gave Hannah pause. "No, I swear, Scout found it this morning. I was going to tell Dad—"

"Wait," Ashley interrupted. "You didn't tell your dad? You didn't call the police?"

Hannah flushed, and she was glad Ashley couldn't see it. "Come on, Ash, it's so boring around here—"

"Oh, screw this, Hannah. You want to play Nancy Drew?"

This time Hannah did giggle. "I was thinking more like the

Winchester brothers, but Nancy Drew works, too. We can try to figure out who it is and what happened for the rest of the summer. If we don't get anywhere, we tell Dad and call the police. The kid isn't going to be any deader than he already is."

This time Ashley laughed. "You're a weirdo, but I guess you're right. Maybe we'll be local heroes. Get our fifteen minutes of fame."

Hannah buzzed with nervous excitement. She had half expected Ashley to ridicule the whole idea and talk her into telling Dad right away. Now that she had a partner, she was psyched. "Okay, but you can't tell anyone, promise? I think it's probably against the law *not* to report it, but if we figure out who it is, we'll be so famous they probably won't care that we waited."

"Why would I tell anyone about something as demented as this?"

Hannah laughed. The note of excitement in Ashley's voice told her she was just teasing. Something rustled the bushes deeper into the woods. Hannah glanced at Ashley; she'd heard it too. A moment later, something scurried away.

Am I really cut out for this sort of thing?

"So, Nancy, where do we start looking for clues?" Ashley asked.

Hannah didn't have to think about her answer—she'd been planning all day. "Step one: the library."

Ashley groaned. "That's like homework. Can't we just, like, interview people? Maybe there are some cute boys that might know something about this?"

Hannah shook her head. "I'm glad you mentioned interviews, partner. It just so happens that was step two. But the first interview is Mrs. Bayole."

14

Ashley groaned again. "*Mama* Bayole, you *are* insane. She might be the one who killed whoever's foot this is! Nuh-uh, no way, not happening."

Hannah shrugged. "No worries, wimpy, I'll talk to her. But that leaves you with library duties."

"It's a deal." She sighed. "But don't get yourself turned into a zombie or something at her house, I don't want to have to solve that mystery too. Not to mention the pain of having to break in a new best friend."

Hannah laughed and punched Ashley's shoulder. "Fair enough, I'll make a note in the case log not to get turned into a zombie. Now let's get back before Dad figures out we snuck out and has a bird."

CHAPTER THREE

Ashley puttered around the house after Mr. Green dropped her off, unable to focus on anything. Both her parents were home, making it an excruciatingly uncomfortable place to be. She glanced at her phone. *Good, the library will be open soon.*

Ashley winced when she heard her father raise his voice from the bedroom. They were both packing for their trip, and it wasn't going well based on what Ashley had heard so far.

She popped in her ear buds and turned up the volume on her phone, the hip-hop drowning out her parents' misery. Ashley knew the trip wasn't just a vacation, it was a last ditch save-the-marriage excursion. No kids allowed. That part Ashley was okay with—she'd get to spend more time with Hannah and not have to think about which parent she wanted to live with when they split up.

"Mom? Dad? I'm going out," she called as she passed by the bedroom.

The door swung open and Ashley pulled out an ear bud.

"Where are you off to?"

Her mother's voice trembled, and her eyes were swollen from crying.

Ashley bit her lower lip, her eyes filling with tears. Anger and sadness fought for control.

"I'm meeting some friends at the park. We'll probably get lunch at May's."

"Okay, sweetie, have fun." Her mother closed the door.

Ashley put her earbuds back in and cranked the volume, storming down the stairs and out the door, choking back an angry sob. Her anger ebbed as she walked and was replaced by a desperate sadness. She slowed her stride, trying to enjoy the waning summer. The thought of returning to school and not being in the same classes as Hannah only pulled her deeper into despair.

The tree-lined streets offered plenty of shade, but the day was muggy and hot. Ashley slowed her pace again, not wanting to be covered in sweat when she got to the library. She turned onto Maple Street, one of the older neighborhoods in Hopeland. The houses were larger and well kept, set back on expansive emerald carpets. This was the land of gardeners and underground sprinkler systems to maintain appearance. Ashley wondered what went on behind the closed doors of these houses. Were there unhappy children whose parents fought? Did the money make it any better?

A chocolate lab puppy, gangly and clumsy, ran toward her from one of the driveways. She smiled despite her glum mood, thinking of Scout when he'd been a puppy. A whistle sounded from the yard, beyond where Ashley could see, and the puppy turned with a sad glance at her, bouncing up the driveway.

A couple of turns later and Ashley was approaching downtown Hopeland. The library was just ahead, and Ashley realized she was looking forward to the cool, dry comfort of the old building. *Beats this three-H bullshit,* she thought, remembering the weatherman's almost deliriously gleeful forecast of "hazy, hot, and humid."

She climbed the steps and entered the library, idly wondering why the door was so big and heavy. It wasn't a fortress, just a library. She made her way to the research room, imagining the stares of the few patrons that were there this early. She felt like an imposter.

Fighting the urge to log into Instagram, she opened the website for the Hopeland Journal and began searching for an article about a missing girl. The website's search function was dog slow and regardless of what keywords she entered, the answer was always the same:

Zero results found. Try another search.

She looked around for a librarian and spotted a thirty-something woman speaking to an older man who looked very confused. The woman's expression was one of sheer annoyance. "So much for your friendly neighborhood librarian," Ashley muttered.

She tried The New Hampshire Union Leader, thinking there might be something there, an opinion piece or editorial about the missing girl. She came up empty again.

Next, she tried Google, but no matter what she put in for search criteria, the results seemed unrelated to what she was looking for.

"Shit," she muttered, louder than intended.

An elderly woman peeked around the corner, about to admonish Ashley, then her expression changed.

"Can I help you with anything?"

Ashley brightened. It was another librarian. *One that doesn't have resting bitch face.*

"Um, yes, that would be great," she said with a smile.

The woman placed the books she was holding on a nearby table and stood next to Ashley.

"What is it that you're looking for that evokes such harsh language?"

Ashley felt the color rising in her cheeks but couldn't hide a grin.

"Sorry about that," she said earnestly. "I just can't seem to find anything in the newspapers, local or state-wide. There's this story my cousin told me," she went on, the white lie forming as she spoke, "about a girl that went missing around here a few years ago. I think it's just one of those …"

"Urban legends," the older woman suggested.

"Yes, exactly. Anyway, I was just curious …"

"Here," the woman said, shooing Ashley out of the chair. "You let Mrs. Cheevers show you how to do it."

Ashley stood and let the woman have her chair. She watched over her shoulder as the woman opened Google's Advanced Search window and began filling in different fields. She hit ENTER and Ashley stared at the results.

"Whoa," Ashly said in amazement. "You're pretty cool for—"

"For an old lady?" Mrs. Cheevers said with a mischievous grin.

Ashley smiled. "No, for a *librarian*."

They both laughed as Mrs. Cheevers scanned the results.

"Well, it looks like your cousin wasn't just spinning a yarn after all."

Ashley frowned, leaning in closer to see the computer screen. The article was from the Hopeland Journal, after all.

"Why didn't this show up when I searched the newspaper's website?" Ashley was half-curious and half-annoyed.

Mrs. Cheevers chuckled in that sort of chuckle that only old ladies seem to have mastered. "Their search engine is ca-ca. Always use Google, honey."

Ashley laughed out loud, then glanced around sheepishly, waiting to be shushed. *Hey, I'm with the librarian. It's okay.*

The back of Ashley's neck went all tickly. *Someone is watching me.* She turned quickly and found herself staring into the face of the other librarian.

The woman jerked back and turned, grabbing the books Mrs. Cheevers had set down on the table.

"I'll just finish shelving these for you, Mrs. Cheevers, unless you need my help with anything?"

The woman's voice was cheery and she wore a smile, but there was something not quite right about the smile. It stopped at her lips while her eyes remained cold and hard.

Mrs. Cheevers turned, her eyes narrowed, deep wrinkles creasing her forehead.

"Thanks, Kristi. I'm just helping this young lady with a school project. We won't be long."

The other woman, Kristi, flashed another cold grin and stepped away.

She was spying on us, Ashley thought, *trying to see what we were looking up.*

Mrs. Cheevers had turned back to the monitor to finish reading the story. She opened her mouth to speak, then paused until the younger librarian walked away.

"The girl's name was Abigail Hart. She didn't live in Hopeland. She was from Silverton but had just moved there a few months before she disappeared. According to the article, Abigail had run into some sort of trouble in Concord."

Ashley had heard of Silverton but it wasn't exactly nearby. *What was Abigail doing in Hopeland?* She made sure the other librarian was still out of earshot. "What sort of trouble?"

"She'd been suspended from school a couple of times. Once, they found drugs in her locker. Marijuana. She swore up and down it wasn't hers. A few weeks later, she was involved in a fight in the cafeteria. Abigail said it was because of the marijuana. The girl she had the fight with was the one she said planted the drugs in her locker."

Ashley grunted noncommittally. *Wouldn't anyone caught with drugs say they were planted?*

"According to the Abigail's parents, she had never been in trouble before. They threatened to sue the school. It looks like they reached a settlement: the Harts would take Abigail out of the school, and the two incidents would be expunged from her record so transfer would be easier."

Ashley stretched her back while she considered this. She twisted her head from side to side, then froze. The other librarian, Kristi, was glaring at her from across the room. She was talking on her cell phone, but her eyes were glued on Ashley.

Who did she call?

Ashley stared back, but the woman would not look away, and her twitching legs started to all-out tremble.

"Are you all right, dear?"

The voice seemed miles away. Then Ashley was sitting in the chair with Mrs. Cheevers hovering over her. She stared up at the old woman.

How did we switch places?

She turned around, but Kristi was gone. "I'm sorry, Mrs. Cheevers, I'm okay. Just got a little dizzy for a minute." She hated the fear in her voice.

"Are you ill? Shall I call someone?"

The old woman's eyes were wide with concern, all the color gone from her face.

"No, really, I'm okay." Ashley turned back to the monitor. "Was there anything else about Abigail Hart?"

Mrs. Cheevers watched Ashley, searching her face for something.

"There's another story" —she gestured toward the computer screen— "about some rumors that there was a cult in Silverton, sacrificing animals. The reporter tried to tie that girl's disappearance to the cult." The old woman rolled her eyes. "It didn't hold any water, just someone trying to get their fifteen minutes of fame by breathing life into the old Satanic Panic nonsense from the seventies."

Ashley nodded. She'd not only heard of the Satanic Panic but had watched a bunch of the old movies that had started it. She stood, her legs still a little wobbly.

"Thank you so much for the help, Mrs. Cheevers. I think I'd be still sitting here staring at 'no results found' if you hadn't come along.

She smiled, genuinely appreciative of the help.

Mrs. Cheevers gave her a long, appraising look.

"You're welcome ..."

Ashley blushed. "I'm so sorry. My name is Ashley. Ashley Wallace." She reached out a hand and was surprised at the old woman's strong grip when they shook.

The old woman smiled, making her look much younger.

"It's nice to meet you, Ashley Wallace, and a pleasure to help out." Mrs. Cheevers' face darkened. "Are you sure you're all right?" she asked.

There was real alarm in the librarian's voice.

Ashley nodded. "I'm fine, really. I might be back to do more research in the next few days, I'd love to have you here to help."

Patches of color flared in the woman's cheeks. "Why, thank you, Ashley. It would be my pleasure."

Ashley said her goodbyes and left, keeping an eye out for Kristi.

Wait until I tell Hannah.

CHAPTER FOUR

Hannah walked slowly down the old dirt road to Mama Bayole's place. The day was overcast but hot, the humidity oppressive. It wasn't the weather that slowed her down, it was the destination.

Dad had driven Ashley home and taken Hannah shopping for back-to-school clothes. The idea of summer ending, school starting, and winter following too soon after had her down. She'd listlessly picked out a few outfits and some school supplies, anxious to get started on the investigation. Now that it was time to talk to Mama Bayole, her enthusiasm had diminished. Disappeared.

For as long as Hannah could remember, Mama Bayole had been at the heart of every scary campfire tale in Hopeland. She knew the stories were probably all made up, but there was that part of her that wondered. She shivered, wishing she had Scout with her, but Mama Bayole had goats and chickens running loose and she didn't want Scout to cause a scene.

From a distance, Mama Bayole's farm looked like something on a postcard. The sprawling house was the centerpiece, with an old New England barn in the background, framed by small fields of corn and tomatoes and other vegetables that Mama Bayole sold at the local Farmer's Market. Hannah knew that because she often went to the market out of sheer boredom. Creepy stories aside, Hannah figured Mama Bayole was just a lonely old woman who liked to mind her own business. The only reason she wanted to talk to her was because of her proximity to the area where Scout found the sneaker. Well, that and the creepy stories she'd heard about the old woman.

As she approached, the postcard picture changed into something else. Something that you might see on a "haunted places" website. Hannah marveled at how rundown the farm was. Her own house was no mansion, but this place didn't even look livable. The front porch sagged under the weight of a few broken-down rocking chairs, half of the windows were boarded up and the house had faded to the point where it had no color at all. Tangled crabgrass clung to the sides, all but obscuring a small basement window. An old wreck of a car—just the shell, really—decorated the lawn, along with an ancient washing machine and refrigerator.

Beyond the house, the fields looked overgrown and untended. The old red barn's paint was faded, and it looked one or two New England winters away from collapse. There was no sign of any goats or chickens, no sign of life at all. She wiped the sweat off her brow and tried to push back the fear that gnawed at her gut. Something was wrong. She didn't know what, didn't know how she knew it, but felt it as strong as any intuition she'd ever had. She turned to head home when she heard a sickly screech.

Hannah looked up and saw the screen door was open. Mama Bayole stood on the stoop. The door slammed shut with another ugly squeal. Bayole pinned Hannah with an intense gaze. "You lost, little white girl?"

Her strange accent was likely behind the stories that she was a voodoo priestess—it sounded Jamaican. Mama Bayole, the stuff of local legend, was about five foot nothing. A strong wind would take her away like an autumn leaf. Her dark skin was creased with decades of wrinkles, but her eyes were sharp.

Hannah took a deep breath and tried not to laugh. "No, ma'am. I'm Hannah Green, from up the road. I want to talk with you if you have a moment."

Mama Bayole's face, stern and hard when she first spoke, melted into a brilliant smile full of small, pearly teeth. "If I has a moment?" The old woman broke into a fit of laughter. "I think I ken squeeze yo in."

Hannah grinned as she approached the porch. "Thank you, Mrs. Bayole."

The woman's face grew serious again. "Just fo'get that 'Missus' nonsense. Call me 'Mama' and we get along just fine."

Hannah tried to put on a serious expression of her own but couldn't pull it off. "Yes, Mama."

Mama Bayole laughed and turned to go inside, waving at Hannah to follow.

They stepped into the farmhouse, and Hannah's good humor evaporated. The house was dimly lit—the wallpaper faded and peeling, with an indistinguishable pattern that had probably been in style when Dad was a kid. The furniture was ancient and in various stages of ruin. That wasn't what bothered her. She wrote those things off to Mama Bayole being a poor, elderly woman living alone.

The smell, that was different.

Hannah hesitated at the doorway while Mama Bayole continued toward the rear of the house. Flies buzzed in the distance. She was unwilling, no, un*able* to take another step.

Mama Bayole sensed she wasn't following. She turned and frowned. "You comin', child?"

Hannah tried to swallow, but her throat had turned to dried parchment. She reached a hand out to the wall to steady herself when Mama Bayole shifted in and out of focus. "Ahh, I just remembered ... My dad ..." She trailed off, lost in the incessant buzzing.

Mama Bayole smiled, but it was a different smile than the one she flashed on the porch. This was cunning, *knowing*. "What about your daddy, girl? Go on, spit it out."

Hannah's tongue stuck to the roof of her mouth and the drone of the flies grew louder. She couldn't think. She looked at the tattered couch in the living room to her right and the idea of just curling up and taking a nap there seemed like a fine idea. She looked back at Mama Bayole and saw her nodding, as if she knew what Hannah was thinking and was encouraging her.

Hannah took a shuffling step toward the living room.

"Go 'head, child, rest your weary self. You lookin' paler than the underside of a catfish. Not that you was an'thing but white when you 'rived. Yo daddy doesn't even know you here, does he?" Bayole cooed.

Hannah took another step, the somnolent buzzing lulling her closer to the couch, closer to sleep. She stopped when a sound rose above the buzzing in her head. She blinked, not sure why she was walking into the living room. Scout's barking grew louder, bringing her back from wherever she'd gone. She brought a shaking hand up to her face and wiped the beads of sweat that had formed on her forehead. Then she looked at Mama Bayole.

The woman was watching her, *glaring* at her. She noticed for the first time how penetrating the old woman's gaze was, how empty her eyes were. The sense of menace she felt was paralyzing until Scout barked again, closer still. Hannah backed up to the screen door as Mama Bayole took a step toward her. She turned and burst through the door, leaping off the porch and sprinting up the dirt road without looking back.

She found Scout running toward her and stopped, gasping for breath. Scout's fur was up, and he was growling in the direction of Mama Bayole's place. Finally, Hannah dared a glance back. In the shadows of the porch, the old woman stood watching. Hannah felt her icy scowl like an unwanted physical touch. Calling Scout, she turned and ran the rest of the way home.

CHAPTER FIVE

Hannah made it home and grabbed a can of Coke from the fridge. Her throat was so dry from fear and the heat she thought it might crack. The Coke was magic. She filled Scout's bowl with water and stepped back as he drank furiously. A strange sound came from the basement. Hannah crept to the door, cocking her head as if it would help her hear better.

Someone's down there.

Dad muttered something unintelligible, and Hannah almost collapsed with relief.

"Dad, whatcha doing?" she called, going down the stairs.

He jumped, stuffing something into the pocket of his jeans like a kid caught cheating on a test. "Uh, just, you know, going through some of these boxes." He took a deep breath and let it out slowly.

Hannah stared, the look of sadness on his face almost too much to bear. "Do you need any help?"

Dad smiled, but it was a sad smile. *He's so lost in his grief. So broken.*

"Sure, if you're up for it. It's mostly clothes and shoes. You know how your mother loved shoes."

Hannah barked out a laugh, grabbed a box and began pulling clothes out, holding some up to herself, then tossing them in whatever pile Dad said they belonged. They worked together in comfortable silence for a while, making good progress.

"How long have you been down here?" It was a good sign that Dad was starting to go through Mom's stuff.

"All afternoon, since we got back from shopping. I lost track of time until I heard you come in. I ... I don't think she's coming back." He blurted the words out, as if saying them out loud might make them not true.

Hannah stopped and looked at him. He smiled again.

"I know this is going to sound harsh," he continued, "but I'm not devastated by that. I'm *resigned* to it, I guess."

Hannah had no response. She swallowed, waiting for him to go on. He pulled a dress out of one of the piles.

"Your mother wore this on a date with me a few years ago. Some event in town, a retirement. She looked stunning. She was always beautiful, but that night, she was ... *radiant*. We danced all night as if the party were for us. It was one of the last good times I can remember.

"Things went downhill soon after. When I saw how bad it was getting, I asked her to go to counseling. She refused, said it wouldn't help. I knew she was right. We limped along like that, tiptoeing around each other. Then she was gone. I hired a detective to find her, but he came up with nothing. It was like she never existed."

Hannah went to him and hugged him. When he pulled away, his eyes were dry, and he had an odd look on his face.

Small steps.

30

They went back to work, getting through a few more boxes of clothes. Like Dad said, shoes, lots of shoes. Hannah wore sneakers or flip-flop unless she absolutely couldn't get away with it.

Will I ever grow into a shoe obsessive?

"Hey, Dad, what do you know about Mrs. Bayole from up the road?" She tried to sound casual, like she was making small talk, but her voice sounded thin, tense.

He stopped what he was doing, a frown crossing his face. "Why do you ask, honey?"

Hannah shrugged, still busy going through Mom's clothes. "No reason. I was out with Scout and saw her, that's all."

He regarded her, maybe picking up something in her voice. *Something that sounded like a lie?*

"Well, I know she lives alone and runs the farm well enough to eke out a living. You know she has a stand at the market, right?" He paused, his forehead creased. "To tell you the truth, that's about all I know. Your mother could have told you a lot more. She used to visit Mrs. Bayole quite a bit before she ..." He cleared his throat. "She'd do some shopping for her, bring her dinner, things like that. There's a lot of talk around town about her, but it's all just gossip, I'm sure. Some people in small towns have nothing better to do than make up stories about people they don't even know."

Hannah raised her eyebrows. "What kind of gossip?"

He frowned. "Oh, you know. The kind of crazy stuff people say about anyone who doesn't look like them, or fit in. I've heard everything from she's some voodoo high priestess to she killed her husband. Like I said—crazy talk."

Hannah shrugged again. "Didn't you once tell me all rumors have a nugget of truth in them?"

Dad laughed. "I probably did say that, but I doubt it applies in this case. If she killed her husband, or *anyone*, she'd be in jail. That voodoo stuff is only because she's black and talks with an accent. Don't pay any attention to it. I'm sure she's just a nice old woman who doesn't like bothering people. Or to *be* bothered."

The last line sounded like an accusation. Or a warning. "You don't think it's weird that she lives all alone on that farm?"

Dad sensed something a little off about her questions. "What's going on, sweetie? Did something happen? Did she say something to you?"

Hannah stared at the ground, clenched her hands into fists. She looked up, avoiding his eyes. "Nothing at all. Just curious. I mean, she is our neighbor."

The sound of her voice was hollow, scripted. His antenna was up now, his parental instinct on high alert. She could see it. Could *feel* it in the air.

He's going to start grilling me.

A car door slammed, followed by footsteps on the walkway.

"Oh, that's Ash. We're gonna hang out, okay?"

Dad watched her, still looking uneasy. "Sure, honey. I'm going to just keep puttering around down here and get some of this stuff cleaned up."

Hannah smiled, gave him a peck on the cheek, and bounded up the stairs.

Hannah walked into the kitchen just as Ashley was sitting down with a bag of chips and a Coke.

"Hey, Ash. Make yourself at home."

Ashley stuck out her tongue. "What are you doing in the cellar? Looking for more body parts?"

Hannah turned and closed the door to the basement. "Be quiet. Dad is down there."

Ashley made a face. "That's even weirder than you being down there alone."

Hannah sighed. She loved Ashley, but sometimes the girl was just crude. "He's going through my mom's stuff, trying to figure out what to throw away."

She watched with a dark hint of pleasure as Ashley's expression crumbled.

"I'm sorry, Hannah," She stood and went to Hannah, wrapping her in a hug. "I'm such a jerk." Hannah pulled away with a smile.

"You really are, but you're my best friend, so I put up with it. Come on. Let's go to my room and talk."

Scout was stretched out on the bed. He looked up lazily at Ash, sighed, and went back to sleep. Hannah wanted to tell her about the weirdness at Mama Bayole's but was more curious about what she'd found at the library.

"First, let me tell you how annoyed I was at having to sit in the smelly library in the summer," Ashley began with an eye roll.

Hannah smiled patiently, waiting for her to get to it. She happened to love the smell of the library but didn't feel the urge to tell Ash that.

"Anyway, I wasn't having much luck when I realized that's what the librarians are for. I went over to an older lady. There was a younger one, but she looked miserable—mad at the world, as my mom would say. I'll get to her." She gave Hannah a look that said there was a *lot* to get to. "I put on my 'I'm a curious bookworm' face and asked grandma for help.

"I put it on thick, Hannah, Academy Award style. I said my

cousin told me an urban legend about a girl that disappeared in the woods.

"Grandma smiled, you should have seen the spark in her eyes. I made her day. Maybe her *year*. Mrs. Cheevers is her name. She Googled it and said, 'Looks like your cousin wasn't just spinning a yarn.' She actually said that—spinning a yarn. Can you believe it?"

Hannah stared at her friend, smiling. Ashley's eyes were bright. Dancing, Mom would have said. *She's really into this.* "What did she find?"

"The girl's name was Abigail Hart ..." She quickly recapped the rest of the story. "Then I started to feel weird, like someone was watching me. I glanced up at Bitch Face and she *was* staring at me, talking on her cell. It freaked me out.

"My legs started feeling shaky. Mrs. Cheevers read more out loud, saying some reporter was trying to tie the disappearance into some of the cult activity that was rumored to be going on in the woods.

"To make it worse, Bitch Face was still staring at me, not even trying to pretend she wasn't. She looked livid."

Hannah giggled. "You're calling out the librarian for saying 'spinning a yarn' then you drop a 'livid' on me?"

Ashely waved her hand at me. Her *whatever* motion. She looked anxious to tell the rest of the story. "The next thing I knew, Mrs. Cheevers was on her feet and I was sitting in the chair."

Ashley paused. She had her moments of drama, but this felt different; Ash was afraid. Hannah waited for her to continue, but she was just kind of staring at nothing.

"Ash, are you okay?"

Ashley focused her gaze on Hannah, then grabbed a handful of chips. "I'm good. What's your big news?"

Hannah sat cross-legged on the bed, absently patting Scout. "I went to talk to Mama Bayole earlier."

Ashley's eyes widened. "What happened?"

Hannah was silent for a moment, unsure how to explain to Ashley exactly what *had* happened. She wasn't sure. "It was weird. She was really friendly at first, and then we went into the house—"

"You what?" Ash interrupted, "Are you crazy? Hannah, what were you thinking?"

Hannah threw up her hands. "What was I supposed to do? She's just an old lady." She paused. *The buzzing.* "Then I started feeling funny. Tired, but more than that: confused, lethargic." She stopped, the memory folding over her. She tried to take a deep breath, but it was all shaky.

The color drained from Ashley's face. "Hannah, are you okay? Did she drug you?"

Hannah shook her head. "No, nothing like that. I had just stepped in the door and it was like my brain got all fuzzy." She didn't really want to tell Hannah the next part. "I felt like I just wanted to take a nap. There was this noise, like flies buzzing, but I'm not sure if it was real or in my head. I started walking toward her couch ... If Scout hadn't barked ..." She burst into tears.

Ashley ran over and hugged her while Scout tried to squeeze into the middle of the embrace. Hannah calmed down, knuckling the tears out of her eyes, unsure of where the outburst had come from. "I'm okay, really. It was just, I don't know, like she hypnotized me or something."

"What if the stories are true and she's some kind of witch or voodoo priestess?" Ashley's eyes were wide.

Hannah tried to laugh, but it came out strangled. "Seriously, Ash?"

"Well, this isn't going to make you feel any better. I really think that bitch-faced librarian was up to something. You know this stuff never scares me."

Hannah thought of all the horror movies she'd watched with Ash; she was always laughing about how stupid the victims were or how corny the monster was.

"This is different. This is real," Ashley whispered.

Hannah drew in a deep breath. "Do you want to stop? Just tell Dad, or call the police?" As intrigued as she was by the mystery, part of her hoped Ashley would say yes.

"Hell, no. This is the most excitement we're ever going to see in this town, unless you want to spend the rest of the summer going to the Farmer's Market or waiting for Marcus Diaz's acne to clear."

Hannah's cheeks burned all the way up to her hairline. She thought she'd kept her crush on Marcus a secret. Even from Ashley.

What if he knows, too?

Ashley laughed and punched her shoulder. "You think I didn't see the way you looked at him when we went to watch the baseball games? You were practically drooling."

Hannah gasped, then started laughing. "I wasn't drooling, but he *is* cute."

Ashley grinned. "I guess, if you like tall, dark, handsome, athletic kind of guys."

Hannah was about to respond when a knock sounded on the door.

"Mind if I come in for a minute, girls?"

She looked at Ashley and shrugged. "Sure, Dad."

The door opened and her father stepped in, his face clouded with worry. "Funny thing about being in the basement—you can hear almost everything through the heating ducts."

CHAPTER SIX

Hannah sat at the kitchen table staring at nothing. They had moved out of her room, Scout following, sensing that something was going on. The silence lengthened and Hannah stole a glance at Dad. He was pacing back and forth, running a hand absently through his hair. He stopped, turned, opened his mouth to speak, then closed it and started pacing again.

"Dad," she began, but he held up a hand to stop her. Finally, he sat at the table across from her.

"I want you to know I wasn't eavesdropping. By the time I realized what I was hearing, I had already heard too much."

"Dad—"

The hand again.

"I need you to tell me what's going on. Where did you get the idea about a missing girl? Why would you bother Mrs. Bayole?"

Hannah gave Ashley a look that said, 'Let me do the talking.'

"It's nothing, Dad, just an old story kids at school tell. We were bored and decided to see if any of it was true. Turns out some of it is. I just went to talk to Mama—Mrs. Bayole because the kids talk about her too. Then I felt weird when I got to her house, lightheaded, and decided to leave. Maybe I'm coming down with something."

She met her father's stare, willing herself not to break eye contact.

He stood again, took another lap around the kitchen, then swung his chair around and sat on it backwards.

"First, I want you to stay away from Mrs. Bayole."

Hannah jerked her head up. Something in Dad's voice was off.

"Second, I don't want you bothering anyone else in town with this. Third, I want you to stay out of the woods."

She stared, mouth hanging open. The woods were her thing. She loved being out there with Scout. "That's not fair." Her eyes went wide. "Unless you know something. Some reason that makes it dangerous?"

Ashley turned to look at him. "Is that it, Mr. Green?"

Dad sighed. He looked like he wanted to get up and run away. Like he wished he'd never started the conversation.

"Girls, I'll tell you everything I know, but you have to promise you won't go running around town trying to find out more."

Hannah was nodding and saw Ashley doing the same.

Dad got up and grabbed a beer from the fridge. He spun the chair back around the right way and sat down. Hannah couldn't help but smile as a memory popped into her head.

She was about five or six, and Dad was tucking her in for the night. She had begged him to read her one more story, but he'd looked at her sternly and told her he would most certainly not. Then he'd cracked a grin and said, "But I will *tell* you a story." He had proceeded to invent a tale so silly that Mom had to come up and break up the fun.

Something about the way he was getting ready to tell this story brought that memory back so vividly that Hannah's eyes filled. She jumped to her feet to get a drink.

"Dad, mind if Ash and I have Cokes?" Her voice was steady despite being overwhelmed with emotion.

"Sure. Just as long as you promise not to operate any heavy machinery or do any parkour when you're all drunk in the middle of the afternoon."

She handed the drinks out and caught Ashley looking at her with a strange smile. *She knows,* Hannah thought. Another example of their strong connection.

"All right. Where do I begin?"

"I inherited this house from my grandfather. He built it himself when he was just a young man, early twenties maybe." He smiled. "I could never picture my grandfather young, building houses. He was so old and frail, even when I was just a kid visiting here."

Hannah had already heard this part of the story, but she listened intently anyway. Partly she let him ramble for Ashley's benefit to get her up to speed. Mostly, she just loved to listen to Dad tell stories.

"My parents used to bring me here every summer and I'd spend all my time in the woods, just like you. When I was about your age, I came here to live permanently." He paused, looking out the kitchen window.

"My parents were killed in a car accident, leaving me, an

only child, with nowhere else to go. I spent my high school years in this very house before going off to college and meeting your mother. Shortly after we married, my grandfather passed away, leaving the farmhouse to me.

"My grandfather used to sit out on the porch with me at night while he told me stories." He looked at Hannah and smiled. "Man, I wish I'd paid more attention to them."

The pained expression on Dad's face made her make a promise to always listen to *his* stories. She was well-schooled in regret and didn't need any more lessons.

"Grampie did a lot of odd jobs when he was younger. One story that stuck with me was from when he worked on a road crew. This was back in the fifties. The roads around here were still mostly dirt. Grampie's crew was hired to work on Route 33."

"Wait," Hannah interrupted. "You mean like where the shopping plaza is?"

Dad smiled. "That's the place. Hard to believe it hasn't been there forever, right? Anyway, Grampie was just a gopher, doing whatever dirty work and odd jobs the more experienced crew didn't want to do. The land the state bought to build the road apparently included some kind of commune."

This time Ashley interrupted. "You mean like hippies? I thought that wasn't a thing until the sixties. Woodstock and sh— stuff."

Hannah shook her head at Ashley's near miss.

"The sixties was definitely when it became mainstream, thanks largely to the music. It started well before then. A guy named Gypsy Boots and a group of followers lived in the Tahquitz Canyon in California back in the forties. He later founded one of the first health food stores." Dad shook his head, as if he realized he was going down a rabbit hole. "Anyway, the same thing was going on here. People were fed up with cities and looking for an alternative lifestyle. The term 'hippies' was coined in the sixties as well, but the people had been around for a while."

Ashley stood and started rummaging through the cabinets for snacks. "Keep going, Mr. Green."

Dad took another sip of his beer. "Grampie and a few other grunts were sent to clean up the commune. The people had moved on after a minor protest. There's one thing New Hampshire has plenty of ..."

"Woods!" they all said together and laughed. It was an old joke between them.

"Grampie said he was more than happy to take that detail. It was hot that summer and being in the shade of the forest was welcome over breaking rocks or hauling gear in the sun. They found the site of the commune easy enough and got to work. There wasn't a lot to do, really, just clean-up work. The group had left behind some makeshift tents, some clothes, mostly a lot of trash."

Dad stopped and smiled. His eyes got a funny look; he was back in time listening to his grandfather telling the tale.

"Grampie said they spent a whole day hauling trash bags out of the woods. The boss didn't bother supervising the work and they were far enough off the actual work site to get away with a lot of goofing off. And the second day's job was literally crap work; they had to take down a couple of outhouses and fill in the latrines. Nasty chore, he told me.

"They got it done in the morning and spent the early afternoon hauling more trash out to the main site to be disposed of. There wasn't much left to do when they got back to the commune. They spread out to search a little deeper into the woods to make sure they didn't miss anything. The crew boss was a real pain in the butt, Grampie said, and they were just kids who didn't want to listen to his lectures."

Dad's face clouded. He looked from Ashley to Hannah, his jaw hanging open a bit.

"Dad, what is it? Mom would have said you looked like someone walked over your grave." Hannah's lips tightened, hoping the mention of Mom wouldn't send him into a downward spiral.

"It's ... I just remembered something. The point I was getting to was that Grampie's buddy found a clearing out in the woods, with some sort of stone altar."

Hannah shot Ash a look, trying to stay calm.

"Wow, Mr. G, that's pretty weird." Ashley had dumped some salsa in a bowl and found a bag of Tostitos. She placed them on the table and sat down.

She's freaked out, Hannah thought.

Dad still looked lost in the past, but Hannah waited, letting him work out what he was going to say. Finally, he did. She wished he hadn't.

"I haven't thought about this next part of the story in forever. Grampie said he got lost in the woods after they split up. They'd all skipped lunch and it was hot. He wandered around for a while and eventually found his way back to the commune site. One of his buddies was already there—the other came staggering out of the trees much later. That last one told how he'd stumbled upon a clearing that was surrounded by brambles. He said he didn't know what made him fight through them, ripping his clothes and getting cut up like he did. But in the middle, there was ..."

Hannah swallowed a sip of Coke to sooth her dry throat. She was scared. Not so much because of what Dad was saying, although it was creepy, but mostly because *he* was scared. She saw it in his eyes, heard it in his voice.

"This guy told Grampie it looked like an altar, a stone altar. There were all sorts of bones around it. They looked like birds and small animals. Hanging from the trees were these ... figures ... made from sticks twisted together."

"Like Blair Witch!" Ashley shouted, caught up in the story as well.

Dad ignored her, his eyes still faraway like he was the one in the clearing.

"There was an old leather-bound book on the altar, but he couldn't read it. He said it looked like French. Then he saw bigger bones, and a human skull. He tore his way through the brambles and eventually found his way back to the commune site. At first Grampie laughed it off, but when they saw how scared the guy was, they agreed to go look. The guy couldn't find his way back to it. They searched until dark but didn't find the clearing."

Dad looked back and forth from Ash to Hannah. His eyes were wide, darting between them. He finished off his beer in a long, desperate gulp.

"I think you girls should stay out of the woods, okay?"

"What do you make of your dad's story?" Ashley asked, her voice unusually soft.

They were out in the backyard playing fetch with Scout. Hannah wanted to make sure they were out of Dad's earshot.

Hannah shrugged, taking the ratty old tennis ball from Scout and tossing it across the yard. "I don't know what to think. Is it possible there's been some weird cult around here for over fifty years?"

It was Ashley's turn to shrug. "I guess it's possible, but they couldn't have been sacrificing young girls all that time, right?"

Scout dropped the ball at Hannah's feet and cocked his head, waiting. She picked it up, grimacing at the drool, and tossed it. It rolled down the hilly part of the yard toward the edge of the woods.

"Dad said there were bones. Maybe they started out with animals?" Hannah ventured.

Ashley nodded. "Yeah, like they were warming up, like those serial killers, you know? They start out pulling the wings off flies when they're little. Then burning spiders under a magnifying glass. Then it's the neighborhood pets. Next thing you know … people."

Hannah stared at Ashley. *Where does she get this stuff?* Both girls liked their share of horror movies, but this was a little over the top. "Have you been watching those weird documentaries again?" She held up her hand. "Never mind, I think we both need to hit up the library again. One of us can research the group of hippies and see if there was anything in the papers about them. The other can scan for stories about missing girls. Not just from Hopeland but the surrounding towns as well, going back as far as we can."

Ashley was bouncing on her toes, back into the adventure. "And maybe back then, more kids just ran away when they got older and people just shrugged it off. But maybe they weren't *all* running away …"

Hannah scanned the yard. "Where's Scout?"

Ashley looked to where the ball was thrown. "I don't know. Maybe he caught a whiff of a rabbit and ran into the woods."

Hannah stared off into the trees and started walking slowly in that direction. She wanted to call for the dog, but something stopped her. Instead, she continued surveying the tree line, making her way to the edge of the yard.

"Hannah, what's wrong?"

Ashley had picked up on her concern, doing the mind meld thing.

"I don't know," Hannah whispered. "Do you hear how quiet it got suddenly?"

All the normal sounds of the forest, crickets, cicadas, even the birds, had gone silent. Ashley nodded.

At the end of the lawn they stopped. The next few steps would take them into the trees. Hannah felt something, an ominous presence in the air, the way you felt the electricity before a thunderstorm. Worse, she felt someone watching them. She stared into the trees, wondering just how close Mama Bayole's property was if you went straight through the woods.

"There's someone in the woods." Her voice came out gravelly. Her throat was closing.

"Let's get your dad," Ashley said, her head moving back and forth, searching.

Ashley grabbed Hannah's arm to pull her back toward the house. A rustle in the underbrush stopped them both. They remained still as the movement in the bushes grew closer. Closer and closer.

Scout bounded out of the bush and they screamed in unison before bursting into nervous laughter.

"Come on. Let's go see what's for dinner." Hannah's voice

was shaky, and she almost *heard* her heart beating.

They headed toward the house, but she turned to stare once again into the trees. Something still felt wrong. Then the sounds of nature picked up and the air returned to normal, like a release of pressure. Hannah let out a sigh and ran to catch up to Ashley.

"Hey, Hannah, can I ask you something?"

Hannah smirked. It was so Ashley-like to just move on from a weird experience right to the next thing.

"Sure, but I'm warning you, if it's about any of the boys at school you think I should be dating, I'm not going to answer."

Ashley looked at her, eyes narrowed, lips a tight line between her cheeks. Her expression was a rare one of seriousness.

"What's up with your dad? He seems different, almost funny again." Ashley raised an eyebrow.

"Is that a bad thing?" Hannah asked, head cocked.

"No, I mean, of course not. It's just, like, suddenly, he's getting back to normal. I'm happy for him, and for you."

Hannah stopped walking and swallowed. Ashley and Hannah were close and told each other everything, but this was such a personal subject, such a hard thing to talk about. Instinctively, she reached out and gave Ash a hug, her eyes welling.

"Thanks, Ash. It really is a good thing, right? I've missed him. Mom, too. It's harder missing someone when they're right there ... but they're not."

They walked toward the house.

"Yeah, I get it, Hannah. I was thinking more along the lines of does he have a girlfriend?" Ash's expression was far from serious. She took off at a run, laughing and screaming. Hannah gave chase, laughing along with her. They crashed into the kitchen, breathless.

"What kind of shenanigans have you two been getting into?" Dad asked with a grin.

He was in front of the stove cooking up scrambled eggs and home fries. Breakfast for dinner was a favorite of Hannah's.

"Oh, we just met a couple of boys from school, told dirty jokes, made plans to meet up after you fall asleep. The usual."

Dad didn't miss a beat with his cooking. "Dirty jokes like the one about the four white horses that fell in the mud?"

"Wow, Mr. Green, you're so hip." Ashley's voice dripped with sarcasm and they all laughed.

"Seriously, Dad, we were just playing with Scout. We didn't leave the yard, I promise."

Dad filled three plates on the counter with food.

"That's good. I was getting ready to call Special Forces to look for you. Come on, let's strap on the feedbag, as the cool kids say."

Ashley snorted a laugh and dug into her eggs. "I think you might want to look up the definition of *cool* before you get yourself in too deep with the nerd herd, Mr. Green."

Hannah sat on the couch watching television while Dad read in the recliner across from her. She couldn't concentrate on whatever silly sitcom was on—instead she watched him. The book he was reading was something about the lost colony of Roanoke. He looked up suddenly, sensing her stare, and smiled.

"What's up, Hannah?"

She looked away, face burning. Since talking with Ash, first about Mom the other night, then Dad earlier, she'd wanted to bring up the subject of Mom with him. She needed to find out what had really happened, but was afraid. *What if it sent him back into a depression?*

"Come on, Hannah, what's bothering you?" His voice was gentle, filled with concern.

Hannah looked up, sneaky tears spilling from her eyes. Dad stood and moved next to her on the couch, wrapping an arm around her shoulder.

"I just ... It's ..."

She took a deep breath and let it out slowly, shakily.

"I need to know what happened to Mom," she blurted, the words coming rapid fire, before she could chicken out.

Dad's arm tensed across her shoulders, then relaxed as he let out a sigh.

"I knew this conversation was coming someday. I guess tonight's as good a time as any."

"Dad, if you don't want to—*can't* go there."

Dad stood and started pacing.

"No, you deserve to know. At least to know as much as I do. I loved your mom, Hannah. I guess I still do. When we first met, I couldn't believe she went out with me. Then when we got serious and I asked her to marry me ..."

He stopped pacing and stared out the window. When he started speaking again, his voice was thick with emotion.

"I was the luckiest man alive. She was so beautiful. On our wedding day, she was a vision ... You've seen the pictures."

He turned and smiled at Hannah, but tears ran down his cheeks. "You look so much like her."

He took a deep breath and wiped his face.

"Things were great between us. All our friends teased us, told us we were the perfect couple. Then we had you, and things couldn't have been better. We were a real family. The teasing grew with us. We weren't the perfect couple anymore—we were the perfect *family*. Mom used to love dressing you up, showing you off. Not in a weird beauty-pageant way, but out of pride. Love."

Hannah smiled. She had gone through the photo albums a million times since Mom had left. At first just to remember, later desperately looking for clues, something hidden in one of the pictures that would explain why she'd run away.

"After she lost the baby, everything changed."

Hannah gasped. She didn't remember Mom being pregnant. *Was it when I was too young to remember?*

"I know, we never told you. I'm sorry for that. We both thought you were too young. Then when she started changing, we drifted apart."

"Oh, Dad, I'm sorry."

He made a sound I couldn't make out. Part laugh, part anguish.

"Why would you apologize, honey? You were so young, so fragile. You couldn't have known. She was only a couple of months along ..."

A memory seeped into Hannah's head. *Coming home from school in tears after being picked on for something. Dad was home from work. He was never home that early. Mom had to go stay with her sister to help with the twins while Uncle Frank was away on business. The next day she came home from school and Mom was in bed. She's just tired, Dad had said. The twins had run her ragged ...*

"She was at the hospital when you told me she was helping Aunt Amy with the twins." It wasn't a question. Her voice came out lifeless. *How could I have been so clueless?*

"We thought it was for the best. There was nothing anybody could say or do to make your mom feel better. I thought she'd get over it in time, but she never did. Eventually she just, I don't know, stopped caring. She didn't want anything to do with me."

Dad stopped talking, his face flushed. Hannah realized with a sick feeling he was talking about sex. She didn't want to know any more. She wanted the conversation over.

"I begged her to go see someone, a marriage counselor, but she refused. Said it wouldn't help. Then she started going out in the evening. She told me she was going to church. She said it helped her cope. I offered to go with her, but she said it was better for her to be alone."

Hannah's stomach clenched and sweat broke out on her head. It was all she could do not to run from the room. *Why did I think I wanted this?* Her hands started to shake, then the tremors spread until her whole body was trembling.

"It seemed to be helping. She became more attentive to you and more involved. She was almost like her old self for a while."

He stopped again, this time with a faint smile on his face and a faraway look in his eyes. Scout raised his head from where he slept next to the couch and whimpered, like he was questioning Dad.

"Remember we rented the cottage on Cape Cod? She seemed happy for the first time since losing the baby. Relaxing on the beach, going out for ice cream, that night we went—"

"To the drive-in." Hannah finished with a laugh. They had gone to see a horror double feature. When they'd gotten back to the cottage, a storm had rolled in and knocked the power out. Dad had kept pretending he heard someone outside, and Mom had freaked out. They had all laughed so much that night. Then something really had crashed outside and they had all screamed. Hannah remembered feeling real fear but still being unable to control her giggles. A shutter had come loose in the wind, and Dad had gone out to fix it. When he'd come in, he'd been soaked from the rain and they had all cracked up again.

Hannah looked up to find her father staring at her. Their eyes met and she knew they were sharing the memory. She offered him a smile, encouraging him to keep going.

"That was the last time I saw her happy, I think. By the end of the vacation, she was withdrawn and agitated. I caught her talking on her cell phone a few times and she would hang up quickly. She said she was talking to Aunt Amy." He let out another strangled attempt at a laugh. "I remember thinking that Aunt Amy was the story we told you when we were lying.

"When we got back from the trip, she started going out every night. She would leave as soon as I got home, wouldn't even eat dinner with us. She'd come in late and she became more and more distant. I confronted her, telling her we had to do something. If not for us, for you. She seemed to get it. She never pulled out of her despair, but she did seem like she was trying again. She went to parent-teacher night; she stayed home to give out candy on Halloween. Then …"

Hannah's memory on this part was clear. Dad might have thought she'd been trying, or maybe he was just saying that to paint Mom in a better light, but she remembered things differently. Mom had been so disconnected by then, so cold and indifferent.

"Then she was gone," Hannah whispered.

Her voice cracked, and hot tears fell frantically. She was caught between heartbreak and anger.

"Then she was gone." Her father repeated the words, his tone somehow making them worse, more hopeless. "I just don't know what made her leave. I mean, leave me, sure, people leave spouses all the time. But, to cut ties with her sister? With her own daughter?"

Hannah looked up.

Dad looked lost; his voice came out in a raspy whisper. "I just don't know why she left."

Her anguish was partly from the story, but mostly because she knew he was lying.

CHAPTER SEVEN

Hannah met Ashley in town at May's Diner, across from Champlain Park. It was about the closest thing Hopeland had to a landmark. The converted train car drew quite a bit of tourist traffic on weekends. The two had watched when May's had been featured on an episode of *Diners, Drive-ins and Dives* a few years ago, officially making it Hopeland's claim to fame.

The diner was the very definition of nostalgic. From its black-and-white checkered floor to the garish red upholstery on the booths, it reeked of the old *Happy Days* reruns she'd watched with her dad. The waitresses wore old-fashioned one-piece uniforms and a fully restored Rock-Ola jukebox stood in the corner. They served breakfast all day, along with burgers and fries, and their "world famous" milkshakes. There was neon everywhere.

Hannah walked in. Ashley took one look at her and jumped up to give her a hug.

"Okay girl, spill it."

The waitress had taken their order and left them alone. The diner wasn't crowded—it was too early for the lunch rush, and the breakfast crowd was long gone.

"That obvious, huh?" Hannah said, eyes locked on the table, unable to meet Ash's gaze.

"You're a human billboard for sadness. What the hell happened?"

Hannah recapped the conversation with Dad. Ashley stayed quiet throughout, letting her get it all out. Hannah's voice dropped to a whisper at times, and it shook at intervals, but she made it through without crying.

"And?" Ashley said when she finally finished.

"And he was lying." Saying the words out loud felt like a betrayal to her father.

Ashley just stared at her and Hannah's face began to burn, her eyes filling. She tried to blink away the tears. *How does she always know?*

"Wait, lying about which part?" Ashley asked.

Hannah sniffed, hoping snot wasn't running down her face. "That's the thing, I'm not sure. I think he knows why she left."

Ashley nodded and Hannah saw her friend's mind spinning, turning this information over and looking at it from every side like a Rubik's Cube.

Ashley played the part of the cool girl at school and her grades weren't the best, but she was smart. Hannah's dad called it "street smart" but it was more than that. She was smart about the things that mattered to her.

Outside, a car horn honked, and someone yelled. Hannah jumped and jerked her head to see, but it was just someone waving to a friend, nothing malicious. The waitress brought their lunch—a cheeseburger for each of them on a plate heaped with fries.

Ashley stared out the window for a while before asking her next question. "What do you think is more likely, another guy or drugs?"

Hannah stopped, a French fry in mid-flight to her mouth. She didn't want to contemplate either scenario. Sure, she'd thought about both, but mostly in the lonely hours of the night when sleep wouldn't come. Throwing the possibilities out there in the light of day made them seem so much worse. So wrong.

"I don't know. It's hard to imagine either one. Toward the end, before she left, she was, like, dead inside. I can't picture it being another guy. I think she would have acted different."

"What about drugs? They can make people act weird, right?"

Hannah shrugged, pushing a fry around in a pool of ketchup. Mom rarely ever drank other than an occasional beer with Dad. She'd never gotten into the whole wine drinking craze and Hannah couldn't remember her ever being drunk.

"It just doesn't seem like her, you know?" She looked up at Ashley. "You were around a lot. What do you think?"

Ashley was back to staring out the window. Hannah assumed she was checking out some boy, that's what she was usually doing. Then her face changed, became confused.

"Ash? What is it?" Hannah turned, following Ashley's line of vision.

She saw a handful of people walking by, a few cars on the road, nothing unusual.

"That lady across the street, wearing the stupid hat and the dark sunglasses—see her?" Ashley raised a finger, as if to point, then thought better of it.

Hannah scanned the street, finally locking in on the woman. "Yeah, so?"

"She's been staring over here for a few minutes. I think it's the creepy librarian that was watching me the other day."

Hannah looked again, committing every detail about the woman to memory. If it was her, it *would* be kind of weird. She did seem to be staring in their direction. Suddenly the woman turned and walked away, as if she'd seen them looking. Hannah noted she was walking in the direction of the library.

"I think it was her, Hannah. You saw her, right?"

Ashley's eyes were wide. Hannah wasn't sure if it was excitement or fear.

Hannah nodded, back to dipping her fries in ketchup and eating them while she pondered the possibilities.

"Hey, so what do you think? You never answered." Hannah was still thinking about her mom.

Ashley had deconstructed her burger and was eating just the meat patty with the tomato.

"About your mom? I get what you're saying, I really do. Don't you think everybody says that in this situation? I think people just don't see what's going on around them sometimes. Maybe they don't *want* to see, you know?"

Hannah looked at her plate. Ash's words hurt. She hadn't meant them to, but words have sharp edges, they can cut whenever they want. Hers also had a truth to them.

I didn't even know Mom was pregnant.

She felt queasy. The remains of her burger and fries, appetizing a few minutes ago, now looked greasy and unappealing. She pushed the plate away.

"Hey, Hannah, I'm sorry. I didn't mean it the way it

sounded."

"I know, it's fine. It's just hard." She offered Ashley a smile. "And you *still* haven't answered."

"Oh, definitely drugs. If she just lost a baby, she probably wasn't feeling very sexy and up to going out and seducing strange men. If she was depressed and maybe started taking something for it, she could have gotten hooked. It happens."

It was times like this that Ashley made Hannah feel like a child. The way she casually spoke about adult topics made her seem so much older. She was right. It made sense. Just because Mom didn't drink, didn't mean she couldn't get addicted to anti-depressants after having a miscarriage.

"You are wise beyond your years, Ashley Wallace. That's a sound theory."

Ash made a face and tossed a French fry at me. "Such high praise. Let's go to the library and see if that was Bitch Face watching us."

They walked into the library, and Hannah instantly had the urge to start giggling. It happened to her any time she was somewhere that she was supposed to be quiet or serious, usually at church or school. When the heavy wooden door slammed shut behind them, she let out a squeal and did start laughing. Ashley grabbed her arm, shaking with laughter as well. They got themselves under control and stepped through the small foyer into the main part of the building, drawing angry stares from those seeking quiet and solitude.

They looked around for Ashley's librarian. The front desk was deserted except for an older man waiting impatiently for something. Hannah couldn't see anyone that looked familiar.

"I don't see either librarian that was here the other day," Ashley whispered.

As they approached the entrance to the research room, they almost crashed into a woman hurrying out with a large volume in her arms.

Ashley gasped. It took Hannah a beat longer to recognize the print on the woman's skirt. The startled expression on the librarian's face turned to one of recognition, then something that looked like fury.

"Excuse us," Hannah mumbled and pushed Ashley through the door, afraid she was going to confront the woman and cause a scene.

Once in the research room, they turned to make sure the woman was gone. Ashley's eyes were wide, and she had a strange look on her face. Hannah understood. She had been looking into the missing girl and that woman had overheard. Then she turned up to watch the two of them at the diner? It meant they were digging up something the woman was afraid of them finding out.

"I don't see the other librarian, and *she* certainly isn't going to help us." Ashley sounded more angry than scared.

Ashley was right; they were on their own unless another librarian showed up.

"It's fine, Ash. We've got this. We'll start over there on the computers and then go old school with the microfiche thingy if we have to."

Ashley held up a fist and they bumped and then settled into their respective chairs. Hannah began feeding words into Google that she thought would pinpoint the commune of hippies Dad had told her about. Before long, she was engrossed, following link after link to the never-ending sources of information in cyberspace.

The names of the sites started out as credible outlets—newspapers and magazines that mentioned the commune in general-interest stories about the fifties and sixties. She kept clicking, following the trail to the more obscure corners of the Internet. She landed on a blog that featured posts about everything from time slips to global warming. She wasn't sure about the credibility of the site, but it was the most useful information she'd stumbled on so far. She was immersed in the story when the small hairs on the back of her neck tingled.

Someone is watching me.

She glanced at Ashley, but she was transfixed by whatever she had dug up. Hannah turned and saw the librarian standing in the doorway. The woman frowned and started walking toward them. Hannah reached out and nudged Ashley.

"Hey, what?" She noticed the woman approaching. "Oh, boy."

The librarian cleared her throat loudly, even though they were already looking up at her. She was clearly reading what was on their screens. She attempted a smile. "Can I help you girls find anything?"

Hannah looked at Ashley, who raised her eyebrows. *Should I?* Hannah nodded slightly.

"I was actually hoping Mrs. Cheevers would be here. She was *extremely* helpful the other day. You know, when you were staring at me while talking on your cell phone?"

The librarian's face hardened, then quickly went back to the forced smile.

"Yes, I do remember seeing you here. I was commenting to

my fiancé how refreshing it was to see a young girl at the library during summer vacation. It doesn't happen often."

Ashley flashed a grin of her own, but the look in her eyes didn't match her smile.

"Is it just as refreshing to see two young girls eating lunch at the diner during summer vacation?"

Her voice dripped with sarcasm and she went so far as to bat her eyelashes at the woman. Hannah's heart was already beating too fast. With the confrontation escalating, her hands and face began to tingle. She licked her lips.

What was Ashley doing?

The librarian's smile faltered again, this time she made no attempt to recover. "Are you accusing me of spying on you?"

Ashley's shrugged. "If the shoe fits, and all that."

This was not going the way Hannah had hoped. She wanted to drag Ashley out of there. The woman was staring Ashley down with a look of annoyance bordering on hatred.

"I think it's time you girls find somewhere else to spend your last days ... of summer, I mean."

The woman plastered the smile back on her face, but there was no mistaking the threat in her words.

"I've got a better idea," Ashley countered. "Why don't you step off and go get Mrs. Cheevers? I've got things to do and I'm sure your *fiancé* is waiting for an update."

The woman stepped closer to Ashley, their faces inches apart.

"I don't think you're going to be seeing Mrs. Cheevers around here anymore. She ... retired."

In the electric silence that followed, a strange mewling sound began to rise. It took a moment for Hannah to realize it was coming from her. She grabbed Ashley and pulled her away from the woman. Ash let herself be led away, but her eyes never left the librarian.

"You might want to be more like your friend. Fear can be a good thing to keep you out of trouble."

Hannah dragged Ashley through the main library and out the front door, finally gulping in a breath. They looked at each other. Ashley's bravado was gone, replaced by confusion and fear.

"Hannah, what do we do?"

They sat in the gazebo at Champlain Park sipping Cokes they'd bought at the convenience store. They had decided walking home along the winding, deserted country roads would be too scary and staying in plain sight was smarter. Hannah agreed to call Dad for a ride later.

"What just happened?" Ashley said, after gulping her Coke.

Hannah looked at her for a long moment. *Did she not remember she was the one that set things in motion?* "I think you poked the bear."

Ash took another long drink of Coke, let out a loud burp, then sighed.

"I thought that's what you wanted me to do. You kind of nodded at me?"

The girls never spoke about the weird telepathy they shared, but rather just accepted it. This was the first time it had been wrong.

"I did, but I thought you were going to ask her for help finding out about the missing girl, not confront her."

Ashley sat up, nearly choking on her drink. "Hannah. I never got to tell you what I did find."

62

Hannah sipped her own Coke, relishing the cool burn on her dry throat. The sounds of children laughing in the park and birds chattering in the trees faded. An eerie calm settled over them and Hannah looked around to make sure the rest of the world was still out there, still moving. She knew one thing for certain: whatever Ashley was about to say was going to put them across a line. There would be no turning back from whatever was going on. They would have to see it through. The thought terrified her.

"First, the Internet is a weird place."

Hannah smiled. No matter the circumstances, Ashley always made her smile.

"Second, I'm pretty sure I know what happened to Abigail Hart, and that it's her foot Scout found in the forest."

Before Hannah had a chance to respond, Ashley dropped the bomb.

"Third, I think there are a lot more feet buried in those woods."

Hannah stared. "We have to go to the police—"

"No! You didn't let me get to four. People think the police are involved."

Hannah glanced beyond Ash, wondering if someone— *they*—were watching. "Ash, come on. Involved in what?"

Ashley stood and paced around the perimeter of the gazebo. Hannah thought it was just her way of working off nervous energy, or maybe adding some dramatic flair to her story. Then she realized Ashley was checking to make sure nobody was listening. This brought it home for her. Ashley wasn't being dramatic, wasn't embellishing anything she read—she was scared. She finished her loop and sat down close to Hannah.

"A cult." The words came out in a harsh whisper. "Religious

fanatics, Hannah. Not devil worshipping exactly, but not far off."

Hannah thought about the story she'd been reading before the psycho librarian had interrupted. The blogger was speculating that the commune was more religious-based than some flower-power bunch of hippies. The theory was they were some distant offshoot of Wicca or more likely something from abroad, South American origin perhaps, or Haitian. Very nature-based but leaning more toward what the blogger referred to as the dark arts.

She told Ashley what she knew.

"It makes sense, Hannah. At least as much sense as this type of thing *can* make. The girl who disappeared had just moved to town from western Massachusetts. Abigail was kicked out of school there a bunch of times."

Hannah got up and did her own lap around the gazebo. Everything on the grounds of the park was bathed in brilliant sunlight, but the gazebo was dark and full of shadows. Hannah longed for that light.

"Not long after she moved here, she began spending a lot of time in the woods. She dropped the whole goth thing, took out her piercings and let her hair go back to its natural color. Her parents thought it was a positive change, despite the time she was spending doing God-knows-what in the woods."

Hannah thought about all the time she spent alone in the woods. *Am I a weirdo?*

"Stop it, Hannah. This was different."

Their telepathy-thing was back in working order.

"Her grades were getting better and her family thought the change was a positive thing. Then she just vanished."

Ashley's eyes grew wide with excitement.

64

Here comes the drama. Hannah was only half amused at Ashley's antics. The other half was just plain scared.

"One rumor—or story, I guess—from a witness that wanted to stay anonymous. They were afraid for their safety. So, does that still count as a rumor?"

Hannah smacked her playfully on the shoulder. Ashley was teasing her, dragging out the big tell. Hannah grinned, but it faded as soon as Ashley continued.

"The story goes that Abigail was seen in the woods with an old black lady, and that lady was the one that ran the late-night rituals. The witness said the girl didn't look right, like she was drugged or something."

Hannah's chest tightened, like a python was wrapped around her, slowly squeezing the air—the life—out of her. The world outside the gazebo shifted, then blurred. Ashley grabbed her shoulders and shook her.

"Hannah, are you okay?"

"You don't think it was Mama Bayole?" Hannah croaked.

"I think it had to be, but there's more. The witness claimed the last time they saw one of these rituals, it was different. It's the reason they left."

Hannah waited, focusing on Ashley's face so things didn't go all shaky again. This was not Ash's usual theatrical pause. This was Ashley trying to grasp what she was about to say.

"They said the ritual involved a blood sacrifice. *Abigail* was the sacrifice."

As Ashley packed her duffel bag, relief washed over Hannah. Ashley's parents were going away for a week and Ash was staying with her while they were gone.

"It isn't a vacation," Ashley had spat, "more like a 'save the marriage' pilgrimage that their therapist recommended. A week away from everything to spend on each other with no pressures and no distractions." Her words were filled with vitriol and desperation. "I won't even be able to call them."

She thinks she's one of the pressures and distractions. Hannah's heart ached.

Ashley had no hope of it working and had resigned herself to having eventually to choose one parent. In a rare moment of vulnerability, Ashley had broken down. She'd confided that she hoped they would stay together until she finished high school. Then she would go off to college and not have to choose.

Hannah wondered how it had happened. Ashley's parents weren't bad people—they just seemed bad with each other. Something had happened at some point that sent them in opposite directions. Or maybe they'd just drifted apart over time. The only common ground they seemed to have left was Ashley, and they both clung to it. Hannah had spent many an uncomfortable evening watching them snipe at each other while trying to show Ashley they loved her more than the other. It was sad and it did look hopeless, but Hannah was a romantic. She secretly hoped this trip would fix something and help them hold it together.

Ashley hoisted the duffel bag, impatient to get out of there. "Ready, fool?"

"Ready," Hannah answered.

They walked downstairs where Ashley's parents waited. They were all packed, their luggage in the car. Hannah looked at each of them, wondering what they were thinking. Were they excited to be going? Scared? Would they spend the week worrying about Ashley? *If they knew what we were getting into, they would.* More likely they wouldn't leave at all.

The ride to Hannah's house was quiet. They were each lost in their own thoughts and Ashley was banging away on her cell phone, thumbs flying. She knew the signal at Hannah's house was nonexistent and she'd be jonesing for social media all week.

Hannah watched the Wallaces from the back seat, musing as she always did about the wonders of genetics. Mr. Wallace was a tall, beefy guy. Not fat, but not too many cheeseburgers away from it. His wife was also tall but built like Olive Oil from the old cartoons. Both had the pale white complexion and light hair of western European descent. Ashley had beautiful skin that looked tan year-round and black, curly hair. Hannah always joked that she looked more like the Wallace's daughter than Ashley did. As she watched, Mr. Wallace's hand snaked across the front seat and intertwined with Mrs. Wallace's, bringing a smile to Hannah's face.

They arrived at Hannah's and Dad came out to say hi and wish them well on their trip. He grabbed Ashley's bag from her and motioned Hannah to follow him into the house, leaving Ashley to say her goodbyes.

"What do you think, Hannah, are they going to be okay?" Dad asked, once out of earshot.

Hannah had told Dad about the trip and she knew he was rooting for them too. *I guess I know where I get my romantic side from.* She thought of Ashley's parents holding hands in the car—something she had never seen them do before.

"I think they are, Dad," Hannah said, nodding as if to confirm.

He smiled and put his arm around her, pulling her in for a quick hug. "That's good, honey."

He sounded sad. *Will that ever change?*

Hannah brought Ashley's stuff to her bedroom, and a few minutes later they heard the car pull out of the driveway. Ashley stepped into the room and Hannah went to her immediately. Ashley's face was streaked with tears and she was shaking. Hannah held her tight, not saying anything, just letting her get it all out. What could she say?

Finally, Ash pulled away. "I'm sorry, Hannah. You must think I'm a big loser baby."

"I *know* you're a big loser baby. Now I actually think you might have a heart."

Ashley sniffled, then laughed. She grabbed a tissue from the box on Hannah's dresser.

"Okay, I cleared out a drawer and some room in the closet for your summer wardrobe," Hannah said, trying to get to a positive side of the situation.

Ashley made a face and started unpacking.

"After dinner, we'll take Scout for a walk and make a plan."

Hannah whispered, she was on the alert knowing Dad might be able to hear her from anywhere in the house. As if to prove her right, Scout came bounding in at the mention of his name. Ashley stopped what she was doing and bent to pat the dog. Scout rolled over for a belly rub and Ashley indulged him. Seeing Ash like this was weird. She wasn't usually very affectionate, but Hannah guessed saying goodbye to her parents was still affecting her.

Dinner was uneventful. Ashley was subdued, still thinking about her parents. Hannah was anxious to get away so they could figure out what to do next. Dad seemed confused by the relative quiet, stopping occasionally to look at each of them like he wanted to say something. Then he'd go back to eating.

They cleared the table and started the dishwasher. Dad moved into the living room and flipped on the TV, looking for the Red Sox game.

"Dad, we're taking Scout for a walk. We'll be back soon."

"Thanks, girls. Remember, stay out of the woods and don't go bothering Mrs. Bayole."

"Sure. Want anything for the game before we go?"

"A beer would be great. Thanks, Hannah."

She grabbed one out of the fridge and brought it to him. He was leaning back in the recliner, watching the pre-game show. The volume was down low, and she knew he'd be napping by the first pitch. She handed him the beer, then impulsively leaned over to give him a kiss on the cheek.

"Love you, Dad. Thanks for letting Ashley stay with us."

Dad smiled and patted her hand. "It's my pleasure. She's a good friend, more like a sister to you. I'm happy to have her. Now go, gossip about girls at school and giggle over boys or whatever it is you two do twenty-four-seven."

Hannah and Ashley walked out to the road with Scout trailing close behind. The night was hot, but the humidity was down and there was a bit of a breeze to make it comfortable. The sun had just hit the tree line, casting the road in shadow. Off in the woods, the crickets and peepers began waking up, filling the air with the music of summer.

I'll never get tired of their songs. Hannah dreaded winter evenings when the only sound was the wind whistling through the bare trees or the cracking of ice.

"Okay, boss, what are we going to do?" Ash finally asked.

They were far enough from the house to start the conversation. Hannah thought about Ashley's question before answering. She'd been thinking about it all day, but still she paused.

"If the blogger was right, we can't go to the police. There's no way we go near Mama Bayole or the library. I—"

Ashley had stopped walking and grabbed Hannah's arm. She was staring at something behind them.

Gooseflesh crept up Hannah's back. *Was someone following them?* She followed Ashley's gaze but was relieved to see nothing unusual. Ashley turned slightly to the left, then back toward Hannah's house again, her lips moving, her face a portrait of concentration. Hannah let her work it out, keeping an eye on Scout sniffing around the side of the road.

"Route 33," Ash finally blurted out.

"Um, what about it?"

Ashley bounced on her toes, her excitement contagious. Scout ran in crazy circles around them, barking. Hannah found herself smiling in anticipation, the jitters of a moment ago gone.

"Route 33, from your dad's story. If you go through the woods behind your house far enough, that's where you end up!"

Hannah frowned, trying to picture it. If Ashley was right, that meant the commune also used to be back there, along with the altar and the bones.

Hannah's voice came out quiet, shaky. "Maybe they never really left, the hippies, or whatever they were. Maybe these sacrifices have been going on ever since."

CHAPTER EIGHT

The girls were sitting on Hannah's bed with Scout curled up on the rug, occasionally looking up at them. Dad was sound asleep on the recliner.

"Ash, I think we're in over our heads. Maybe we should tell Dad and let him decide what to do."

Ashley looked at her like she was crazy. "You want to quit? Now? This whole thing was your idea. Now it's getting interesting, and you want to bail?"

"Interesting? Ashley, it's getting *dangerous*. People are being killed. We might already be in danger."

"Danger, shmanger. When did you get all chicken-shit?"

This was just like Ashley. Once something was edgy or just a bad idea, she was all over it. Resorting to name-calling and pressure to get Hannah to go along was nothing new either.

"I don't think it's being a chicken to not want to get killed. Think about it. I mean *really* think about it. You might end up on that stone altar with Mama Bayole or the crazy librarian or someone worse standing over you with a knife. Is that *interesting?*"

Ashley sighed, but Hannah knew she was getting through to her.

"You're right, it is getting dangerous. If we tell your dad before we know exactly what we're dealing with, we might be putting *him* in danger. Especially if he goes to the police and they are involved. They won't be after us at that point."

The words shook Hannah. Ashley was right, but at the same time, she couldn't help but wonder if she was sincere or just playing Hannah to get her way. Whatever Ashley's motive, there was no way Hannah was willing to put Dad in harm's way.

"Okay, okay, but we have to be careful. We make a plan and we both stick to it. If anything gets weirder than it already is, we go to Dad. Deal?"

Ashley flashed a triumphant smile, quickly replaced by a serious look. She held out a hand, trying hard to maintain her solemn expression. "Deal."

Hannah slapped her hand away, grinning.

Ashley tried to look shocked but couldn't keep a straight face. They both laughed, the tension between them disappearing like ripples on a lake.

"So, what's the plan?"

Hannah saw something in her friend's expression that hadn't been there before. This had taken on some importance to her. It wasn't just Ashley looking for an adrenaline rush—this had significance. Maybe in some weird way it was tied to the emotions she was dealing with regarding her parents' faltering marriage, but Hannah wasn't about to pry.

"We have two leads to follow up on. First, the witness. He

must know something more than what he wrote on his blog. No way would he dare print everything he knew. Second, the friend of my great-grandfather that was on the road crew. There might be something else he was afraid to tell his coworkers. If he's still alive," she added, "I guess he'd be pretty old."

Ashley was nodding. The look in her eyes was unnerving.

"Sounds good. It makes sense that you follow up on your great-grandfather's friend. I can try to track down the blogger."

"I'll talk to Dad in the morning and see if I can get the name of the guy. If he's still alive, I'll find him."

Ashley stood and paced around the room. She stopped and snapped her fingers. Scout opened one eye, then went right back to sleep.

"I'll take your bike over to the West Meadow Library in the morning. I can do all the research there and not have to worry about psycho-bitch. Hey, do you think we should check on Mrs. Cheevers? What that crazy librarian said ... You don't think they'd hurt an old lady?"

Hannah replayed the confrontation in her head. *I don't think you're going to be seeing Mrs. Cheevers around here anymore. She ... retired.*

Ashley was right—it sounded ominous.

"I'll add that to my list. I'm not quite sure how, but I'll figure it out." Hannah said.

She was almost as excited as Ashley again. At the same time, a weariness came over her and she yawned. It wasn't even that late, especially for summer vacation, but she was exhausted.

"What do you say we kick Dad out of the living room and find something mindless on TV? All this mystery solving is taking a toll on me."

"Good idea, maybe we can find *The Babysitter* or something." She laughed and ran out of the room.

Hannah followed. "Or maybe we can find that reality show about the crafty teenager that kills her annoying friend."

The next day, they split up early to tackle the jobs they had agreed upon. After breakfast, Ashley rode Hannah's bike to the West Meadow library, while Hannah hung around the kitchen, trying to figure out an angle to get the name of Grampie's friend out of Dad. She couldn't think of anything clever, so she went with the straight-on approach.

"Dad, that was quite a story you told about Grampie. I can't picture him as a young man, hanging out with his posse on a road crew."

Hannah pictured the great-grandfather she knew from pictures, a kindly old man. Frail and gentle-looking. It *was* hard for her to think of him any other way.

"Grampie was something," Dad said.

He was smiling, his eyes far away. Hannah already knew how much he adored the man who had raised him, and even if she hadn't, his expression in that moment spoke volumes.

"I thought of something while I was watching the game last night but I—"

"Watching the game?" Hannah cut in. "Dad, I don't think you made it to the National Anthem."

He laughed, a sound she would never get tired of hearing after it had been absent for so long.

"Wait here," he said, putting down his coffee.

Hannah finished up the dishes while Dad went to the

basement. She heard him rummaging around in the boxes he had been going through the other day. A few minutes later, he bounded back up the steps and into the kitchen, beaming, carrying an old, dusty book of some sort.

"Grampie kept a kind of scrapbook/journal thing. I stumbled across it the other day. I'd never seen it before."

They sat at the table and Dad started flipping through the pages. He stopped at a faded old newspaper story with a grainy picture of three men holding shovels. His fingers moved over the picture like a man reading braille. Hannah waited, knowing Dad was reliving his memories with his grandfather. Finally, he looked up, his eyes shiny.

"This picture was in the local papers when the road was being built."

He spun the book around so Hannah could see better. She read the caption, and, as she'd hoped, it contained their names.

"What a gang. I wonder which one of these guys is the one who stumbled into the clearing and found the bones?" Hannah said.

She hoped it sounded like innocent curiosity. Dad reached across the page and tapped the face of the African American man in the middle. He was the biggest of the three, almost a full head taller than the others, and as wide as an NFL linebacker.

"Big Jake, Grampie called him. I'm not sure why."

Hannah laughed and once again scanned the caption. Ezekiel Jacob Mather.

"The guy looks like he could have built Route 33 all by himself. They all look so young ..."

"Your grandfather was actually the oldest of the bunch. Big Jake was the youngest, if you can believe it. He lied about his age to get on the crew. He was only sixteen. When he came to Grampie's funeral, he still looked larger than life. Other than the gray hair, he really didn't look much different."

Hannah's heart quickened. He might be local if he showed up for the funeral, and he might still be alive.

"He and Grampie must have been close friends if he came back here for the funeral."

Dad pulled the book away and started flipping through the pages again. He stopped on one toward the back and spun the book toward her. There in front of me was the same man, fast-forwarded fifty-something years. He was pouring soup from a ladle into a bowl held by what was clearly a homeless person. He was a mountain of a man, broad and thick, not fat. His hair was gray and his brown skin lined with wrinkles, but his eyes shone with an ageless inner strength. The headline above the picture read:

Jacob Mather Celebrates Thanksgiving by Giving Back

The article went on to talk about Jacob's work with the homeless community. He spent every Thanksgiving and Christmas at the shelter, feeding those less fortunate. He organized clothes drives and had even started a program that had vans driving around the city each night to round up anyone they found sleeping outside and offer them a warm place to rest. As inspiring as the article was, Hannah's eyes were drawn to one thing—Jacob's location. Concord, NH.

"Wow, Dad," Hannah said impressed, "Grampie's old pal is quite a guy. Do you keep in touch?"

"No, not really. A card at Christmas, you know …"

"What about the other guy?" Hannah asked.

Dad frowned. He looked at her for a long minute before saying anything.

"That was Sam Nichols. They called him Sammy-Five. I guess everybody had a nickname back in those days." Dad laughed, but it was a sad laugh. "He disappeared that summer, the summer they worked on the road crew. I remember Grampie telling me that story, too."

Hannah folded her arms, chilled despite the heat of the day.

"What happened?"

"It wasn't long after the whole thing with Big Jake getting lost and saying he found that weird clearing. Jacob and Sammy were hanging out. Jacob was obsessing over the incident in the clearing, swore he would find it this time. They left for the work site at sunrise. The road still wasn't finished, but they knew how to skirt the barriers and get there by car. They went into those woods drunker than a couple of sailors on shore leave and spent the day stumbling around the forest until they were sober."

Dad shook his head, a sad smile creeping across his face. Hannah wondered if he was thinking about his grandfather telling it. She remembered the promise she'd made about listening to Dad's stories.

"At some point, they got separated. They met back at the car just before dusk. Grampie told me Sammy was never the same. Started showing up drunk for work and got kicked off the crew. He went on drinking binges that lasted days, always babbling about someone being after him, that they were going to get him. They found his car down a steep embankment off the Route 33 site. It had rolled over a bunch of times and finally landed at the bottom where it burned."

Hannah stared open-mouthed at Dad. That was not where she'd thought the story would end up.

A mild breeze came through the kitchen window, carrying the smell of pine, and for just a second Hannah thought there was a whiff of smoke there. "He died?"

"The strange thing about it is they never found Sammy's body. No bones, nothing."

"Could they have burned in the fire?" Hannah asked, not really believing it.

"It's possible, but nobody thought so. Even when they cremate bodies, there are chunks of bone that survive. Nobody believed the fire was hot enough to completely incinerate him."

Hannah could not believe what she was hearing. *Another potential disappearance?*

"What did Grampie think happened?"

"He said he didn't know. There were stories that old Sammy was faking his death to try to collect insurance, other theories that his body was thrown from the car and eaten or dragged away by animals. Nobody believed any of it according to Grampie."

"What *did* they believe?"

"Grampie thought the most likely explanation was that he did fake his death, but not for the insurance. He did it so he could disappear and start over. Or get away from something."

"Wow. Who knew Hopeland was such a hotbed for weird stuff? I mean, other than the whole 'Burning Wagon' on Halloween, not much happens here." Hopeland had a tradition every year of sending a burning wagon down Black Hill Road. It had something to do with Hopeland's history as a mill town, but she couldn't remember the details.

Dad stared out the kitchen window, that strange look on his face. The sun had changed angles and was streaming in on him. For a second, she saw Dad as a young man, just like the guys in the picture. Then he looked normal, maybe older. She shook her head, trying to clear the image.

"I guess I never thought about it, but there have been a lot of bizarre things that have happened around here," Dad agreed.

She waited, but he didn't say anything more.

Hannah walked down the road toward town, wishing she had her bike. She also wished Ash were with her. She'd tried calling but figured Ash wouldn't pick up if she was in the library. Then Hannah smiled.

Who am I kidding? It would be just like Ashley to talk on the phone at the library.

Scout trailed behind her, sniffing at whatever dogs sniff at. It was the kind of day where dogs should be out sniffing, and kids should be out being kids. The sun was a golden ball against a backdrop of dazzling cerulean. It was hot, but the humidity was low, and a gentle breeze rustled the vibrant green leaves and carried all the aromas of summer. Hannah smirked at her 'adult' thoughts and tried to commit the feeling to memory so she would be able to record it later in her journal.

There was no good day to track down an old man and dredge up his past, she thought, but that was exactly what she was going to do. The library was off-limits, but she was headed for the convenience store where an old-fashioned telephone booth stood in the parking lot. An equally old-fashioned telephone book hung on a steel cord in that booth, and it was there that she hoped to find Jacob Mather's number.

She approached Sanderson's Market, checking to make sure Scout was still nearby. A car rolled up the road behind her and she kept an eye on Scout, afraid he might wander into the street. The car was taking forever to pass, and she felt a tickle of unease. The sun reflected off the windshield, making it impossible for her to see the driver. It was probably just some ancient person who shouldn't be driving, or someone battling the sun, but ...

Finally, the car drew up next to her. It was a late model she didn't recognize, too sporty for an elderly driver, and the windows were tinted dark enough that she couldn't see in.

She had the feeling that the driver was staring at her, she looked up and down the road, searching for the closest place to run to safety if the car stopped. It slowed more, matching her pace. Scout whined and got right next to her, hackles spiking up.

Maybe it's someone that needs directions.

Her heart was almost audible, it was beating so hard. She swallowed, her throat gone dry, and prepared to take off running. Then the car roared away in a screech of burning rubber.

Hannah exhaled, unaware she'd been holding her breath. Scout barked at the car and Hannah watched it turn off the main road and out of sight. She waited, still ready to bolt if it appeared again, but everything was quiet. The sound of the engine was gone, replaced with the buzz of the heat bugs. She walked unsteadily toward the phone booth, unable to shake the fear that had taken hold of her.

The enclosure was a throwback to times gone by—a tall glass booth with bi-fold doors for privacy. *It looks like an upright coffin,* she thought, her musings of a perfect summer day replaced with dread. She stepped inside and was hit with a blast of stale, oppressive air that reeked of old cigarettes and body odor. She grabbed the phone book and began flipping through the pages, pulling the steel cord taut so she could get as close to the fresh air outside the booth as possible.

As expected, there were a ton of Mathers. Hannah's eyes slid down the page to the letter 'E' and there it was—*Ezekiel*. She took a deep breath and exhaled slowly. Part of her had hoped that this would be a dead end and that Ashley would also come up empty. Then they would turn this whole thing over to the police and be done with it. She would salvage the rest of the summer and stop stressing out.

She shivered when a car sped by, but it was not the same one that had rolled by so menacingly moments before. Thinking of the car made her wonder if Ashley was safe. Part of the bike ride to West Meadow was on a long, winding country road. It was secluded with nothing but woods on either side.

She shook the thought away and pulled out her cell. Before she chickened out, she dialed Jacob's number.

"Hello." The deep baritone voice boomed through the phone. Hannah immediately recalled the picture of Mather pouring soup into the homeless man's bowl, and a smile crept across her face.

"Hello, is this Mr. Mather? Mr. Ezekiel Jacob Mather?"

"Yes, who is calling, please?" he rumbled.

"Um, my name is Hannah Green, I'm Brian's daughter."

There was a long pause, followed by booming laughter. Hannah pictured the actor from that movie where the guy built a baseball field on his farm, and her smile widened.

"It's a pleasure to hear from you, Miss Green. I must say, this is quite a surprise."

Hannah froze, unsure what to say next. Mather filled in the silence, his voice hushed with concern.

"Is your father all right?"

"Oh, yes, Mr. Mather, Dad is fine. That's not why I'm calling. I, uh …"

"Come now, Hannah. You've made it this far, tracking down my number, gathering the nerve to call me. Finish the deal."

She couldn't stop smiling. The way his words spilled out of the phone, Hannah felt him grinning at the other end.

"I was wondering if I could ask you something. My dad told me a story about his grampie and you and Sammy-Five working on the road crew—"

Thunderous laughter from the phone silenced her.

"Hannah Green, you certainly have a piece of your great-granddaddy in you. Let me ask you something first."

"Um … sure, of course."

"Why does Sam Nichols get the benefit of his nickname of youth, but I'm burdened with the old-man moniker of Mr. Mather?"

Again, Hannah heard the smile in his voice and before she was able to stop the words from spilling out, she said, "You're right, Big Jake, now may I ask my question?"

She pictured him doubled over at the other end of the phone and laughed along with him.

"Ask away," he finally managed.

"Well, Dad told me about you finding a clearing in the woods when you were working on the road crew. I was wondering if I could talk to you about that."

An ominous silence was the only response. She waited, glancing at her phone to make sure the call hadn't dropped.

Finally, she heard a long, heavy sigh.

"Does your dad know you are calling? Never mind. Of course he doesn't."

Hannah waited again, sensing the man struggling with his decision.

"I'll tell you whatever you want to know, but not over the phone." He breathed, the whimsy gone from his voice. He just sounded old.

"Okay, thank you Mister—I mean Big Jake, but I'm not old enough to drive."

"I'll come to you. Is there somewhere in Hopeland we could meet? Is May's Diner still there?"

"Yes, the diner would be perfect, but only if it's not too much trouble."

"I'll meet you there at 9am tomorrow morning." The line went dead with a soft click.

Hannah looked at her phone again, only realizing at that moment her hand was shaking.

CHAPTER NINE

Ashley arrived at the West Meadow Library hot and sweaty. *If anyone told me I'd be visiting not one but two libraries over the summer, I would have told them to see a shrink.*

"Yet, here I am," she muttered, locking Hannah's bike to the rack out front.

The West Meadow Library was smaller than Hopeland's, and not nearly as quaint. As much as Ashley complained about libraries, she did appreciate the architecture of old buildings. West Meadow's library had a newer, more functional style. It looked like every other library, town hall, or elementary school built in the seventies.

She entered the building and spotted tables with computers off to one side. She silenced her cell phone and sat down heavily in one of the utilitarian wooden chairs. *Hopeland at least has comfy seats*, she thought, and began her research.

Most of the information they'd found was from the same source—the mysterious blogger who seemed to know an awful lot about Abigail Hart. She spent the first hour reading and re-reading all his posts that mentioned anything about Abigail or cults. Satisfied she had learned all she could, Ashley focused on getting in touch with the blogger. Unfortunately, his website contained no contact information, no "About" section, and nothing that helped Ashley find his identity.

Ashley looked around, the short hairs on the back of her neck tingling. It was the same feeling she'd had when that bitchy Kristi had been watching her. The library was fairly crowded, but everyone seemed engrossed in their books or browsing. She shook off the feeling as paranoia.

Smiling at the thought of Mrs. Cheevers besting her by simply using Google, she opened the search engine and began typing. The Internet was an endless "how to" manual, and Ashley used that to her advantage. She bounced from site to site, reading about domain names, website creation, and hosting. Not long after, she had an email address.

Ashley licked her lips as she typed a note introducing herself to the blogger.

Hi there!

I've been reading your posts about Abigail Hart. Crazy stuff! I live in Hopeland and had never heard about it.

Can I ask you some questions?

Thanks,
Ashley

Bouncing in her seat, she hit "send" and started to close out of the browser windows she had opened. She left her email open until she was done and was about to "x" out of that as well when a new message popped into her inbox.

> Hi Ashley,
>
> Thanks for reading my blog. I've pretty much said everything I have to say on the subject, though. Trying to put it all behind me, you know?
>
> Xfiles666

He thinks I'm one of the cult trying to track him down, Ashley realized. She thought for a moment, then replied.

> Hi Xfiles666,
>
> I totally get that. It's just ... I don't want to say too much, but some weird stuff is going on in Hopeland now. I'm scared.
>
> Ashley

She waited. Five minutes passed. Ten. *I scared him off,* she thought.

"Five more minutes," she whispered. The reply came in four.

> What kind of weird stuff?

Ashley pondered her answer. The wrong one would mean radio silence. She decided two-stepping around the issue wasn't going to work. *Full steam ahead.*

My friend's dog dug up a human foot in the woods behind her house. We think it's Abigail's. She's neighbors with this creepy old lady. We're both scared.

This time, she didn't have to wait for a reply, it came almost immediately.

I saw them bury her body in the woods. There's a kind of mutant tree, I call it the Siamese Pine. I hid behind it and watched them bury her. It was creepy, terrifying; the sun was rising behind them and I was only about thirty yards away. Where did your friend's dog find it? Never mind. Can you meet tomorrow?

Ashley took a deep breath and replied. After a few more messages, they'd agreed to meet at the West Meadow Library. Ashley would arrive at noon and sit at one of the tables in the middle of the library. Xfiles666 would decide when he got there whether or not he'd approach her.

The feeling of being watched hit her again, and she jerked her head around. Again, nobody was paying her any attention. She closed out of her email and stood, sneaking glances around but seeing nothing unusual. She went to the ladies' room before her long ride back to Hannah's.

She was sitting in the stall when she heard the bathroom door open. Next, she heard footsteps on the tile floor, moving slowly. Ashley assumed it was an old woman, but her radar was up after the weird feelings of being watched. More footsteps, somehow sneaky, then the door opened and closed again.

Ashley quickly finished up and booked it out of the bathroom. She looked around the library again, searching for two things—either an old woman moving slowly, or someone that looked suspicious. Everyone was reading at a table or wandering in the stacks. She ran outside to double check that Hannah's bike was still there, thinking maybe it was someone making sure she was in the bathroom so they could snatch the bike. Just as Ashley got to the bike rack—the bike was exactly where she had left it— she heard a car gunning it out of the parking lot.

That's the person that was just in the ladies' room.

The day was blistering hot, the sun beating down on her from a cloudless blue sky. Still, she shivered.

CHAPTER TEN

Later that afternoon, Ashley sat across from Hannah at the edge of the backyard sharing the results of their day. Ashley's research had been just as productive as her own. Her friend quickly recapped her day at the West Meadow Library.

"I still don't know his or her real name, or if the person is young or old. I'm gonna say *he* for the sake of discussion." Ashley paused, gathering her thoughts, searching for the right words. "He seemed really scared at the beginning, and only a little less scared at the end. We're meeting tomorrow, back at the library. I have no idea where he is coming from. Oh! The domain registration lists New Hampshire, so I assume he's not far."

Ashley's eyes were wide as she spoke, her words tumbling out with reckless abandon. It wasn't her usual dramatic storytelling. She was clearly too excited for any drama.

"He said for me to sit at a big table in the center of the library with my back to the entrance. He would decide when he gets there if he wants to talk or not."

89

Hannah sighed, massaging her temples. It seemed way over-the-top, some half-assed spy shit. *Unless this is more dangerous than we think.*

"I don't know, Ash. It doesn't sound safe. Meeting a complete stranger by yourself?"

Ashley shrugged. "I'll be in the middle of the library in the middle of West Meadow in the middle of the day. What could go wrong?"

She flashed one of her grins, but it didn't hold the confidence an Ashley grin usually did. Still, Hannah knew Ash was probably right but couldn't help worrying. The thought of that car …

"Hey, did anything weird happen while you were out?" she asked.

Ash snapped her gum and stared at her for a minute before answering. Her grin had slipped, replaced with a dark look, something close to fear. She recovered quickly.

"What did you do, call the psychic hotline or something? I was getting to that. Saving the best for last, you know?"

It was Hannah's turn to stare. If something similar had happened to Ashley that meant the car that had driven by had not been just some random creepo checking her out—it had something to do with the commune and the foot Scout had found. It meant someone, or likely more than one someone, was watching them.

"Go ahead, Ash, spill it."

Ashley looked at Hannah, an oddly concerned expression on her face. Hannah realized her words had come out sounding helpless and full of dread. Ashley's eyes widened again as she switched to storytelling mode. She relayed what had happened in the restroom, then stood and stretched. There was grass stuck to her shorts and her hair was a mess from bike-riding.

Hannah leaned back so she was lying flat on the grass, staring at the sky. The day had remained perfect, the kind of day you took for granted in the summer but longed for in the short, dark days of winter. The smell of earth and grass and pine filled her with an odd sense of nostalgia. For what, she didn't know. Maybe just the recent past before this mystery started. Had she really been bored a few days ago?

"Maybe someone came in to brush their hair or fix their makeup?" Hannah said finally, her voice overly hopeful.

"I thought about that." Ashley said hastily. "Before I ran outside, I scoped out the bathroom, trying to … I don't know, recreate someone walking in? The sinks and mirrors are just inside the door. The stalls are all the way across the bathroom. The person took way too many steps to go to the mirrors, but never made it to the stalls. The only trash barrel is right next to the door, too." Ashley shivered.

Hannah looked up at her friend. Ashley was backlit by the sinking sun, but her face was clearly visible. She didn't like what she saw. Ash's face was lined with worry, brows furrowed, lips tight. It made her look older, frailer.

"I think whoever it was walked over to the stalls and bent down to see where I was. I don't have any way to prove it, I just *feel* it. They never got close enough for me to see their shoes or anything, but I'm sure that's what they did."

She plopped back down on the grass. Hannah was relieved; she didn't want to see that expression on her friend's face anymore.

She finished the story, telling Hannah how she ran out of the library thinking Hannah's bike was getting stolen. And about the car.

Hannah sat up. There was no way this was a coincidence. Somebody was following them, watching them both. She told Ashley what had happened on the way to the phone booth.

"What did the car look like?" Ashley asked, head cocked.

Hannah described the car—silver-gray with tinted windows and fat tires, like on the old muscle cars you see in the movies. Ashley's eyes widened and Hannah knew it was the same vehicle.

"Did you see who was driving?"

Hannah shook her head and recounted the conversation with Jacob to get Ashley up to speed.

"That's it, Ashley. Time for us to get out of this. Something is going on and it's way too dangerous for us to be playing detective anymore."

Ash's face fell. She was devastated.

"Come on, Hannah, we're close to figuring this out."

Hannah wasn't used to the whine in her friend's voice. "No way, this is serious. People are missing. Dead. We're being followed, watched. This is too much. We're in over our heads."

Ashley stood again and walked to the stand of pines that marked the beginning of the woods. She used the trunk of a tree to lean on, her head hanging down. She looked like she had just run a race and was trying to catch her breath—either that or she was trying to push the tree over. After a moment, she turned and walked back, rubbing her hands together. Hannah smiled, knowing they were now sticky with sap.

"One more day," she said calmly. "I'll meet the mysterious blogger at the library, you meet this Jacob guy. Then we compare notes and decide who to tell."

As determined as Hannah was not to give in, something in Ashley's expression softened her resolve. Hannah imagined being Ashley, possibly on the brink of having to choose which parent to live with. Her conviction crumbled, replaced only with the desire to give Ashley something to focus on. As scared as Hannah had been earlier, a part of her wanted to figure this thing out too.

"If our parents ever find out we went to meet total strangers—"

Ashley cut her off by jumping on top of her and pinning her to the ground. "Thanks, Hannah."

For a minute, she thought Ashley was going to cry. Instead, her friend tore up a handful of grass and sprinkled it on Hannah's face. Hannah twisted her head back and forth, attempting to escape the shower of green while laughing at the same time.

CHAPTER ELEVEN

Hannah woke the next morning to a gloomy, drizzly day. A cold front had rolled in overnight, bringing with it a fantastic thunderstorm that had ruined her sleep. The lightning had been almost constant at one point, the flashes so brilliant they left tracers in her vision. The house had shaken with the rumbles of thunder, as if they were in the belly of an angry, hungry beast. A couple of times the lightning had struck nearby with vicious cracks that left the girls afraid but screaming with laughter just the same. Throughout the night, even as the thunder had faded to a distant growl and the lightning mere blinks, the rain had continued to pound the house.

Dad was up early making pancakes and toast. He had a meeting in Boston and would be gone for the day.

Hannah breathed a sigh of relief. *At least I won't have to make up a lie about what Ash and I are up to.*

They ate breakfast in near silence, subdued and tired. Dad left first, and then the girls dressed quickly. They weren't happy about having to go out walking, or riding in Ashley's case. The sky was dark and threatening, more rain was almost guaranteed.

Luck was with them, however, and the rain petered to mist as they were preparing to go their separate ways. Hannah stalled, having difficulty finding the words to say goodbye.

You're being an idiot. It's not like we're going off to war.

Ashley spoke first. "Keep your cell phone handy, all right?"

Hannah nodded, inexplicable tears pooling in her eyes.

"Be careful, Ash, okay? Anything feels wrong, get help, start screaming, dial 9-1-1. Whatever."

Ashley tried to put on her tough-girl face, but it wouldn't cover the concern in her eyes. "They're the ones that need to be careful, whoever *they* are. Right?"

Always the tough one. It made Hannah smile and she instinctively gave Ashley a hug. Without another word, she turned and headed for town, tears slipping down her cheeks as she heard Ash pedal away.

The walk to town was nerve-wracking. Every car that approached was the one from the day before. Every person she didn't recognize was watching her. Every rustle in the bushes by the road was someone following her.

By the time she reached the diner, she was frazzled. She scanned the restaurant but didn't see Jacob, and he would be hard to miss. Hannah walked up and down the length of the diner, looking at the pictures on the wall that made up a mini history of the place. In one, waitresses in short-shorts and roller-skates brought food out to the cars and hung trays on the windows.

She finally sat at a table in the corner and took the side of the booth facing the door so she could watch for Jacob. The waitress came over and she ordered toast and orange juice. She hated spending her babysitting money frivolously, and was still full from Dad's pancakes, but thought she should order something.

The waitress brought her food over and she picked at it, constantly glancing toward the door. The air was stuffy, the fans spinning lazily overhead not doing much to help. The normally welcome scent of bacon and eggs was making her nauseous. Her phone said 9:06 and she was beginning to think that Jacob wouldn't show. Her stomach clenched when she realized whoever was watching her might have somehow found out she'd spoken to Jacob and—

A shadow passed the diner's window and all the bad thoughts that were spinning in Hannah's head disappeared. Jacob stepped into the restaurant and immediately Hannah relaxed. Somehow, this was going to be all right. She stood with a smile and waved him over.

"Miss Hannah, I presume."

He reached a catcher's mitt-sized paw out to shake her hand. Hannah watched her own hand disappear into his, his rough calluses and strong grip giving her assurance.

"Jacob. Pleased to meet you, and thank you for coming."

A smile lit up his face, making him appear much younger than Hannah knew he had to be. She moved to sit but he remained standing, and his smile faded.

"Would you mind if we switched?" He gestured toward the seats. "The Wild Bill Hickok thing."

Hannah had no idea what he was talking about but moved to switch seats with him. The waitress came over and Jacob ordered coffee and a slice of apple pie.

"Never too early for pie, girl. Besides, it's really just a Danish in a different outfit." He winked.

Hannah laughed and watched Jacob's face split into that smile that she was already growing to love.

"What did you mean by the Wild Bill Hickok thing? Wasn't he a cowboy or something?"

Jacob leaned back, the chair groaning beneath him. "Wild Bill was a jack of all trades. Gambler, gunfighter, actor, lawman, he did it all. The story goes that whenever Bill was playing poker, he'd always face the door, keeping his back to the wall. The one day he didn't, he was shot from behind and killed. The poker hand he was holding was two pair: aces and eights. If you ever hear someone referring to a dead man's hand that's what they mean. Not that I think you'll be the poker-playing type, of course."

Hannah pondered his words. Her first thought was that she could sit and listen to him tell stories all day. Her second was that he was afraid of something.

The waitress brought his coffee and pie and Hannah waited until she was out of earshot before speaking. "Big Jake, my dad told me the story his grampie told him about your days on the road crew. Is there anything else you can tell me about the clearing—the one where you found the bones?"

Jacob's face clouded, matching the skies outside. The wrinkles deepened, making him appear ancient. "Hannah, this stuff you're getting into, it's dangerous. I really think we should tell your father."

"I'm already in pretty deep. Dad is going through a tough time since my mom disappeared. He doesn't need anything else to worry about. I want to see it through."

The words were out before she could stop them. Jacob studied her. She watched him spinning what she'd said over in his head. Finally, he nodded.

"Before I say anything more, how much do you already know? Besides the story your daddy told, what else have you heard?"

Hannah recounted everything from Scout finding the foot to their research at the library, the weird behavior of the librarian, and finding the blogger that Ashley was meeting with. Jacob listened while devouring his pie and sipping his coffee.

"Oh, I almost forgot. There's this old lady that lives near me that I went to talk to, Mama Bayole."

Jacob's hand froze in mid-flight as he was about to take another sip of coffee. If he'd looked afraid before, now he was terrified. He placed the cup on the table and Hannah couldn't help but notice the tremors.

"What did you say her name is?" His booming voice was reduced to a gravelly whisper.

"Mama Bayole," Hannah answered.

"That's not possible," Jacob replied.

Hannah waited, her expression imploring him to continue.

"She was in the clearing that day. That was over fifty years ago, and she had to be in her eighties then."

Hannah sat stunned, unsure of how to respond. Jacob looked smaller, his fear somehow diminishing him.

"I told you this was dangerous," he said sternly.

"Dangerous is one thing. This ..." Hannah stammered, unable to express her disbelief.

Or am I this afraid because I do believe?

"Listen, Hannah. It was nice to meet you, but you need to end this. Do you understand?" Frown lines spread across his face like cracks.

Jacob signaled for the waitress and reached for his wallet. Hannah's fear morphed into anger. Kids were missing, dead, and he was just going to walk away?

"You're a chicken," she said, her eyes wide, boring into his. "A big man like you and you're just a scared little rabbit."

Her face burned and her hands trembled, but Hannah's gaze never wavered. She was angry, and the anger of the righteous is something to behold.

"You don't have any idea what you're dealing with, girl." All friendliness was gone from Jacob's voice.

"Then why don't you tell me? At least do that much before you run off with your tail between your legs."

Hannah braced for an angry tirade. Instead, he smiled. It wasn't the grin he'd flashed earlier that could brighten a room, though. It was a sad smile, born of misery and regret. The waitress came over and Jacob surprised Hannah by ordering a refill on his coffee.

"You've got more than a little bit of your great-grampie in you, and that's a compliment."

The waitress came back and filled his mug. He nodded thanks and sighed deeply. He looked tired, old.

"I'll tell you what I know, and what I think. God help me if any harm comes to you because of it. I've already lost one dear friend because of this …"

"You mean Sammy-Five?" Hannah interrupted.

Jacob leaned forward, placed his elbows on the table and put his face in his hands. The table shook and his coffee splashed over the rim of the mug as he rubbed his face.

"Yeah, Sammy-Five. No doubt in my mind he's dead and I'm the reason."

"What about his car and never finding the body?" Hannah asked.

"I'll get to that but let me start at the beginning. The day in the clearing. Your dad told you what he knew, but he didn't know everything. There was more than the altar and the bones. That old witch was there. It was like she'd been waiting for me.

"The really weird thing is ... when I first made it through all those bushes to get to the clearing, I didn't see her. I saw the altar, but it was empty. The air was different, the scent of pine and honeysuckle were gone. It was a stale smell—a *bad* smell, evil. When I looked again, she was there, only it was a *different* she."

Hannah waited for him to continue, not understanding.

"She was lying on the altar, but she was young, beautiful. I couldn't believe my eyes. I thought it must have been the combination of the summer's heat and a long day of mucking out latrines. I walked toward her in kind of a stupor. This happened sixty years ago but I remember it like it was yesterday." He smiled that sad smile again. "Who am I kidding? I have trouble remembering what I did yesterday, but I *do* remember this. A sudden wind tore through the clearing. It was hot and humid that day, and the air wasn't moving, but still that wind came. It ripped leaves off the trees and pulled all the old, dead ones from the ground. They swirled around the woman like a tornado. Then it just stopped, and all those leaves fell back to the ground. There she sat, old and wrinkled and evil."

Hannah understood why he'd left this part of the story out—his friends never would have believed it.

Jacob took another drink of his coffee and continued. "It was then I noticed the ground was littered with bones. There were all these weird figures made from twisted sticks hanging from the trees. Not a single one of those got blown down in the wind. Still, I walked right up to the old lady, as if she were pulling me toward her, reeling me in. I stood in front of her, waiting.

"She looked at me for a good long while before saying anything. Then she asked me if I knew why she'd brought me there. She was close enough that I smelled her breath when she spoke. It was like the air from an open grave. Vile. I just shook my head. My throat was so dry I don't think I could have uttered a word if I'd tried.

"She said, 'You are chosen, Ezekiel Jacob Mather. Chosen to do great things.' I shook my head again. Everything was wrong. How did she know my name? The air around her was shimmering, like when you look down a road on a hot day. There was nothing but silence. No birds, no insects buzzing, nothing. My head was all full of cotton. I knew, somehow, I knew I was on the verge of something irreversible. *Irrevocable.*"

He paused. Hannah watched his eyes, riveted. He was back there, in the clearing, reliving that day. She licked her lips, wanting him to go on but *not* wanting him to.

"I grew up poor. That's why I lied about my age to get on that crew. My folks were about to lose their house. The money I made helped them hang onto it. There were no fancy birthday or Christmas presents growing up. The year I made my First Communion, my folks gave me a small silver cross, and I thought of it like treasure. I wore it everywhere.

"When that old witch reached out to touch me, I pulled that cross out and held it in front of me. I don't even remember thinking about it, I just did it. She flew backwards against the altar. I didn't wait around to see what would happen next. I turned and ran, tore through those bushes, ignoring the cuts and scrapes I felt. You can bet I held onto that cross.

"I heard the old lady laughing as I was crashing through the brush. I ran until I found my way back to the rest of the crew, the old witch's laughter in my head the whole way. I still hear it sometimes, when I'm feeling low. Like she still wants something from me. But I didn't really think she was still alive."

He put his head down but not before Hannah saw tears in his eyes. He reached up to his collar and pulled on the silver chain around his neck, fingering the small cross that hung there.

"Wait, how do you know it was Mama Bayole? Did she tell you?"

Jacob looked exhausted. The story had physically worn him out. His face was haggard, his eyes sinking into their sockets.

"She never told me, not with words, but there were things in my head after that day, things she put there. Her name was one of them."

Hannah thought back to her visit to Mama Bayole's farmhouse. *What would have happened if I had lain on that couch?*

"You keep calling her an old witch. Is that what she is?" Hannah already knew the answer.

"I'm sure of it. I've never been more sure of anything in my life."

"What about Sammy-Five? Dad said you ... you went back there, to the clearing?"

An expression of such deep sorrow and remorse crossed Jacob's face that Hannah had to look away.

"Yeah, I went back, and Sammy paid the dues for my bad judgment. It was like I had to go back, had to find that place. That *godless* place. Something else I think she put in my head. I resisted most times, but I realized too late that alcohol made it harder ... it weakened my resistance. That night Sammy and I drank too much, and she had me."

Tears spilled freely down his face and splashed onto the table like raindrops. Hannah's heart broke for him.

"We went into those woods and I managed to find the spot. We wriggled through those bushes and brambles and into the clearing. It was just like I remembered it. The same stink of evil, the same unearthly quiet, all the bones and those stick dolls.

"And her. Sitting on the altar. It scared me sober just seeing her. I grabbed hold of my cross and I swear it was warm between my fingers. I believe the power of the Holy Spirit was flowing through that cross, protecting me. It wasn't enough to protect Sammy, though. I was bigger and stronger than him, but I couldn't drag him out of there. The whole time that ... witch ... she just laughed.

"I left him there, Hannah. Left him with her. When I pushed through the brush to get out of there, I heard noises ... I heard ..."

Jacob stood suddenly. His hands were balled into tight fists. He was breathing hard and sweating. Hannah thought he might be having a heart attack. He threw a twenty on the table.

"Let's finish this outside, I need some fresh air."

He didn't wait for a reply, just walked out. Hannah followed. They ended up at the gazebo. The day had started brightening, the clouds thinning to reveal patches of blue as the sun struggled to make an appearance.

"I think she took him, took his *soul*. I don't remember much after that. I think I got lost in the woods, or maybe I passed out for a while. Next thing I know it's getting dark and I'm back at the car. Sammy comes stumbling out of the woods some time later looking like death on toast. He was shaking and his shirt was covered with vomit. He wouldn't speak to me.

"I drove him home and he was never the same. Took to drinking day and night, got kicked off the crew. I tried to talk to him, tried to get through to him. I even brought a priest to his house. By that time, I had vowed to never drink again and given myself to God. I knew that was the only way to keep her from getting me.

"Father Paul and me went to Sammy's place. He wouldn't answer the door, but I knew he was there. I broke the lock and we went in. The place stunk—there was rotten food everywhere and spilled booze and ... there was puke all over the place. Even through all that stench, it was evil I smelled. Sammy was in bed, just lying there, eyes open.

"We tried to talk to him, but he would just mumble occasionally. Not to us, but like he was having an entirely different conversation with someone else. I knew it was her. Father Paul, he sensed it too. He began to pray over Sammy. He splashed holy water on him, and Sammy screamed like it was acid. Father Paul kept at it.

"It wasn't an exorcism, not exactly, but it was in the same neighborhood, I guess. It went on for hours. Finally, Sammy started sweating like I had never seen a man sweat. It was pouring out of him in rivers, I swear. And the stench." Jacob shook his head. "His clothes were soaked through and he was screaming, all the while Father Paul was praying and splashing holy water.

"Sammy arched his back so just his head and heels were touching the bed. It was just like in the movies. I was terrified but couldn't move, couldn't turn away. Then he went limp and collapsed back onto the bed. He woke up a few minutes later, smiled, and asked us when we'd got there.

"Father Paul left him with a set of rosaries and a crucifix. We planned to go back the next day. When we got there, his car was gone. You know the rest, they never found him."

Hannah stood and walked to the railing of the gazebo. The sights and sounds of summer surrounded them. Two kids she recognized from school tossed a Frisbee back and forth. Families with toddlers laughed at the playground, while some teenagers played basketball and tennis on the courts. Hannah longed for the normalcy of it.

"What do you think happened to him?" she whispered.

"On good days, I think he took those beads and the cross and kept them with him and he burned that car so she'd think he was dead." He smiled wistfully, then stood and joined her at the railing. "I picture him somewhere nice, maybe near a beach, a bunch of grandkids running around. Him in an old lounge chair, watching it all, holding those rosaries and never, ever thinking of that day in the clearing."

Jacob was crying again, and Hannah reached out and placed a hand on his arm.

"And on bad days?" Hannah whispered.

He bit his lower lip and his body hitched with sobs. It took a minute for him to get control of himself.

"I think she got him."

"After Sammy came out of the woods that day, I never took another sip of alcohol. I devoted my life to the church because I believe it was the cross that saved me. The power behind the cross, I mean. Maybe it was a selfish reason, but I think, I *hope* I did a lot of good over the years. Even still, sometimes she calls me."

Hannah rested her small hand on the big man's arm and gave it a squeeze. "I'm sure you do a lot of great work."

Jacob patted her hand and tried to smile. He looked so old, so beaten.

"Jacob, I don't know what to do next."

"I'm scared for you. That old witch, living just down the road from you. She already tried to get you once."

Hannah turned and slouched against the gazebo railing. She'd come looking for answers, looking for something that would make everything better. Instead, she was burdened with such a sense of hopelessness she didn't know what to say or do.

"I think I need to go to the police, but the blogger said some of the people in this thing are the police," she said. "What is it, a cult of some sort?"

"I don't know what it is, Hannah, but that old witch oversees it. I don't think it's entirely natural," Jacob replied.

Hannah realized he had never said Mama Bayole's name, as if saying it aloud would give her more power. She also realized he was trying to bring up the one thing we hadn't talked about yet.

He continued, "Because there's no way the old lady you encountered is the same one I did, unless ..."

"Yeah, unless." Hannah nodded. Unless she really was a witch or was somehow using the sacrifices to live longer. She refused to say it aloud.

She looked out over the park again, searching for an answer somewhere in the brightening day. *Was it possible one or more of the people at the park had something to do with this? Was one of them watching me and Jacob right now?*

At that moment, the sun burst through a break in the clouds, bathing everything in a glorious light, but Hannah went cold and she felt the color drain from her face. Jacob noticed and went to one knee to look into her eyes. For a bizarre second, Hannah thought he was going to propose.

"Hannah, what is it?"

"Ashley," she managed to squeak, unable to get enough air to speak.

"Calm down, girl. Breathe. That's it. What about Ashley?"

Everything around Hannah was starting to go gray until her entire scope of vision was Jacob's worried face.

"Ashley ... She went ... to meet the blogger. What if ..."

Jacob stood with a slight groan and put his arm around her, leading her to the steps of the gazebo.

"Tell me where she went, we'll go get her," Jacob said, the strength returning to his voice.

CHAPTER TWELVE

Ashley pedaled along the winding country road, trying to keep her eyes everywhere at the same time. On two occasions, she almost rode right off the road and down an embankment. Each time she heard a car approach from either direction, she found a safe spot to pull over and let it pass, studying the car and driver as it went, searching for anything suspicious. It would be easy for someone to, well, to do whatever they wanted on this lonesome stretch between two small New Hampshire towns.

Maybe I'm not cut out for this shit.

She arrived safely, but mentally strained. As she locked Hannah's bike to the rack, she rotated her head to relieve the stiffness in her neck and shoulders. It wasn't from the bike ride—she could make that ride in her sleep—it was stress. A dull throb ebbed in her temples, the result of her clenching her teeth. The sheen of sweat wasn't the healthy sweat of physical exertion—it was the rancid sweat brought on by fear.

With a final look around, she went into the library. She

checked her phone but had no messages and she was a few minutes early. She found a display of new releases and randomly grabbed a couple of books to distract her while she waited. One last look at her phone—she remembered to mute it—and she made her way to one of the tables in the center of the room as instructed. The library was sparsely populated compared to the day before.

She took a seat, flipped open one of the books, and stared at nothing, waiting.

The main door opened, then closed slowly with a heavy click. Ashley resisted the urge to turn and see who came in.

It's him, you know it's him. She had no idea how much time had passed since she'd sat.

"Ashley?"

The voice was barely a whisper—she learned nothing from it. She nodded. The chair next to her scraped on the waxed floor. Her heart had grown wings and was fluttering madly in the cage of her chest, trying to escape. She bit her lower lip and turned to face him.

That's it?

She suppressed a lunatic giggle. The man beside her was as average as a man could be, straight out of central casting for a middle-aged white guy. Relief coursed through her. She didn't know what she'd been expecting, but it wasn't this.

"Hi. I'm glad you decided to meet me." She smiled at him, but he didn't return it. He just stared. "Anyway," she stammered, "I thought we'd start off by comparing notes—"

He cut her off. "I don't want this to take long, okay? I just need you to tell me where you found the foot."

Get out! Run!

The thought exploded in her head. One minute she was processing his statement, the next minute every alarm in her body was going off. The relief she'd felt only moments ago was gone, replaced with throat-closing panic. She fidgeted for a few seconds, trying to focus on anything but her rising fear, trying to calm down. She flipped closed the book that was on the table, knocking it to the floor with a crash that sounded like an explosion in the quiet of the library.

A flash of anger crossed the blogger's face, then he bent to retrieve the book. Ashley grabbed her phone, and her fingers flew across the touchscreen. She opened one app, then quickly switched to the camera. She tapped the button rapid-fire, taking a few pictures of the blogger as he was sat back up with the book in his hand. She put the camera on the table and flipped the cover of the second book open to hide it just as the blogger turned to her.

She took the book from him and placed it on the table mouthing a silent apology. "Listen, I've been thinking, maybe we should just call the police—"

"No. At least one of them is a cop. We go to the police and we might be the next bodies buried in the woods." His voice had risen above a whisper to a shrill hiss.

Ashley swallowed, her mind spinning. "What is your name? I—"

"No names." His voice was loud. He stopped, looking around. When he spoke again it was in a whisper but somehow more menacing than a scream.

"No names, I already told you that. You haven't been paying attention at all, have you?"

Ashley's eyes darted across the table, sure her phone wasn't visible, sticking out from the corner of the book cover. Of course it wasn't.

"I told you my name," she said softly, afraid to provoke him.

The muscles on the sides of his jaw bulged and his lips tightened to hard slash. "I'm done playing games with you."

Ashley stood. "I'm leaving—"

But she didn't. His next words froze her, the muscles in her legs turning to stone.

"We have Hannah."

CHAPTER THIRTEEN

"West Meadow Library." Hannah replied. She still felt lightheaded, disconnected from the events, a spectator watching the story play out.

They crossed the park, heading back toward the diner. Jacob stopped beside a mammoth boat of a car and pulled out a set of keys. Despite Hannah's fear, she couldn't help staring at the car with a bemused expression.

"You could start gathering animals two by two," she said, glancing up at him.

Jacob stopped, key poised over the lock, then erupted in a booming laughter. Hannah was helpless but to laugh along with him.

"You're all right, girl, and you're gonna *be* all right."

Somehow, the shared laugh and Jacob's words brought her back.

He opened the door for her, and Hannah tumbled into the enormous front seat. With the gait of a much younger man,

Jacob went around to the driver's side and climbed in, rocking the car on its springs. The engine started with a roar and they pulled out, heading toward West Meadow. Hannah kept turning around, watching for any sign that we were being followed but saw nothing.

"You know I have a rearview mirror, right?" Jacob said with a grin.

Hannah offered a sheepish grin of her own and shrugged. She knew she was overreacting, but that didn't stop her from calling Ashley's cell every few minutes. Ashley didn't pick up.

She's at the library, probably getting a lot of good information from the mysterious blogger.

It was no use—nothing was going to calm Hannah down until she saw Ashley with her own two eyes. She felt Jacob glancing at her but kept her gaze on the road, trusting him to use the mirror to make sure they weren't being followed.

They turned onto Maple Street and Hannah saw the library. She craned her neck to get a better view of the area next to the granite steps where she knew the bike rack was. *It's there!* It was chained to the rack. The sense of relief was overwhelming.

"That's my bike," Hannah said, her voice shrill and panicky. "She's here, she's okay."

"That's good," Jacob replied, his own voice steeped with relief. "That's real good."

Jacob parked the car and Hannah bounded out, nearly falling. She ran toward the door, not waiting for Jacob. Once inside, she breathed in the smell but didn't savor it the way she normally would. She glanced at the center table but didn't see Ashley. Walking as calmly as her buzzing nerves allowed, she searched the rows for her friend. The door opened and closed,

Jacob had entered the library.

Hannah reached the far end of the library, crossed to the opposite side, and started looking through those rows. As she came full circle to the front doors, dread wrapped her in its embrace. Her chest tightened and she darted her eyes back and forth, trying to search the library again. Jacob was standing by the librarian's desk. He turned his palms upward with a shrug, then engaged the librarian in conversation. Hannah went to the middle table where she noticed there were open books, and something else.

With trembling hands, she picked up the cell phone, seeing all the missed calls on the screen. Ashley's phone never left her hand. Hannah's heart rate doubled, tripled. She leaned against the table. Her mind reeled back to a day she'd found a baby rabbit in the woods. It had been just lying on the trail, listless, hadn't even tried to hop away when Scout had nudged it with his snout. She'd picked it up in her cupped hands and felt its tiny heart beating so fast Hannah thought it would surely burst. That's how her own heart was beating now.

The restroom! She grabbed onto the thought like a lifeline and searched the library to find it. When she did, she threw open the door. The room was empty. Fighting back panic and unable to stop the flow of tears, she went back out and joined Jacob at the desk.

His expression told her everything she needed to know. Ashley was gone. Hannah's world pitched like the deck of a ship in turbulent waters. Jacob thanked the librarian, then took Hannah by the arm and led her outside.

"Hannah, you need to pull yourself together."

She heard the words but couldn't quite grasp their meaning.

She kept her hand protectively on Ashley's cell phone, as if it were a link to her. Hannah's eyes were locked on her bike. Without saying a thing, she went to the rack and spun the combination lock. It took her a couple of tries—it was hard to see the numbers through her tears. Jacob helped her put the bike in his trunk, and then they got into the car.

She turned in her seat, willing Ashley to be standing on the library steps as Jacob pulled away.

CHAPTER FOURTEEN

Hannah sat in the living room, her eyes bouncing back and forth between Dad and Jacob. The tension was a physical thing, making the air heavy and oppressive. They'd told Dad everything, taking turns spilling out parts of the story. He was angry and worried—his first instinct had been to call the police. Hannah, with a lot of help from Jacob, was able to talk him out of it. At least for the moment.

Dad ran his fingers through his hair and paced the small room. "This is unbelievable. A young girl, a girl I'm supposed to be responsible for, is missing. Give me one good reason not to call the police."

Hannah looked at Jacob. *He's not going to answer and incur the wrath of Dad.* "According to the blogger—"

Dad cut Hannah off, hands raised in exasperation. "The blogger might be the one that has her. Of course, he doesn't want the police involved."

Jacob spoke up, "Brian, I think—"

"And you!" He whirled to face Jacob. "I can't believe you would be willing to put these girls in harm's way. What were you thinking?"

Jacob leaned forward, cupping his chin. Hannah stood and put a hand on the big man's shoulder.

She leveled her gaze at Dad, putting on her most adult expression. "I know you're upset but this isn't helping Ashley. I dragged Jacob into this looking for help."

Dad's face crumbled. His shoulders slumped and he staggered to the couch. His next words were almost inaudible. "Why didn't you come to me for help?"

Hannah's heart cracked. The desperate emptiness in his tone brought a wave of despair over her. She couldn't speak.

"Brian," Jacob said softly, "kids don't always want to go to their parents."

Dad silenced him with a glare.

"I'm sorry," Hannah whispered. "You're right. I should have come to you. I just … things were finally starting to get back to normal."

Dad winced, then wrapped Hannah in a hug.

"I know, Hannah, I know. I just realized I'm more upset with myself than with you. If I had been there for you, you *would* have come to me."

He let her go and the three looked at each other for a long moment.

Jacob broke the silence. "Hannah, I think your father is right. We need to involve the police. Every second we waste might make it harder to find her. I don't doubt some of them are involved in this thing, but what choice do we have? We can't find her ourselves."

Despite her initial misgivings, Hannah *would* feel a lot better knowing the police were looking for Ash.

"Thank you, Jacob." Dad breathed. "Now we're talking sense."

"Before you call, there's one more thing," Hannah said.

Jacob flashed her a look, but she ignored it.

"We think Mama Bayole might have something to do with this."

Hannah quickly filled in the parts of the story Jacob had left out, as well as what had really happened when she went to talk to the old woman. Dad was incredulous.

"You two ... you don't really believe it's the same person? She's an old lady, harmless ..."

Jacob stood, rising like a mountain out of the chair. He straightened his shoulders and met Dad's gaze.

"I have no doubt it's the same woman and she is *not* just an old lady. You are free to believe what you want to believe, but I have seen her power firsthand. Whatever you do, don't underestimate her, Brian." His booming voice was that of a street corner preacher.

Dad shook his head and ran his fingers through his hair. "And what do you propose I tell the police? How can I tie Mrs. Bayole to any of this without sounding like a complete lunatic?"

Dad had a point, but Hannah's heart swelled just knowing he was *trying* to believe her. All they really had was the blogger—nothing pointed to Mama Bayole except Jacob's story and the weird incident Hannah had at her house. The police weren't going to listen to either of those.

"The foot," Hannah blurted.

Dad and Jacob stared at her, waiting.

"We show them where I found the foot. It's close enough to Mama Bayole's property that they'll have to question her."

Jacob and Dad exchanged a glance and they both shrugged. Dad reached for the phone.

"It's as good a plan as any," Jacob said. He didn't sound very hopeful, and he was back to absently playing with the cross. Dad was speaking quietly into the phone, constantly running a hand through his hair. Hannah was biting her nails, something she hadn't done since Mom disappeared.

"They're sending an officer over now," Dad said as he hung up the phone.

Hannah remembered she had Ashley's cell and pulled it out, figuring the police would want it. She sat on the couch and clicked on PHOTOS, knowing most were probably of the two of them. Her eyes widened when she saw the first picture. Her thumb flew across the screen, scrolling through the next few.

"Dad. Jacob. You have to see this," she breathed.

She brought the phone over and showed them the photos Ashley had taken that day at the library. Whether just to document the meeting or because she'd suspected something was wrong, Ashley had managed to get several pictures of the blogger. It was clear that he hadn't known she was doing it based on the odd angles. Some only had a portion of his face in the frame but others were better. Good enough to give to the police.

He looked to be in his forties, longish brown hair, a few days of beard growth. Nothing remarkable.

Hannah had another idea. She clicked on Ashley's email but there was nothing there. No unsent text messages either. Then she saw the icon for voice recordings.

She opened the app and there was a new recording from

earlier in the day. She looked up at Dad and Jacob. Their faces each held a pain Hannah recognized. She felt the same raw ache in her heart. In the distance, the sound of approaching sirens.

Dad motioned with his hand. "Go ahead, Hannah. Play it. Before they get here."

She pressed PLAY.

> Ashley: Listen, I've been thinking, maybe we should just call the police—
>
> Male Voice: No. At least one of them is a cop. We go to the police and we might be the next bodies buried in the woods.
>
> Ashley: What is your name? I—
>
> Male Voice: No names. No names, I already told you that. You haven't been paying attention at all, have you.
>
> Ashley: I told you my name.
>
> Male Voice: I'm done playing games with you.
>
> Ashley: I'm leaving—
>
> Male Voice: We have Hannah.

There was a long pause. Hannah thought the recording was over but saw on the timer display there was more. Finally, Ashley spoke.

THE CLEARING

Ashley: Bullshit.

Male Voice: We got her before she even got to town.

Ashley: What ... what do you want?

Male Voice: We just need to know where you found the ... foot ... so we can dispose of it properly.

Ashley: That's all?

Male Voice: That's all. That happened a long time ago. No need to dig up the past. Pardon the pun.

Ashley: You promise if I show you where the foot is you'll let me go? You'll let Hannah go?

Male Voice: Of course. You were just insurance for each other. Neither of you would have helped unless it was to save the other. Make no mistake— if you try anything funny, Hannah will be as gone as her mother.

Ashley: Okay, just don't hurt us. If we go now, we can be at the spot in the woods by noon. Then Hannah and I can be back at her house by one, before her dad gets home and starts to worry.

They heard papers rustling and chairs scraping, then silence.

It took Hannah three tries to close the app her hand was trembling so badly.

"It's almost one o'clock now," she said. "They might still be out there."

She jumped up and headed for the door just as a police car pulled up out front.

"Hannah, wait. We have to tell the police." Dad's voice was hoarse.

As her dad went to open the door and greet the officer, Hannah raced toward the back door with Scout at her heels.

Fueled by adrenaline and instinct, she gave no thought to whether Dad or the police would follow, or what the consequences might be if they didn't. She was energy and willpower, running faster than she thought possible. She'd already passed the edge of the yard and was entering the woods when she heard the *thwack* of the screen door behind her. She barely registered Dad's shouts.

Hannah darted into the trees, following a path she had forged over the years, veering around thickets and leaping over fallen logs, never slowing. The only sounds were those of her breathing, her pulse in her ears, and Scout scrambling to keep up.

She bounded up a small hill, almost slipping when she crested it and began running down the other side. She approached an outcrop of rocks, one of the countless formations that gave the state its nickname. Hannah finally stopped and leaned over, hands on her knees, trying to catch her breath. Scout plopped to the ground next to her, panting.

The forest was eerily quiet. The pine trees that surrounded her barely whispered in the occasional breeze. She moved around some rocks near a large pine tree and pushed aside a small pile of branches. The foot was gone.

Hannah scrambled around frantically, first making sure she was in the right spot, then looking for signs that an animal might have dragged it away.

A few minutes later, she heard approaching footsteps and Dad calling her name. It broke her heart how panicked his voice was. She yelled to him, signaling her location. He stumbled down the hill and knelt by her, grasping her in a fierce hug. A police officer followed a few seconds later as Hannah got to her feet.

"Just … what the heck … is the meaning of this?" The cop was red-faced, breathing hard. And he was not happy.

"Officer, I told you, Ashley Wallace is missing." Dad replied.

The officer held up his hand, giving Dad a stern look. "Let's slow down a minute, please. My name is Officer Benson. You're Brian Green. Who are you, Miss?"

"Hannah Green," she answered. All the fight was out of her, the adrenaline rush spent, and her spirit crushed at the significance of the foot being gone. They were too late. Ashley was gone, too.

Just like Mom.

"All right, Hannah. Your dad told me during our little jog through the woods that your friend has gone missing. We're going to find her—that I promise you. You need to help me, okay?"

Something in the man's earnest tone gave Hannah a spark of hope, and she looked up at him for the first time. He was about Dad's age but bigger, like a football player. He removed his hat to reveal a military-style buzz cut. Mom had once told her the old saying "the eyes are the window to the soul" and Hannah believed it. This man's eyes spoke of honor and conviction. She trusted him instantly and nodded in agreement.

"Atta girl. We'll get to the beginning of the story eventually, but why don't we start with the reason you think she's out here?"

Hannah realized she'd left Ashley's phone back at the house.

"It was on the recording. The man that took her made her show him where the foot was, but it's gone." She motioned to the pile of pine boughs when something caught her eye.

"What recording? Did you say a foot?" Benson said, looking from Hannah to Brian.

Hannah ignored him and went to the tree, bending down, unable to believe what she was looking at. She picked Ashley's necklace off one of the branches and held it out to Officer Benson.

"I gave this to her for her eleventh birthday. She was here." Hannah broke down, sobbing and falling into her father's arms.

Dad held her, telling her it was going to be okay and that they would find Ashley.

"I think she's at Mama Bayole's, Officer Benson. We have to go there. Right now."

She pulled away from Dad, swatted the tears from her face, and started back toward the path. Officer Benson stepped in her way.

"Whoa, whoa, whoa. Just a minute, Hannah. I'd said we'd find her but I'm not a mind-reader and you're not making a lot of sense right now."

Hannah's eyes narrowed and her lips tightened. She watched a lot of crime shows—she knew how quickly the trail went cold in kidnapping cases.

"We might not *have* a minute." She said more calmly than she felt. "We need to get to Mama Bayole's. Are you coming?"

Hannah stared him down, satisfaction coursing through her when she saw the corners of his lips twitch in a near-smile. More important, his expression also held something that might have been respect. He stepped aside and waved his hand with a flourish that would have been comical in another situation.

"Lead the way."

As they made their way back to the house, Hannah told Officer Benson the short version of everything that had taken place since Scout had dragged the foot out of the woods. He was trying to take notes while they walked. It wasn't going well. She smiled inwardly thinking of the chicken scratch he would have to decipher later for his report.

They got to the house and were surprised to find Jacob gone. Hannah went to the living room to let Officer Benson listen to the recording but couldn't find Ashley's phone.

"Dad, did you or Jacob grab the phone?"

Hannah remembered dropping it on the couch after they'd listened to it. She quickly searched under the cushions and bent to look under the couch itself, but it was gone.

"Jacob must have taken it. I wonder why he left," Dad said. He sounded casual but his face was tense. "Let's go, we can figure it out later."

"Okay, folks, let's go visit Mrs. Bayole and I'll call this in." Officer Benson sounded more authoritative when he wasn't gasping for breath.

They followed Benson out to his cruiser, and he opened the doors to let them in, Dad in front and Hannah in back. She had never been in a police car before, and she looked around in uneasy wonder. Benson got in the driver's seat, flipped on the bubble lights and gunned the engine, peeling out in the direction of Mama Bayole's farm.

They arrived at the farm moments later. Hannah's stomach clenched just thinking about going back into that house.

I can do it for Ashley.

Benson and Dad climbed out and Hannah realized she couldn't open the doors from the inside. Electric panic paralyzed her, and she didn't breathe until Benson let her out. It was too much like being trapped, and she wondered if Ashley was feeling that way, wherever she was.

"Now listen, folks, you need to let me do the talking. We are not going to go in there and start throwing out accusations, are we clear?" Benson was fully in charge now.

Brian and Hannah nodded in unison and they started up the dusty driveway. Before they got to the porch, the screen door screeched open, and Mama Bayole stepped onto the porch.

The old witch, it's like she was waiting for us.

Hannah's chest tightened. She'd read about the Salem Witch Trials and how Giles Corey had been pressed to death. *More weight.* The memory of almost walking zombie-like to that couch chilled her. She shook the thought away.

"Lookie here, now. Miss Hannah, Mr. Green, and Hopeland's finest. Isn't this a day!"

Her voice made Hannah's jaw tighten. Fingernails on a blackboard, Mom would have said.

"Afternoon, Mrs. Bayole. Mind if we visit for a few

minutes?"

Hannah noticed Officer Benson's tone had changed dramatically. He was speaking with a down home inflection, no doubt trying to appeal to Mama Bayole's simple lifestyle.

"Well, I was fixin' to have tea and crumpets with the queen of England, but I reckon we can set a spell." She cackled at her own wit, sending a ripple of anger through Hannah. The old woman was playing the same game as Benson, only her part was the helpless old redneck lady.

She waved the trio up to the porch and hobbled over to one of the rocking chairs. Hannah watched as Dad and Benson walked up the rickety stairs, expecting them to fall through to who-knows-where. Hannah followed, the memory of her last visit still heavy on her mind. After talking with Jacob, she knew the old woman was someone to fear.

When they were all seated, Mama Bayole smiled at Officer Benson. "Well, you're not here for my moonshine recipe, so am I under arrest?"

The old woman's gaze shifted to Hannah and they locked eyes. Mama Bayole's look was somehow penetrating and empty at the same time.

She has no soul.

The thought came unbidden, jarring Hannah. Still, she refused to lower her eyes.

Benson offered a friendly smile. "We're looking for a girl, Ashley Wallace. She's staying with the Greens while her folks are away, and we seem to have misplaced her."

"Lordy," Mama Bayole cackled, "why would some little white girl come over to old Mama Bayole?"

"Nobody said she was white," Hannah said quickly, harshly.

"*I'm* white, and I came over the other day, remember?"

Did I just say that? Hannah's words carried equal amounts of righteousness and bitterness. Despite her fluttering heart, she held Mama Bayole's stare.

"Sure, I remember you, girl. You were *so* tired that day, yes, you was. Looked like you was gonna just lay yo' head down and close those pretty eyes. See you feeling better?" She regarded Hannah with a knowing look.

Benson spoke up, "Mrs. Bayole, have you seen Ashley Wallace?"

Mama Bayole pulled her eyes from me and smiled again at Officer Benson. "No, sir. Ain't seen no one until you folks. I'll be sure ta keep an eye out."

Officer Benson stood and tucked his notebook back in his front shirt pocket. "Actually, I was thinking we might look around?" He motioned to the appliance graveyard on her lawn. "Lots of places for a kid to hide, if she had a mind to. I'm sure a respectable farm like this has some outbuildings—a barn, or some sheds? Maybe we could just, you know, walk around, call her name?"

Mama Bayole struggled to her feet, placing a hand on the small of her back. Hannah couldn't help but think it was exaggerated. "You can go ahead and play hide-a-seek, sure thing. I'll go fix some iced tea and when you finish, you can come in and wet your whistle, look around the farmhouse too. I don't get many visitors and it would do an old lady some good ta entertain proper."

Officer Benson tipped his cap and said that would be fine. They left the porch and watched Mama Bayole retreat into the house.

Hannah followed Officer Benson and Dad around to the back of the property. A handful of chickens scattered when they rounded the corner, squawking at the disturbance. Hannah spotted a barn, a small chicken coop, and two sheds.

"Let's check the barn first. Everybody stay together, and nobody touches anything. Clear?" Benson's tone left no room for debate.

They nodded and crossed the tangled crabgrass that made up the yard. The two-story barn was an eyesore and probably a safety hazard. The door hung on rust-worn, broken hinges and the clapboard was rotted through in several places. The swayback roof looked one New Hampshire winter away from collapse.

They started around the outside perimeter of the building, seeing nothing more interesting than the remains of a tractor and some farming equipment that belonged in a museum. They arrived at the front of the barn, and Hannah glanced at the farmhouse. A curtain twitched in one of the downstairs windows—Mama Bayole was watching their every move.

They stepped over the threshold into the barn, pausing to allow eyes to adjust to the dim light. The whispery flutter of wings above them meant swallows were roosting in the old building.

The inside of the barn was in worse shape than the exterior. Hannah gagged at the reek of stale hay and rotten wood. One entire side was just the remains of horse stalls in various states of disrepair, from broken fencing to complete collapse. The other was a maze of junk stacked floor to ceiling.

They wound their way carefully through decades' worth of old furniture, boxes, saddles and other riding gear, and just about anything else a person could own and dispose of. One wrong move would send the entire contents of the barn tumbling down around them like dominos.

Nobody spoke until they had gone up and down each row, returning to the center of the barn. They congregated around a rickety wooden ladder that led to what used to be a hay loft, she assumed.

Benson looked up for a long moment and sighed. "I guess it's me."

He stepped toward the ladder and placed a foot on the first rung. The crack of the wood snapping echoed through the empty building, sending the swallows into a frenzy. Hannah put a hand on Benson's arm.

"Let me go, I'm way lighter."

Benson looked at the broken rung, then at Dad, who nodded.

Benson turned to her. "Be careful, understand?"

She took the flashlight from Benson and without thinking about it, stepped over the broken rung and began climbing. She kept as close to the edge of each rung as possible, knowing they would be weaker in the middle. Splinters burrowed into her hands as she climbed. The wood under her feet was spongey and with each step, she pictured her body plunging to the barn floor below. Thinking of Ashley, alone and afraid, was all she needed to keep going.

At the top, she scrambled to the relative safety of the plywood floor. She again heard the flapping of wings but didn't see any birds. Hannah wondered if the sound had been bats all along.

Random shafts of light crisscrossed the loft through holes in the walls and roof, a frenzy of dust danced crazily in each one.

She clicked on the flashlight and shone it on the floor, checking to see if the boards looked strong enough to walk on.

"Everything okay, honey?" Dad called from below.

Hannah jumped and nearly stumbled backward through the opening.

"So far, so good," she hollered down.

The air was thicker up here, oppressive in its heat. The stench of rotten hay and something else, some underlying foul smell Hannah couldn't identify, made it hard to breathe.

Death.

She shone the flashlight around but quickly realized there was nothing to see.

Decomposed hay and bird crap littered the floor, some old ropes and pulleys hung from the support beams, and birds' nests crouched in every rafter. There was nowhere to hide.

"I'm coming down!"

At the bottom of the ladder, she jumped to the barn floor. She handed the flashlight back to Officer Benson and wiped her hands on her shirt.

"Nothing up there but a lot of old hay and even more birds' nests."

She followed the others out of the barn, blinking at the brightness of the day. They made their way to the first shed and it only took a few minutes to realize it was another dead end. It looked to be only about ten feet by ten feet and was filled with run-of-the-mill farm and garden tools—rakes of all sizes, shovels, a wheelbarrow with no wheel, and a few deadly looking sickles hanging on the walls.

The next shed was larger and newer. It had a ramp leading up to the door and a recent model tractor inside. Oddly, there was also what looked like a souped-up golf cart. Work gloves hung neatly on pegs and more tools lined the walls, mostly saws, axes and a shiny new chainsaw that chilled Hannah, bringing memories of too many horror movies she'd watched with Ashley.

As if reading her mind, Benson said, "It looks like a horror movie starter kit in here."

They laughed. Hannah knew the laughter was forced, a nervous reaction. *Whistling past the graveyard.* All her mother's old sayings were coming back to life.

They made a cursory check of the chicken coop, but it too was in such disrepair that there was nowhere to hide a single chicken, much less Ashley Wallace. Benson stopped on the way to the back porch. Hannah followed his gaze to a ramshackle bulkhead off the back corner.

They walked gingerly up the stairs one at a time, afraid their combined weight would be too much for the decaying wood. Mama Bayole waved them into the house from the back door.

Hannah hesitated. *What if she casts her spell on all three of us once we go in?*

Dad held the door, giving her a questioning look until she followed.

Once inside, Hannah immediately became lightheaded. She was psyching herself out and struggling to stay calm. Mama Bayole ushered them into the small kitchen and motioned for them to sit. The table and chairs were straight out of every seventies sitcom she'd watched with her dad. Stainless steel legs with yellow vinyl seat covers and the tabletop was some sort of Formica variant popular back then. The cabinets were plain wood, thick with coat after coat of paint. Plates filled the sink and flies buzzed around a cat's dish on the floor. There was no cat in sight. She watched the flies land on the side of the bowl, then take flight again, their somnolent hum too loud. She dragged her gaze away and shook her head to clear it.

Mama Bayole brought over a pitcher of iced tea and four glasses, eyeing Hannah with that cunning gaze. She filled each glass then sat at the table.

"Did you find that po' white girl out there?"

Her tone was mocking, and anger replaced Hannah's anxiety. Officer Benson spoke before she had a chance.

"No, ma'am. If we haven't already put you out too much, would you mind if we looked around the house a bit? We can't without your permission, of course, so please don't feel like you have to."

Mama Bayole waved dismissively at Benson. "Oh, go on. What's an old woman like me got to hide? You think I'm smuggling dirty magazines or something?"

Benson obliged with a laugh and stood. Hannah noticed he hadn't drunk a sip of his iced tea, none of them had.

We're waiting for her to drink first.

Dad followed Benson to the living room. The house was small and the hallway narrow. Claustrophobic. It took no more than a few minutes to confirm the house was empty.

"Where's the door to the cellar?"

Benson's tone was casual, but Hannah detected a note of suspicion.

"Basement's been closed off since I bought the place. The wood stove heats the place fine in the winter and the last owner moved the fuse box up to the front closet and the water heater too."

"What about the bulkhead?"

Benson was in full cop mode now. He sensed, like Hannah did, that something was off about the old woman's story.

Mama Bayole began laughing—a grating, cackling sound that set Hannah's teeth on edge.

"You go 'head and try that ole bulkhead. If you can even get the doors to pull, the spiders 'ill get you."

Benson smiled but there was no humor in it. His eyes remained deadly serious. He'd caught a scent and was going to follow it. "Well, that sounds like a challenge, Mrs. Bayole. I think I might just go do battle with those spiders."

Mama Bayole's laugh dried up and her eyes narrowed. "Don't say I didn't warn ya." Her tone was flat, humorless. Almost threatening.

Hannah and her dad followed Benson out the back door and down the listing steps. Hannah didn't know if Mama Bayole was lying about the cellar or not, but she was certainly telling the truth about the bulkhead.

The wood was splintered and rotting, the paint faded to an unrecognizable color. The hinges and handle were nothing but rust. She didn't doubt spiders would be there if they were able to budge the door.

Benson reached down and yanked the handle, stumbling backward when it snapped off in his hand. He caught his balance before taking a comical fall on his butt, and Hannah was a little disappointed. She faked a cough to cover her smirk.

He stepped back up to the bulkhead and wedged his hands under the lopsided door. Dad moved in next to him and did the same. Benson counted three and they pulled.

The door came away from the frame with a wet ripping sound, revealing a stairway piled with old boards and cinder blocks, and half-filled in with dirt. There was a door at the bottom of the stairs that once led to the cellar, but there was no getting past the debris, not without a couple hours of back-breaking work to clear the way.

"Well, I guess that settles that." Benson sighed and turned to Hannah. "I think it's time we call this in and make it an official missing persons report."

CHAPTER FIFTEEN

P ain. Darkness. Silence.

Ashley blinked but nothing changed. The pain remained, the darkness was impenetrable, and the silence unbroken.

As panic took its icy grip on her, another sense kicked in. The smell was horrible, some gruesome mix of pain, blood, sweat, and hopelessness. Her breath came in ragged gasps, and she tried to sit up. It wasn't the explosive agony in her head that stopped her, though it was bad enough to—it was the feel of the chains bound to her wrists.

She squeezed her eyes shut tight, taking in a deep breath despite the stench. She refused to fall victim to fear. Whatever had happened was bad, but through the foggy headache she couldn't remember anything, but fear would only make it worse. She pictured a brick in her mind, then another. With each breath she took, more bricks built up her wall, and fear was on the other side of it. She remained still, eyes shut, breathing slowly and building. When the wall was complete, she opened her eyes and forced her thoughts backward, before the pain.

She was in the library, talking to the blogger who wasn't really the blogger. That, she had figured out pretty quickly. She'd done her best to get evidence, snapping pictures with her phone and turning on the voice recorder.

She smiled in the darkness, praising her own cleverness. Then what?

We have Hannah.

Ashley gasped at the memory. She closed her eyes again, visualizing the wall. It was solid, holding back the terror that relentlessly tried to get through.

She'd agreed to go with the fake blogger to show him where the foot was. He'd promised that was all he wanted, and he would let Hannah go. They'd left the library together. Then the darkness had begun.

Ashley's head throbbed. The more she tried to think, the worse the pain. *Fight through it.* She looked at her wall, so strong, keeping all the bad thoughts and crippling fear away from her.

She spent the next few minutes trying to feel her way around in the darkness. She was on a crusty mattress that rested on a bed frame of steel or some sort of metal. The wall she touched with her foot felt like rock.

Am I in a cave?

The idea held a horrible power. Ashley pictured it as a battering ram, bashing her wall repeatedly.

Another memory of the day crept into her mind, fleeting and murky, but something to focus on, to cling to like a life preserver. It was the woods, where she and Hannah spent a lot of time, usually with Scout tagging along. But this had been different. There had been no jingling collar or happy barking, and there had been no Hannah.

"Find the spot or you'll end up on the wrong side of the dirt yourself."

Ashley started, the memory coming clearer, like a shape through the fog. The guy had taken her to find the foot. She remembered stumbling around in the woods, his hand on her upper arm like a vise, sometimes stopping her from falling, other times shoving her forward. Had they found it?

They must have, otherwise they'd still be out there looking.

There was something else, but it wouldn't come. Her stomach clenched and her heart pounded in her temples. She willed the last piece of the memory to come, but it wouldn't. She tried to stop, to think of something else, anything else, but it was no use.

She glanced inwardly at her wall. It was still there, but was that mortar crumbling between the bricks?

She began to scream for help. She told herself it was the logical thing to do, but that voice seemed to come from the other side of the wall. She screamed forever, until her throat ached, and her mind went numb, and she lost consciousness.

Ashley is on a crowded beach with Hannah. It is daytime, but very, very dark, the sun hidden behind the blackest, gloomiest clouds Ashley has ever seen. There were people running around and laughing, but Ashley can't hear them. She looks toward the beach, sees the waves crashing, but they, too, are silent. She tries to point but sees her hands are tangled somehow in her beach towel. The clouds part and a blinding shaft of sunlight blinds her ...

She woke up. It wasn't sunlight blinding her, but light from where someone had opened the door to her prison. The shape was silhouetted, and Ashley was unable to see who it was.

Then the light glinted off the something in the person's hand. It was a hypodermic needle, and it was moving toward her shoulder. She closed her eyes and saw her wall come tumbling down.

CHAPTER SIXTEEN

Hannah sat in the living room while Dad put on a pot of coffee in the kitchen. Officer Benson tried to call the station on his cell but, of course, didn't have signal. He went out to the car to radio it in.

Dad returned to the living room and went to the window, then turned to face her. "We have to tell him everything. You know that, right?"

Hannah waited, expecting more, *hoping* for more, so she could think for a minute longer. "What about—"

"Hannah, stop it. Ashley is missing. She may be in serious danger. *Everything*, understand?"

His words hit her like a slap, and she recoiled at his tone. *Is he blaming me for something?*

"Dad …"

Hannah gulped in a breath and broke down, sobbing. It was all too much. She shouldn't have to make such adult decisions. *Why didn't I just call this off instead of letting Ashley talk me into continuing?*

The thought of Ashley, alone and scared, maybe hurt, crushed her. She refused to let her thoughts take the next step.

Dad was next to her, holding her, telling her to calm down. Hannah noticed he wasn't saying everything would be all right.

"I'll tell him everything, but without the phone we have no evidence. Dad, what happened to Jacob? He wouldn't just leave?"

"I asked Officer Benson to send a car to his house to check on him." Dad replied.

Hannah took in a shaky breath. *What have I dragged Jacob into?* Her whole body was trembling, and her face and hands were all tingly. She tried to speak but her throat was closing. Then the room began to shrink and tilt to one side. Blackness filled her peripheral vision. She heard Dad calling her name from far away, like he was at the other end of a long, dark tunnel.

Then everything went dark.

Ashley and I are at Hampton Beach. The day is hot and sunny. A breeze blows in from the water. Waves crash. Kids are running around, playing football and tossing frisbees. Ashley watches people walking by with a critical eye. She turns to me and says, "Is there a four-tattoo minimum to walk on this beach?" We both laugh. I reach into the cooler and pull out and old-fashioned bottle of Coke. It's one of the ones with the green glass. The label is hanging off from soaking in the water. I put it to my forehead, and it is blissfully cool ...

Something cool touched Hannah's forehead and she tried to open her eyes. She was holding a bottle of soda to her head. *No, that wasn't right.* She tried again and squinted, able to make out Dad's concerned face. She blinked and her confusion began to clear. She was lying on the couch. Dad was holding a wet facecloth to her head. Not a bottle of soda.

"You fainted, honey. Are you okay?"

Hannah nodded and tried to sit up. She was still a little unsteady but remembered her last thought before she fainted. She saw Officer Benson standing beside Dad.

"Did you find Jacob?" Hannah's voice was crackly, her throat sandpapery. Dad handed her a glass of water and she drank greedily, savoring the relief on her parched throat.

"Jacob wasn't home yet. No sign of him or his car. I had them run his plate and issue a BOLO."

Hannah had watched enough cop shows to know that meant "be on the lookout." She wanted to cry but had no tears left.

"Dad, Officer Benson, what are we going to do?"

Dad started to respond but Officer Benson cut him off. "*We* aren't going to do anything. You're going to stay out of this and let me do my job."

Hannah bit her lip, unsure she should say anything.

Screw it. This is Ashley, and now Jacob. She realized how much she'd come to like Jacob in just a short time.

"What if some of the police are part of whatever is going on?"

"Hannah." Dad gave her a withering look.

"It's all right, Mr. Green." He knelt in front of her, so his eyes were at the same level as hers. "Hannah, I understand your concern, but at this point it looks like the person that put that idea in your head is the one that's part of it. I've probably breached protocol a couple of dozen times already, letting you tag along to Mrs. Bayole's. I'd appreciate your cooperation on this. It won't help if you can't trust me and hold something back."

Hannah nodded. He *had* let her tag along. *Maybe he did that because he knew we wouldn't find anything.* She didn't know what to do. She just wanted Ashley back.

An idea struck her, and she started to speak, but decided against it.

"You're right, Officer Benson, I'm sorry. Please find Ashley and Jacob."

Benson spoke with Dad for a few more minutes, giving him his card before he left.

"I promise I'll do everything I can, we'll find them."

Benson shook hands with Dad and gave Hannah a tip of his cap, which she found endearing. She almost called after him but held back. She watched him drive away before turning to Dad.

"Do you think we should try to call Ashley's parents or wait a while?"

Dad sighed. "I already tried the number for the hotel. I left a message, asking them to call back. Hopefully she'll turn up before they call."

Dad's voice was flat, defeated. Hannah's mind was spinning. She needed to check something but knew he'd never let her leave the house alone. He solved the problem for her.

"I'm going to take a shower, okay?"

"Sure," she replied, trying to sound casual.

He trudged upstairs and as soon as he was out of sight, Hannah wrote him a note and put it on the kitchen table where he'd be sure to see it. When she heard the shower turn on, she grabbed Scout's leash and headed for the door. He'd be mad, but this was important. "Let's go," she said, and Scout followed her outside. *Why didn't I get my bike from Jacob's trunk?*

She was a block from the library when she saw a couple of

boys walking toward her. Her heart skipped a beat. She wondered what she looked like after the day she'd had.

"Hi Hannah. How's your summer going?"

Marcus Diaz offered up a crooked smile and Hannah blushed. The other boy, Kenny Driscoll, looked at Marcus funny, then said hi to her.

"Hi Marcus, Kenny. You know how it is in Hopeland. You almost start to miss school out of sheer boredom."

What a dork, Hannah chided.

Marcus laughed. "Yeah, I hear you."

Kenny bent down to pat Scout, and Hannah suddenly understood she hadn't thought this through—she couldn't bring Scout into the library. "Hey, can you guys do me a favor?"

Marcus's face lit up and she pictured the handsome boy he would be when his acne cleared. Her heart did that funny double-beat thing again.

"Sure, Hannah, anything."

Kenny rolled his eyes. That's when it clicked. Hannah realized that Marcus might like her. Her face burned.

"Um, well, I have to check something really quick in the library. Would you mind hanging out with Scout for a few minutes?"

Marcus smiled. "Sure, we'll take him over to the park and snag a tennis ball. Meet us there when you're done."

Kenny looked at Marcus and started to argue, "I thought we—"

Marcus cut him off. "Never mind, Kenny. This'll be fun."

Hannah smiled. "Thanks, I mean it. I appreciate the help."

Marcus smiled his own goofy smile and Kenny punched him in the shoulder.

"I'll be back in a few."

She turned and practically skipped to the library. *Wait until I tell …*

For just a moment, she had forgotten why she was there. Guilt and sadness washed over her as she climbed the steps.

She opened the door and stepped into the cool, dry air of the library. She hadn't noticed how muggy it was outside until she was free from its oppressiveness.

She had almost told Officer Benson about the librarian but had held back at the last minute. She turned the corner and there she was; the librarian that had thrown them out the other day. Instead of fear, a white-hot anger surged through her, making her pulse pound in her temples.

The woman stared at her with a confused look before recognition spread across her face. She started toward Hannah. Clenching her fists by her side, Hannah stepped forward to meet her.

"I thought I told you and your friend to stay away?"

"You can't kick me out," Hannah hissed, stepping closer. "Just try it and see what happens."

Blotches of red formed on the woman's cheeks. She opened her mouth to reply but something made her stop. Her eyes darted back and forth around the library. Hannah looked around, too. The tables in the main area were pretty full, a lot of people trying to escape the heat and humidity for a while. The woman took a step back and smiled. It was the expression Hannah would expect on a shark sizing up its prey, but Hannah didn't break eye contact and look away.

"You're pressing your luck," the woman said through her fake smile, before adding, in a sickly-sweet voice, "Let me know if

I can help you with anything."

Hannah continued to stare her down, filled with a righteous fury. She turned and walked toward the computers without looking back. Hannah sat at one facing the desk so she could keep an eye on the librarian. Aces and eights, she thought with a determined smile.

Her fingers flew across the keyboard. The librarian was on her cell phone, no doubt talking to someone about Hannah.

Mama Bayole? The guy who took Ashley?

Hannah turned her attention back to the computer screen. She logged into Ashley's email. They knew each other's passwords for just about everything. She was looking for the thread between Ash and the blogger.

After finding it, she scanned the conversation, searching for anything that would help her figure out who he was or what had happened to Ashley. Several of the emails talked about where the body was. The blogger claimed he knew, and Ashley was trying to get him to tell her. It was that piece of information that he used to convince her to meet him.

Hannah reread the emails again. He had danced around the location, giving Ashley hints to prove he knew the woods and where the body was buried. She focused on a comment in one of his early emails to Ashley, trying to force a memory to the surface.

There's a kind of mutant tree, I call it the Siamese Pine. I hid behind it and watched them bury her. It was creepy, terrifying; the sun was rising behind them and I was only about thirty yards away.

Hannah had hiked practically every inch of those woods near where Scout found the foot over the years, and there were plenty of weird tree formations. It might be any of them. Half the forest was pine trees.

146

Wait … something clicked. "Siamese Pine," she whispered.

Hannah remembered a walk she'd taken one day, early in the morning. Scout had woken up and needed to go out. The sun was just up, burning the morning fog off the lawn. Hannah had decided it was too beautiful to go back to bed, so she'd thrown on her sneakers and a sweatshirt and just started walking.

At one point, she'd heard something moving around off the path in the thickets. She'd made Scout stay with her and went to investigate. It had been a deer, a fawn just rooting around, enjoying the morning, same as she was.

Scout had barked and Hannah had been sure the deer would bolt, but instead it just looked at them for a few minutes, decided there was no danger, and walked deeper into the forest. Hannah had followed, amazed by the calmness of both the fawn and Scout, after his initial bark of excitement. The deer had led them well off the path, stopping occasionally to graze before moving on.

They'd been deep into the forest when Hannah had heard more rustling. Another deer, a full-grown doe, had broken through the underbrush and approached the fawn. They'd nuzzled each other and Hannah had realized it was the mother. They had both looked at her and Scout, and then darted off into the woods.

She remembered finding her way back to the path and stopping by a pine tree, or rather a pair of pine trees that had grown together for about four feet before splitting into two trunks.

That must be what the blogger was talking about.

Hannah got up to leave, making sure she logged out of Ashley's email and cleared the browser history. She glanced at the librarian and saw the woman was still glaring at her. Hannah gave her the biggest fake smile she was able to muster and waved to her, resisting the urge to flip her the bird. The woman's face went red again and her lips tightened. Hannah laughed and exited the building.

She ran down the library steps and across the street to the park, pausing to watch Marcus and Ken play with Scout. They had indeed gotten a tennis ball and were playing keep-away, letting Scout get the ball every couple of tosses, then chasing him around like lunatics.

Hannah smiled. *This is what summer should be.* She jogged toward them.

Marcus saw her coming and walked over to meet her.

"Hey, Hannah. Your dog is awesome. He's better at keep-away than Kenny."

Hannah laughed and Ken gave Marcus the finger.

"Thanks for hanging out with him, I really appreciate it." Hannah looked around. The park was emptying out. She thought of the long walk home and the car from the other day.

"It was no big deal. Hey … um …"

Marcus glanced at Ken who was watching him with a weird look of amusement. Marcus was already flushed from roughhousing with Scout, but a deeper red was rising up his neck, and burning his cheeks and ears.

"Well, we could walk you home if you want?"

Hannah almost gasped. Partly with relief but mostly with … something else. Ashley was missing, Hannah was getting ready to go look for a dead body in the woods, and now Marcus was offering to walk her home? *Perfect timing.*

"Sure, that would be nice."

What? She'd meant to tell him she had things to do. *How did it come out as "that would be nice."*

Hannah's cell phone buzzed, and she looked at the screen, already knowing it was Dad and he'd be frantic. "One sec," she said to Marcus and accepted the call. "Hi Dad—"

"Are you okay? Where are you?"

"I'm fine. I just had to get out of the house. I'm at the park and a couple of friends from school are going to walk me home." She smiled at Marcus and mouthed "thank you," then finished the call with her father. "Thanks, guys. I do have to get home."

They started walking but realized Ken wasn't coming.

"Marcus, I ... uh ... just remembered my mom wanted me to cut the grass. I gotta go, sorry."

Hannah couldn't believe it, seeing through the thin facade. Ken was Marcus's wingman. Now she was going to have to have a one-on-one conversation. The thought made her throat start to close. Somehow with the three of them, it was different. This was more ... personal. Practically a date.

"Oh, okay Ken, I'll text you later?"

Ken waved and set off in the other direction, across the park. Marcus and Hannah started walking toward her house.

Despite all the things Hannah should have on her mind, her only thought was what it would feel like if Marcus slipped his hand around hers.

"So, what were you doing at the library?"

She almost stopped walking. *Well, Marcus, Scout dragged a human foot out of the woods and me and Ashley, you know Ashley, right? Anyway, she's been kidnapped by some cult, but I'm still trying to find the rest of the body that used to be attached to the foot, you know?*

"Just researching a story I was thinking about writing?" she stammered.

"That's cool. I didn't know you liked to write."

She shrugged. The truth was she *did* like to write but usually just messed around with poems or wrote in her journal. This *would* make a great story.

"I don't know. I've been thinking about it, you know? Not much else to do around here, right?"

Marcus laughed. "It's not so bad. I used to live in Boston. There was a lot to do, but I don't know—it was so crowded and noisy. There were always sirens, twenty-four-seven. Police, fire engines, ambulances. It never stopped. I kind of like it here."

Hannah thought about what he said. She'd always romanticized city life, but he made a good point. Would she really want to be around all those people all the time? To have to take Scout on leash walks and pick up his poop in a bag instead of romping in the woods? Having to worry about crime … She stopped at this one, the irony not lost on her.

"I guess it's not so bad," she relented, "Maybe if we at least had a movie theater, somewhere to go at night?"

"Yeah, that would be cool, I guess. They have those concerts at the gazebo sometimes. The bands usually suck but it's something to do."

Hannah nodded. "I think I saw a sign for one of those coming up."

"It's next weekend. I was thinking …"

Hannah's palms were sweating. *Please don't hold my hand now.*

"Maybe we could go together, get an ice cream after? It's not as cool as a movie." His tone was odd, like he was trying to sound both enthusiastic and casual at the same time.

"I'd like that." Hannah said, thinking how cute he sounded. Then she realized he was asking her out on a date. *I'd like that? I couldn't come up with anything cleverer than I'd like that?*

"Great, it's a—"

"Date?" she finished. Her face on fire, eyes darting sideways. He was blushing, too. And he had that goofy smile going.

"Yeah, I guess so. I mean, I was hoping—"

They rounded the corner of Rough Timber Lane and Hannah stopped, blinking in shock, then she took off in a dead run toward her house.

She bounded past the police car and through the front door. Officer Benson and Dad turned at the same time. Scout began barking outside the door and she opened it to let him in, realizing Marcus was also standing there.

"Is everything okay?" he whispered.

Marcus looked totally confused and more than a little nervous.

"I … I don't know. Come on in, Marcus." Hannah nodded toward Dad and Officer Benson. "Dad, Officer Benson, this is Marcus Diaz, my friend from school." Before anybody asked a question, she continued. "What's going on?"

Benson and Dad looked at each other and she knew it was bad news.

Oh, my God … Ashley.

Her knees went wobbly and the room was doing that tunnel vision thing again. She staggered to the couch and sat down hard, putting her head between her knees. Dad was next to her instantly, gently rubbing her back.

Benson cleared his throat. "Hannah, this has nothing to do with Ashley." It was like he'd read her mind. "One of our other officers found Jacob's car out on Route 33."

Hannah's head snapped up. *Route 33!* She was overwhelmed with mixed emotions—glad there was no bad news about Ashley, but afraid for Jacob's safety. She couldn't even look at Marcus.

"The car had a flat tire. It's being towed to the station now. Jacob wasn't with the car."

"Maybe he started walking to get help?" She hated the desperation in her voice.

"We've got cars combing the area and foot patrols in the woods around where Jacob's vehicle was found. No sign of him yet."

Hannah stood quickly, too quickly, because the room tilted like a ship in rough seas, and she almost fell.

"Was Ashley's phone in the car?"

Officer Benson shook his head. "The initial search came up empty. The strange thing—your bike wasn't in the trunk. I was going to bring it to you."

Hannah stared at him, not comprehending what that might mean. A coughing sound from behind her broke her train of thought. Marcus.

"Uh, maybe I should go?"

"I'm sorry, Marcus. Things are kind of weird right now. Can I talk to you when things settle down a little?"

Marcus nodded and backed toward the door, unsure of what to do. Dad stood up and pulled out his keys.

"I'd feel more comfortable dropping you off," he offered.

Officer Benson also headed for the door. "I'll keep you folks posted."

Hannah followed Dad and Marcus to the car, and they drove across town in awkward silence.

When they got to Marcus's house, Hannah got out of the car

with him. "I'll explain everything, I promise," she said.

Marcus nodded and said goodbye, then jogged up his driveway. Dad gave her a knowing look when she got back in the car, unable to hide the hint of a sad smile. They pulled out and Dad made a U-turn, accelerating toward home and more uncertainty.

"I went to the library and logged into Ashley's email. I think I know where the body is."

Dad turned to look at her, trying to keep one eye on the road. "Hannah, we talked about this. We need to let Benson know."

"Not yet, Dad, please? What if I'm wrong and we waste his time digging in the woods when he could be looking for Jacob and Ashley?"

His lips pressed together, then he began biting the lower one. "All right. If we find anything, we call him immediately. Got it?"

Hannah nodded. "Got it."

"And Hannah ..." he paused, swallowing hard, "please don't go running off like that again." He reached a hand across the seat.

"I won't, "I'm sorry," she said, and squeezed his hand.

She stopped at a small clearing to get her bearings. That spring morning seemed like forever ago, and she began to panic, not seeing anything familiar. *What if I can't find it?* Closing her eyes, she tried to think back to that day. She pictured the deer stopping to nibble on some wild blueberry bushes. Opening her eyes and spotting some wild blueberry bushes on the far side of the clearing, she started walking again, confident she was still on the right track.

Shovels clanked together behind her as Dad adjusted them

on his shoulder and followed. Scout bounded out in front, catching the scent of something. Hannah reached the other side of the clearing and pushed her way through some bushes, feeling the pull of the brambles on her clothes and ignoring the scratches they left on her skin. Ahead, she saw a small group of pines. She didn't have to close her eyes to picture the deer prancing through the pines. They were close.

Hannah slowed her pace, looking in all directions for a sign. There it was, up ahead. Not a sign but the tree itself. She saw the unique fork of the two trunks. She broke into a run and stopped at the tree.

... the sun was rising behind them ...

"Which way is east, Dad?" she practically screamed.

Dad pointed and Hannah slid to the opposite side of the gnarled Siamese Pine, looking east. In her mind's eye, she pictured the woods at dawn, the sun rising above the horizon, splitting the twin trunks. The sound of shovels cutting through earth, dirt being tossed aside. The body on the ground, waiting for its unholy burial.

Hannah turned to her father. He had been quiet the whole time, letting her find her way. Her lip quivered and she turned away.

... and I was only about thirty yards away ...

"Dad, go stand over that way, toward those rocks. Count off thirty paces."

He stared at her for a moment, his face filled with concern. Then he walked in the direction she'd pointed, turning back often to see if she wanted him to adjust his path. She told him to stop, the image of him with the shovel too close to the picture in her head. She shook it off and ran to him. Then she walked in a slowly expanding circle until she found what she knew would be there. The ground was disturbed, like an animal had been digging.

Scout began sniffing loudly, his head jerking back and forth to follow the scent. He pawed at the ground where the disturbance was. Dad grabbed him by the collar and pulled him away. Hannah grabbed a shovel and started digging.

"Hold Scout, let me—" Dad began, but she silenced him with a look. She had to be the one to do it.

Dad held Scout while she dug. The earth was soft, pliable from decades of fallen leaves and pine needles. After a few minutes, sweating rivers, she stopped when her shovel hit resistance.

Maybe it's just a root and this is all just a wild goose chase.

She knew better. Using the blade of the shovel, she carefully raked the dirt aside. She saw what looked like a swatch of tattered denim and, under it, the glistening white of bone.

Hannah watched Dad and Officer Benson talking in hushed voices in the kitchen. Benson was becoming a fixture in the house. Scout was lying in the corner, one eye open, watching with doggie curiosity. Something Benson was saying pulled Hannah from her malaise.

"What did you just say, Officer Benson?"

Hannah was up off the couch, joining them in the kitchen. Benson looked at Dad, then back at her.

"I'm being taken off the case. It's being reassigned to Officer Dietrich. I'm here unofficially. I wanted to tell you in person."

Hannah watched him, seeing the unease in his body

language—the way he shifted his weight on his feet, the way he wouldn't make eye contact.

"It's just like the blogger said, isn't it?" Her words came out as a mixture of fear and reverence.

"Hannah, we don't know …" Dad trailed off and he just shrugged.

"Listen, Hannah, Brian. I don't know why I was pulled but between you and me, it doesn't smell right. I can't help you in any official capacity but what I do on my own time is my business. I promise you both I'm still working on this. I have to go. Officer Dietrich should be stopping by shortly."

Hannah thanked the man and went to her room while Dad and Benson shook hands and said a few more words. When had *Mr. Green* become *Brian*?

Dad knocked on her door a few minutes later and peeked in. "You okay?" he asked softly, almost cautiously.

She shrugged. The truth was she was scared—for Ashley, for Jacob, for herself and Dad. *How could this be happening?* A few days ago, she'd just been a bored teenager in a small town. Now she was mixed up in some cult that sacrificed kids? It was too much to think about.

"I know what you're thinking, but we have to work with Officer Dietrich when he shows up. Either this whole thing is just a coincidence and Dietrich is on the level, or …"

Hannah took a deep, composing breath. "Or he's part of it and we have to be careful."

Dad nodded, wearing a wan smile. "Exactly. I'm going to try calling the Wallaces again before Dietrich gets here."

He kissed the top of her head and walked out, leaving her alone with her thoughts. Finding Ashley was the only thing she cared about. She felt guilty thinking that with Jacob missing too, but how much could she deal with?

Something gnawed at her brain about the search at Mama Bayole's farm, but she couldn't bring it to the surface. Trying to force it was giving her a headache. Mom always used to tell her to stop thinking about something if she wanted to remember it. Get busy with something else and whatever it was will just pop into your head, she'd always said. That was before she'd gotten weird. Thinking about Mom made Hannah's head ache even more, like she was missing something else.

She left her room and wandered out to the backyard. Scout followed and she began a lethargic game of fetch with him, waiting with dread for Officer Dietrich to show up. Despite Dad's words, Hannah knew in her gut that Dietrich was involved and that he wasn't going to help. He had been assigned to keep an eye on them.

Was he the one on the other end of the phone with the woman in the library?

Something else that bothered Hannah was the blogger. Why had he been so willing to help if he was part of it? He wasn't that hard to track down, but he had insisted on meeting in a public place. He was scared.

An idea began to form, crystalizing into something that shook her. What if the person that met with Ashley *wasn't* the blogger? What if someone had found out about the meeting and used it to get to her?

She heard a car approaching and her stomach tightened. She knew she had to keep up the appearance of cooperation, but she was terrified. What was to stop this Dietrich from just taking her and Dad if he really was part of it? Hannah's only consoling thought was Officer Benson. They couldn't do anything to her because Benson knew what she knew.

"Hannah, come on in. We need to talk."

She tried to channel the Hannah that had stood up to the librarian. The tough-girl side of her. The *Ashley* side of her. With new resolve, she went into the house.

Dietrich was a short, barrel-chested man whose uniform clung to him like a second skin. He had the look of an athlete that had let himself go at middle age. There was still muscle there but residing under a layer of too many steak dinners and bottles of wine. The man's head seemed too small for his blocky body and he had dark, beady eyes.

The eyes are the window to the soul.

Hannah didn't trust him.

"Hannah, this is Officer Dietrich. He is taking over the case for Officer Benton."

"It was Benson, sir, with an S."

Hannah smiled at Dad's slyness.

"Nice to meet you, Officer Dietrich. Do you have any news on Ashley?"

Dietrich folded his meaty arms in front of his chest, testing the limits of his uniform's stitching.

"Right now, we can't really consider it a missing persons case since it hasn't been twenty-four hours."

Hannah started to protest but Dietrich held up a hand to stop her.

"But that doesn't mean we're not following up, don't worry. We sent a car to her house to make sure she didn't go there. Sometimes kids do that when their parents are away. The librarian in West Meadow remembers Ashley and a man being there but didn't hear or see anything unusual. Unfortunately, there are no security cameras in the library or outside it."

"So, you have nothing."

She almost whispered it, her heartache making it hard to speak. Dietrich frowned, as if he had just realized that they did, in fact, have nothing.

"Like I said, we're just getting started. There's a team on the way to exhume the remains. We may need you to lead them out there."

"What about Jacob?" Dad asked.

Dietrich turned to Dad, his face tight. He seemed to be getting impatient with all the questions.

"He still hasn't shown up at his house and nothing has turned up in the woods around where they found his car. We suspect he called somebody for a ride and is still with that person."

"Are you sure the department has the capacity to handle all of this?" Dad's voice was accusatory, and Dietrich bristled. He pulled his shoulders back and took a step forward. Hannah knew he was trying to intimidate them, and it was making her angrier.

"I'm not sure what you mean by that, Mr. Green, but I suggest you keep those comments to yourself and let me do my job."

"It wasn't a comment—it was a question," Hannah snapped. "And a reasonable one. When is the last time you had to do anything more than get a stuck cat down from a tree?"

She couldn't believe she'd said it and instantly regretted it. Dietrich was fuming, his face nearing a dangerous shade of purple.

"Hannah, you know it's the fire department that rescues

cats," Dad said, his voice dripping with sarcasm.

Hannah burst into tears. "I'm so scared, I'm sorry I said that. Ashley is my best friend …"

It was the only thing she could think of to do, Dad was going to make it worse—she saw it on his face. He was mad, too. Dad had a very long fuse, but when he reached the end of it, look out.

Dietrich wasn't completely placated but at least he didn't look like his head was going to explode. Dad seemed to realize the dangerous ground they had ventured on. He put an arm around Hannah's shoulders. She didn't know if was meant to be comforting or protective.

"I apologize, Officer, this has all just been so stressful. Forgive us. Can I get you some soda or water? When the crew gets here, we'll be happy to show them where—"

Just then more cars arrived, saving them all from the awkward scene.

CHAPTER SEVENTEEN

"You made quite an impression on Officer Dietrich." Benson was sitting on the couch with a bottle of soda in his hand, grinning. "He was fit to be tied when he got back to the station."

They were gathered in the living room, Dad and Benson drinking root beer while Hannah sipped a Coke. She was exhausted and needed the caffeine to stay awake. It was making her jittery—she was on her third one. The crew had taken the body just before dark, cordoning off the area before they left. They would be back early the next day to make sure they hadn't missed anything.

"Sorry about that," Dad said, not meeting Benson's eyes. "I guess we were a little hard on him."

Benson shrugged and downed his beer. Dressed in street clothes—khaki shorts and a Springsteen T-shirt—he didn't look like a cop. Even his face was more relaxed, as if the uniform made him harder somehow.

"Dietrich is a dink, whether he has anything to do with

what's going on or not. Kind of a Napoleon complex, I think."

Hannah giggled despite her anxiety and weariness. She was getting punchy and would have to sleep soon. A few things were still nagging her, but she couldn't quite grasp them, something about the blogger and some *other* thing about Mama Bayole's.

"Dad, I need to go back to the library in the morning and check Ashley's email."

She silently cursed their remoteness, wishing for the millionth time they had Internet access at the house. Benson looked confused, and then his face brightened.

"I've got my laptop in the car. It has satellite Internet—you can check it now."

Dad fetched a couple more sodas just as Benson came back in with the laptop. He took a minute to get it connected to the Internet, then handed it to her. She logged in to Ashley's email and saw there were new messages. More than one was from the blogger.

Hannah read them quickly, her eyes widening. Her hands trembled, not from the caffeine but from what she was reading. Her heart hammered at a dizzying rate.

"What is it?" Dad sounded concerned and she wondered how awful her expression must be. Dread settled over her like a heavy cloak.

"It wasn't the blogger that Ashley met. He couldn't make their meeting because his car wouldn't start. He was afraid someone might have done something to his car as a warning. He had it towed to the service station and the mechanic said somebody messed with the engine. He got scared for Ashley and emailed her."

She handed the laptop back to Benson and let him and Dad

read the messages.

Hannah motioned for Benson to let her have the computer again. "I'm going to reply and tell him what happened to Ashley. He still might know something. May I?"

Officer Benson stood and paced around the room. He stopped abruptly and sat next to her. "I think that's the right play. Go ahead. I just want to read it before you hit SEND, okay?" Then he said, "Wait. Send it from your own email account in case they somehow hacked Ashley's. How else could they have known about the meeting?"

Hannah nodded and Benson looked to Dad for his approval. Dad looked shell-shocked. "Benson, what are we going to do?"

Benson ignored the question and watched while Hannah typed a reply. She said Ashley had gone to the meeting and had been taken and that he might be in danger as well. She asked him to meet. When she finished typing, she looked over to Benson. He scanned the email and gave her a thumbs-up. Letting out a weary sigh, she hit SEND, and then sat back, waiting. She hoped the guy would be watching his email because he was worried and would respond promptly.

Dad stood and began pacing while Benson settled in next to Hannah, watching the screen for a response. Scout jumped up and began to growl. A second later, Hannah heard a car coming up the road. It sounded like it was crawling by and she went to the window. Benson jumped up and flipped off the living room lights, joining Hannah at the window. Dad moved toward the front door. A low rumble came from Scout, matching the sound of the car's engine.

Hannah looked up and down the road but saw no headlights. Then she spotted the glint of metal reflected in the moonlight and realized the car was driving with the headlights off. She struggled to follow its progress, using her ears as much as her eyes. When the car slowed in front of the house, Benson sprang into action, pushing past Dad out the front door and sprinting down the driveway. Hannah and her dad followed with Scout at their heels, barking wildly.

Benson got within twenty yards of the vehicle before it sped off, engine roaring and tires screeching. The three stopped at the end of the driveway and watched the car disappear. Hannah's eyes had adjusted to the dark, but she still couldn't see more than the occasional wink of metal in the distance. She retreated to the house with Dad and Benson and turned the lights back on.

"Did either of you get a good look at the car? All I could tell was it was a dark color. Looked like a late model, and the engine sounded like an eight cylinder. That narrows it down to about a million cars in the state. I couldn't see the plate at all."

Benson sounded defeated. Hannah realized what a mistake she'd made by not getting the license plate number of the car that had followed her the day she'd walked to the library. *Maybe this would be over already if I had.* Then she looked out the window again and dread crept over her. "Officer Benson, your car."

Benson closed his eyes and shook his head. "Now they know I'm helping you."

"I'm sorry, Rick," Dad said, "I should have had you pull around back."

"I didn't think they'd be watching you at this hour." Benson sighed, then his voice tightened. "We need to know who *they* are."

Hannah ran over to the couch and grabbed the laptop. No new messages. She wondered if the blogger had disappeared like

Ashley and Jacob.

Would some dog be running out of the woods with one of his shoes in a few years?

Her thoughts were blurry, and her eyelids were too heavy, like they had weights on them. The day had taken its toll. The lack of response from the blogger was the icing on the shit cake. Her eyes began to close as she tried to watch the screen, willing a new message to pop up. Then she was out. She vaguely remembered Dad carrying her to bed.

Hannah woke the next day to the aroma of bacon and eggs, still wearing yesterday's clothes. Glancing at the clock, she was shocked to see it was after nine. The sleep had done nothing to rid her of that bone-tired feeling. She dragged her aching body out of bed and shuffled into the kitchen.

"Good morning, Hannah."

She jumped at the voice, blinking in confusion. It was Officer Benson, also still in last night's clothes, sitting at the kitchen table. Dad was manning the stove but turned around to say good morning.

"Did something happen?" Hannah was beginning to assume the worst. She couldn't comprehend why else Benson would still be here.

"No, honey, Rick offered to spend the night just in case, you know." Dad turned and pulled a huge frying pan full of scrambled eggs off the stove. "Let's eat."

Dad was oddly chipper. *And when had Officer Benson become Rick?* An idea tugged at her brain, but she dismissed it as crazy. "Did you check for a message from the blogger?"

Dad and Benson exchanged comical expressions.

"Some cop you are," Hannah quipped and went to the laptop. Still nothing. That couldn't be good. She joined Dad and Benson at the table, and they ate in silence.

"The librarian." Hannah blurted out through a mouthful of eggs. "The librarian is one of them. Officer Benson, you can arrest her, make her talk, make her tell us where Ashley is."

Why didn't I tell him sooner?

Officer Benson kept eating but Hannah saw his mind working. He took another forkful of eggs. "I'm off work today, but I'll go by the library in uniform and see what she knows."

"Do you think she'll talk?" Dad's voice held the same note of hopefulness Hannah was feeling.

Benson had resumed shoveling eggs into his mouth. None of them had eaten dinner last night. Hannah watched Benson, waiting for a response. A weird expression came over his face. It looked like excitement. "I think I might be able to persuade her to help."

Hannah glanced at Dad, relieved for the first time since Ashley went missing. Benson stood up and drained his coffee.

"I'm going to go home, shower and change, then head to the library. I'll leave the laptop. Call my cell if you get a message."

She thanked him and Dad walked him to the door. They spoke in quiet tones for a moment, then Benson squeezed Dad's arm and headed out.

"I could use a shower and a change of clothes. Leave the kitchen, Dad, I'll clean up after."

Dad just grunted. He was busy feeding Scout the last of the bacon. He got up and poured a fresh cup of coffee, tousled Hannah's messy hair, and walked out the back door. Scout followed.

Hannah showered and dressed quickly, throwing a baseball cap on to avoid having to do her hair. She ran back to the laptop, noticing that Dad had already cleaned the kitchen on her way through. Still no message. Her worry was turning to anger. She was losing control of her emotions.

Hannah looked out back for Dad but didn't see him. She heard movement from the basement. She went down, and sure enough, there was Dad, going through more boxes. Hannah stood next to him and watched him pull out different objects, examine them, then place them in one of three other boxes on the ground.

"Thanks for picking up the kitchen, Dad. I would have taken care of it."

He was staring at a small figurine of a ballet dancer. He looked at Hannah and seemed surprised to see her there. "Oh, it's fine, Hannah. Just trying to keep busy."

"What's that?" she asked, realizing she had never seen it before.

Dad smiled his sad smile. His real smile had disappeared with Mom, replaced by this ghost of smiles past. "It's just something I bought for your mom when we were dating. We went to the ballet once ... one of our attempts to add some culture to our lives." He laughed, but it held the same sadness as his smile. "It was awful. The single most boring thing I've ever sat through. I gutted it out for your mom. We went for drinks after and she told me she hated it. Boy, did we laugh at that." He held up the figurine. "I bought this as a joke, to remember that night. Not the ballet part, the laughter afterwards."

His eyes filled up and Hannah looked away. She couldn't handle any more sadness. She had to be strong for him. She placed a gentle hand on his arm.

Just then, a brilliant shaft of sunlight pierced the room, enveloping Dad's face in dazzling yellow light. Hannah glanced up at the small rectangular window and something clicked.

Get busy with something else and whatever it was will just pop into your head.

She closed her eyes, returning in her mind to the first time she'd gone to Mama Bayole's house; the sagging porch, the colorless paint, and the unruly grass growing all around the aging farmhouse. It popped in her head, just like her mother said it would. That first time at Mama Bayole's she had marveled at how high the grass had grown, so high that it covered the *cellar window*.

Mama Bayole had told them that the previous owner had moved the hot water and electrical upstairs and sealed the door. The bulkhead was impassable, filled in with dirt and bricks and debris. Hannah had seen the small cellar window intact, though. If the basement was sealed off, why hadn't they boarded up the windows? It might just be an oversight, but her gut told her otherwise. There *was* a cellar, and that's where Ashley was.

A shrill ringing interrupted Hannah's thoughts and jarred Dad from his memories. He looked at her, wiped his eyes, and ran up the steps to get the phone. Hannah followed, wondering if Officer Benson was calling with news. When she got to the top of the stairs, Dad was holding the phone to his ear with one hand and running the other through his hair. Whatever news he'd gotten was not good. After a few hushed words, he hung up and turned to her.

"That was Dietrich. Jacob is at County Memorial in stable condition. He was dumped out of a car at the ER late last night, unconscious."

Hannah watched Dad drive away, feeling as alone as she ever had. When he'd insisted she go with him to see Jacob, Hannah had done something she hadn't done since she was a grade-schooler—she'd faked sick. The relief she'd felt at Jake being found had been indescribable. She hadn't realized it until that call had come but she'd been sure that Jake was dead. As much as she wanted to see him, she needed the time to herself to figure a few things out. Grudgingly, her dad had left Hannah behind and gone to meet Benson at the hospital. Not before he'd made Hannah promise a dozen times that she'd be careful.

Now that he was gone, panic seized her. It started as a single thought: *what if they come for me?* From there, the seed had taken root and blossomed into an unhealthy flower. She was paralyzed with fear, unable to even think about what to do next.

Her eyes fell on the laptop Benson had left behind and the veil of panic lifted just enough. She went to it and logged into Ashley's email. When she saw a new message from the blogger, the veil lifted more.

> Hannah,
>
> So sorry for not getting back to you sooner. When I didn't hear anything yesterday, I feared the worst and took an extra sleeping pill to calm down. The pills knocked me out and I just woke up to find your email.
>
> I'm so sorry this happened. It's my fault for being afraid. Always afraid. I'm done

with that, it's cost me too much, too many years. I'll meet you or go to the police, whatever you want. This needs to end.

Susan

Susan! The blogger was female.

I should have known. It made sense. There was a phone number under Susan's name. Hannah went to the phone and dialed the number.

"Hello?"

The voice was tentative, Susan's fear palpable. Hannah knew at that moment, from that one word, how hard this was for her. She heard a click and was afraid Susan had hung up.

"Hi, Susan? This is Hannah Green."

"Oh, thank God." Sobs and sniffling filled the receiver for a moment before Susan spoke again. "I was so afraid for you."

There was another click.

"Susan, please, I don't know what to do. I think one of the police—"

"Stop! Don't say anything. Meet me at the gazebo in Champlain Park. Thirty minutes."

The line went dead. Hannah knew she was afraid of someone listening, of the phone being bugged. She wondered about those clicks. Hannah grabbed the laptop and her cell phone, threw both in her backpack and headed for the door. Scout scurried over, ready for the next adventure.

As they walked toward town, Hannah was careful to watch for approaching vehicles. Her panic had subsided but not disappeared. It was too easy to picture a car or van pulling up, grabbing her. Making her disappear.

What would Dad do without me?

She brushed the thought away before it turned to panic. She stopped to retrieve her cell from the backpack. Having it handy made her feel better. She thought of how clever Ashley had been to use hers to leave clues behind and a crippling sadness threatened to consume her.

No. I will not give up.

Instead, she thought about Susan and the courage it took to stand up to people she knew were murderers, risking her own safety for a couple of strangers. That was the kind of person Hannah aspired to be. For some reason her thoughts drifted to Mom. What kind of person was she? Had she just upped and abandoned her family? Had she fallen into the false security of drugs? Was there something else?

Then, a darker thought—what was Dad lying about?

She was close enough to Champlain Park to see the gazebo, but too far to tell if anyone was in it. She picked up her pace, urging Scout to keep up. As she approached, Hannah spotted a lone figure standing against the railing, looking out over the park. Despite the cloudless blue sky and the happy families laughing in the park, the woman's silhouette evoked a heavy sadness in Hannah. A feeling that she was heading toward some awful inevitability slowed her steps.

This is what a death row inmate walking the last mile feels like.

The woman turned in her direction and everything changed. An odd sense of comfort filled Hannah. Something about the woman's face, her stance, her *presence*, made her believe everything was going to be all right. Hannah raised a hand to wave and the woman responded with a smile so beautiful that

Hannah couldn't stop a goofy grin from spreading across her own face.

Before she could climb the steps to the gazebo, the woman rushed down and wrapped Hannah in a hug. The smell of her hair reminded Hannah of her mother and she realized how badly she missed her. Not just since she was physically gone, but for so long before that. Hannah returned the hug and let out her grief.

Eventually, she pulled away and looked up at the woman. Susan was around forty with blonde hair and blue eyes. She was stunning.

"Thank you for coming."

The woman smiled again, and Hannah realized she wasn't just pretty. She had actress or model beauty. Hannah couldn't look away.

"I'm so sorry this is happening again. I was afraid I was going to be too late." The woman looked around, searching the park. Then her words finally sunk in.

"How do you know you're not?" Hannah asked, dread weighing her down.

"The ceremony is tonight. We have to do something *now*." Hannah watched Susan's face crumble into a portrait of pain and fear.

"I don't understand," Hannah whispered.

Susan grabbed her shoulders and Hannah tried to take a step back. *Was I wrong about her?* Scout moved closer, emitting a low growl. Susan sensed the change in mood and pulled her hands away, holding them up defensively.

"I'm sorry, it's tonight. The Ritual of San Sakrifis. The blood sacrifice."

CHAPTER EIGHTEEN

Susan drove fast, but not fast enough to attract any unwanted attention from the police. Hannah kept her eyes everywhere at once, watching for a cruiser or any suspicious-looking car. Scout hung his head out the window, ears and jowls flapping in the breeze. During the ride, Susan told Hannah about the ceremony, her own eyes darting between the road and the rearview mirror.

"The Ritual of San Sakrifis is what Mama Bayole claims keeps her alive. It's a sacrifice to the Great Spirit."

"You mean Satan? The Devil?" Hannah said, her voice querulous.

"No, it's closer to paganism than it is to devil worship. Think hybrid nature-based beliefs with some voodoo thrown in. Mama Bayole says she's well over a hundred years old and believes she stopped aging once she discovered the ritual."

Hannah thought back to Jacob's story. If Mama Bayole was telling the truth, it *had* been her back in the clearing over fifty years ago.

"This ritual, does it take place in the woods?" Hannah asked.

Susan glanced sideways at her. "It does, in a clearing surrounded by thick trees and underbrush. It's nearly impossible to find if you don't know it's there. There's a stone altar in the clearing, and all these creepy stick figures hanging in the trees. They're supposed to be symbolic of the entities that Mama Bayole believes in. The ceremony itself is pagan but very close to what you may have seen in witchcraft movies."

Hannah's head snapped toward Susan, a horrifying thought occurring to her. "Susan, were you part of one of these ceremonies?"

"I was," she said, her voice amazingly calm. "It was my last night as one of Mama Bayole's followers. Until that night ... It was different. I would meet with her and we would talk and pray a little. I would help her at the Farmer's Market, things like that. She was, well, like a mother, or a grandmother, I guess."

"What about the others? Did you ever hear about the ceremony from them?" Hannah hoped that Susan might help identify the other members, specifically the fake blogger that had taken Ashley.

"That's the thing. Until that night, I didn't really know there *were* others, at least not that many. I was new. The ritual was going to be my initiation, I guess."

She stopped speaking and Hannah glanced at her. Tears rolled down Susan's cheeks. *How could someone like Susan even get involved with Mama Bayole?* She was pretty, seemed smart and good-hearted. It didn't make sense.

Susan seemed to read her mind. "I was lost. My parents both died within a few months of each other. I was devastated and decided to go to therapy to help me with my grief. My therapist was nice. I *thought* he was helping, but he *wasn't* nice. He … he ended up messing my head up worse."

Hannah closed her eyes. It wasn't unusual for bad men to take advantage of broken, confused women. Especially ones that looked like Susan. "Did he, you know … did he …" She trailed off, she couldn't say it out loud.

"No," Susan said, knowing where Hannah was going. "He didn't rape me. It was more a matter of him preying on my vulnerability, I guess. I'm not sure it's much different."

A few days ago, the worst thing in Hannah's life had been dealing with Mom leaving. Now everything had gone wrong, one thing after another, dominos crashing down on her. It was more than she could take. She turned to stare out the window, watching the trees rush by her. She longed for her old, boring world.

Susan continued, "I met Mama Bayole at the Farmer's Market and we got to talking. She was so nice, comforting. I made a point to go to the market for the next few weeks just to talk with her. We were becoming friends. She seemed to understand my sadness. She invited me to her house for tea after the market one day."

Hannah waited for Susan to go on. When she remained silent, Hannah looked over at her. Susan was staring straight ahead at the road, but Hannah got the impression she was seeing something else.

"Something happened when you went into the house, didn't it?" Hannah finally whispered.

Susan blinked, her eyes sliding toward Hannah then quickly back to the road. "Yes, I think so." She paused again, biting on her lower lip, her eyes still distant, troubled. "Something didn't feel right as soon as I entered the house. I know it sounds like I'm rewriting history, but I really do remember wanting to get out of that house. It felt suffocating, claustrophobic. *Wrong.*"

Hannah nodded, a chill running through her. *That awful buzzing.*

Susan said, "I felt sleepy suddenly, and there was a sound—"

"The flies," Hannah nearly screamed.

Susan started, turning again to look at Hannah. "Yes, the flies. They were… hypnotizing somehow. It was almost like there was something underneath the buzzing sound that I was trying to hear, a voice maybe." She shook her head. "Mama Bayole changed, too, when we entered. She didn't seem like the kindly old woman I'd been meeting at the Farmer's Market. She seemed sly, sneaky. I felt like *I* was the fly and she the spider who'd lured me to her web. I would swear she'd drugged me, but I hadn't had any food or drink from her."

Susan slowed as they arrived at Hannah's house and she was disappointed to see that Dad wasn't back yet. She was anxious to find out if Jacob was okay and if Benson had gotten any information out of the librarian.

I'll call as soon as Susan finishes telling her story.

Since they weren't sure who, aside from Benson, on the police force was trustworthy, Hannah didn't know what they would do even if Benson had found something out.

They went inside and Hannah got them Cokes. They took them out to the back porch and sat on the top step. Hannah watched Scout do what Dad called his perimeter check, sniffing around the edges of the yard. Susan continued where she left off.

"Mama Bayole began to speak. I honestly can't tell you a single thing she said. Her demeanor changed again, and she seemed both agitated and manic—it was very strange. She was always so calm, laid back. We had a cup of tea, and then she said it was time to go. Any apprehension I'd had was gone. She handed me a duffel bag and we went out to the shed in her yard. The next thing I knew, this golf cart was rolling out of the shed with Mama Bayole behind the wheel. It was the oddest thing I'd ever seen. Until later that night."

Hannah remembered the golf cart from when they'd searched Mama Bayole's property with Officer Benson. It seemed like a lifetime ago.

Scout had meandered to the far end of the property. He stopped sniffing and looked off into the woods. He remained motionless, crouching, his ears back. Then he turned and started toward Hannah and Susan. Hannah exhaled a sigh of relief. For a minute, it had looked like he was going to bolt into the trees, chasing something.

Or someone.

"She drove us through the woods on a path that was barely there. Branches were whipping my face and arms. After a while, maybe as long as thirty minutes, but it was hard to tell, she stopped. She had been silent the entire time, concentrating on driving. I sure wasn't going to distract her and end up in a ditch or smashed into a tree.

"We got out and she started rummaging through the duffel bag. When I tell you we were in the middle of nowhere, I'm not kidding. It was so dark I could barely see her, and she was only a few feet away. She handed me something and told me to put it on. I held it up and felt afraid of her for the first time. It was a scarlet robe with a hood. One of those pointy-shaped KKK-looking things, so your face is covered too. I put it on, and she pointed to a small opening in the bush that I swear hadn't been there before.

"I went through a small maze of thick bushes, mostly feeling my way. At some point, I realized there was light ahead, torches, and I saw other people dressed in the same robes. I wanted to go back but also, I didn't. I was calm, but it was a peculiar calm. I know that doesn't make sense. Looking back, I definitely think she'd put something in my tea. She was no different than Dr. Maxwell."

Susan paused, steeling herself to tell the rest of the story. Hannah waited, still unable to believe all this had happened within a stone's throw of her house.

Scout joined them on the porch and curled up at Hannah's feet. She noticed he was watching the woods, though, and wondered if there was someone out there after all.

"I wandered over to the middle of the clearing to where the others were standing. When I got there, they kind of parted to make room for me, and that's when I saw the altar, and the girl. She was tied down, covered with a sheet."

Susan finally broke down. Her body shook uncontrollably, the sobs threatening to rip her apart. Hannah jumped up and ran into the house to grab a box of tissues. She handed Susan the box and put a hand on her arm, unsure of what else to do or say. Susan blew her nose and took a deep breath. She gave Hannah a nod, took another deep breath, exhaled shakily, and finished the story.

"She was still alive. The night was warm, but the poor girl was shaking so much it almost looked like a seizure. Then everyone turned and another figure entered the clearing. She wore similar robes, but black instead of red. Instead of a pointy mask, she wore what looked like the head of some animal. It had antlers, or horns, I'm not really sure. I knew she had to have put something in my tea, otherwise I would have lost my mind right there. As it was, I felt like I was in shock, kind of half asleep, dreamy-like.

"Mama Bayole began to pray, or chant. It wasn't English, I don't know what it was. The group responded—*I* responded, even though I'd never been told what to say, I just knew. We all kneeled while she continued chanting. Then she asked for the gifts." Susan took in a long slow breath, her eyes closed. "The gifts were symbolic, I guess. A knife and a chalice, carried to Bayole by two of the others. It was like a mockery of a Catholic mass. You know, how someone brings the wine and communion up to the priest? She kept praying, or chanting, and it was like the buzz of the flies in her house …"

Susan couldn't go on, she was sobbing, gasping for breath, reliving a nightmare. Hannah rubbed her back and handed her more tissues, but there was no comfort she could offer. She waited for Susan to settle down.

"Mama Bayole finished. I think she was sort of blessing the knife and the chalice. She walked up to the altar, the followers parting and making a circle around it. She pulled the sheet off and …" Susan slammed a fist down on the step, either in anger or anguish. Scout had moved to the grass at the bottom of the steps, and at the sound of fist hitting wood scrambled to his feet. Seeing no danger, he loped up the steps and sat next to Susan. She reached out and stroked his fur.

"She was awake, Hannah. That poor girl was awake. Her eyes were open and I'm sure she was drugged, I pray she was, but there was *awareness* in those eyes. She knew what was happening.

She began to scream and thrash, desperate to escape. I've never seen anyone so afraid in my life. Mama Bayole was still speaking, but in a very low tone that I couldn't make out. The girl stopped struggling and went silent, either from resignation or because Mama Bayole was hypnotizing her or something."

Susan turned to face Hannah, still absently patting Scout.

"The girl went completely still and tilted her head back."

Hannah gasped, and Scout rumbled a low, throaty growl. She knew what was coming and didn't want to hear it.

"Mama Bayole leaned over and stared into the girl's eyes. She placed the knife and the chalice on the altar, as she whispered something. A prayer, I guess. Then she placed one hand on the girl's forehead and the other on her belly. She raised her head and began chanting louder." Susan paused, her eyes faraway, face grim. "The air grew still. I'll never forget the eeriness I felt." She grabbed her elbows, hugging herself to suppress a shiver. "Then the girl tensed. So did Mama Bayole's. And I saw …"

Hannah placed a hand on the woman's shoulder, causing her to start. "It's okay, you don't have to—"

"Yes," Susan cut her off, "I do. I saw that poor girl grow old before my eyes. And Mama Bayole began to look younger. It was like she was stealing her vitality. I could almost see it flowing through Mama Bayole's arms. Within a few minutes, the girl was just a dried-up husk and Mama Bayole looked twenty years younger. It wasn't the girl's vitality. It was her childhood she stole—her youth."

CHAPTER NINETEEN

Susan's final words came out in a whisper, sending a shudder rippling through Hannah like a cold wind. The vision of Ashley suffering the same fate was too much. Hannah's throat squeezed shut. She tried to draw in a breath. The air whistled in her lungs like a tea kettle at full boil. She watched flocks of strange, black birds fill the woods in front of her. Then Susan was shaking her, holding the cold can of soda against her neck. Scout was bouncing in crazy circles around them. The birds disappeared and Hannah gulped in air.

"I'm okay," she croaked.

Hannah sat in stunned silence. She'd known the ritual involved sacrifice, but what Susan had described? Somehow that part hit her harder than the actual killing. It was so much more ... *unnatural.* Hannah was used to seeing reports of violence and murder every night on the evening news, but this was *Supernatural* territory. Suddenly Susan's screen name made sense.

Susan took up the story. "After the ceremony, people started drifting around the clearing. I made my way over to the edge, outside the reach of the torchlight, and snuck into the heavy brush. I ditched the robe and tried to find my way out of the woods, but I think I just kept going in circles. I'm not sure if they came after me, not sure if they even knew I was gone." Susan's eyes were wide and bright, her fingers restlessly twirling her long hair. "Eventually I was too tired to keep walking. I found this weird rock formation that had a small gap that I squeezed into and slept there. Or tried to. The night got cold and I wished I'd kept the robe. Every time I heard a twig snap or a branch rustle, I was sure they'd found me.

"As soon as the sun came up, I tried to get my bearings. I began to think I was never going to get out of there. Then I heard a sound, not a normal woods sound. I was about to call out, but something, some instinct, made me stop. I crept closer and realized it was someone digging. I watched them bury that poor girl. It was awful. Her skin was so white it looked fake, like it was an Egyptian mummy, not a real person.

"I was so scared hiding behind that tree. I waited for them to finish, certain they were going to find me. It seemed like forever before they left. I saw the direction they went and finally found my way out. My car was still at Mama Bayole's. Everything was. I left it there and never went back. The only thing I wanted, the only thing I cared about was a locket my grandmother gave me. It had an old picture of her and my mom. I was wearing it when I went into the woods that night but when I reached for it, it was gone. I lost everything that night."

Hannah waited for several moments, a horrible vast silence between them, before realizing Susan was done. The whole thing was surreal.

"I have to call my dad. He was going to meet Officer Benson at the hospital. They'll know what to do."

Susan nodded. She seemed out of it, drained from the exertion of reliving that night, in shock. The sound of a car approaching caught Hannah's attention.

"Oh, that must be them now."

She was about to go meet them when Scout uttered a guttural snarl. The fur on his back was up and he was baring his teeth, looking more vicious than a lab should. Susan snapped back to reality.

"What's up with him?"

Hannah listened to the rumbling of the car's engine. She recognized its animal-like growl. Its menace.

She motioned to Susan, pointing to the woods. "We have to run."

Hannah grabbed Scout's collar and pushed him toward the tree line, pulling Susan along by her shirt. She ran straight toward the woods, trying to keep the house between them and whoever was in the car out front. The three plunged into the woods, and Hannah guided Susan and Scout up a small, tree-lined rise. Shafts of sunlight pierced the shadows in the woods, and the sound of something scampering through the brush caused Hannah a split-second of panic. They ducked behind a tangled patch of bushes that offered a decent view of the house. Hannah held Scout's collar in a death-grip, rubbing his ears to keep him quiet.

Two men circled around the house. They walked up onto the back porch and knocked, calling out. Hannah watched in shock as they looked around, then opened the door and stepped inside. Despite everything she knew about how dangerous these people were, she stood and moved toward the house, caught up in a dangerous fury.

They can't just do that. They can't just go in my house. She felt violated.

Susan grabbed her and yanked her roughly to the ground. "No," she said through clenched teeth, "I know how you feel but you can't do anything."

Hannah nodded, fighting back tears of rage, or *out*rage. Her jaw was tight, teeth grinding. Susan let her up and they watched in silence, occasionally seeing silhouettes pass by the windows as the men went through the house. Hannah cursed, knowing they would find the laptop and her cell phone. After a long while, the sound of an engine roaring to life broke the quiet calm of the woods and the car sped off. Hannah caught a glimpse of dark paint as it disappeared up the road.

She stood but Susan grabbed her again. "What if only one of them left?"

Hannah pulled free and started toward the house. "We can't just stay out here forever," she called back. She didn't turn to see if Susan followed. She didn't care. Hannah entered through the back door, hearing Susan's tentative footfalls on the steps behind her.

Surprisingly, the house was not trashed. In fact, everything looked exactly as she'd left it.

Not everything, she corrected. Benson's laptop was snapped in half, the monitor part dangling from the base by a few tenuous wires. The cell phone was smashed, and the landline's cord had been cut.

"We have to go, Susan. Can you drive me to County Memorial?"

"Of course," Susan said quickly.

Susan looked a good many steps beyond afraid; she looked paralyzed with fear. She was fading, retreating to some safe place in her head.

Hannah took the woman's arm and led her toward the door, telling Scout to stay. They jogged to Susan's car, Hannah looking up and down the road for any sign of the intruders. She got in the passenger side while Susan dug out her keys. Susan's hands shook as she tried to put them in the ignition. Hannah jerked her head back and forth, convinced the men would come back. Finally, Susan got the key in and turned it. Nothing but an ominous click.

"Oh no."

They must have cut the cables to the battery. Susan was losing it. Had lost it. She was trembling so badly Hannah felt the car shaking. Hannah jumped out and ran around to the driver's side, opened the door, and tried to ease Susan out. Hannah guided her, but Susan's legs collapsed, and she fell to the ground in a limp pile.

"Susan, please. Get up."

Hannah tried to grab Susan under her arms and pull her to her feet, but she wasn't strong enough. Tears of frustration leaked from her eyes. Everything that had happened, that *was* happening, boiled inside of her. Instead of breaking her, it fueled her, strengthened her.

"Susan, get up, I need your help!"

Hannah raised an open palm, thinking of all the times she'd seen a slap to the face bring somebody out of a stupor on television. She couldn't do it. Instead, she knelt and took Susan's face in her hands, forcing the woman to look at her.

"Susan, I know you can hear me. I know you're afraid.

You've been through such terrible things. Giving up isn't going to make those things go away. It's only going to let them keep happening to other people. To *me*."

Hannah let her hands slip from Susan's face. She stood and looked up and down the road. The sun had already sunk low, dipping below the tree line in the west. Hannah shivered.

It will be dark soon.

She finally coaxed Susan to her feet, but the woman was listless, not speaking, like she was Hannah's puppet. Hannah led the near-catatonic woman into the house and sat her on the couch.

She had two options. One was to walk toward town and use the nearest phone to track down Dad and Officer Benson.

She chose the other one.

Hannah tried the phone one last time, hoping that maybe it was just a glitch. It was no glitch, of course. The phone was dead, the silence maddening. She slammed it down, then grabbed her backpack and threw in the few items she could think of to bring: a flashlight, a coil of rope, a large kitchen knife, and a souvenir Red Sox bat she'd won at a Sea Dogs game. It was the only weapon besides the knife she had.

She scribbled a note to Dad explaining as much as possible, and stepped out onto the back porch, aware of the gathering darkness. This was normally Hannah's favorite time of the evening. The sky still clinging to bluish brightness while shadows lengthened and encroached. The peepers and crickets coming to life, beginning their evening symphony.

Tonight, the shadows held danger, not wonder, and the

dying light in the sky was like sand running through an hourglass. Even the sounds of the night were threatening instead of melodic.

"I'm going with you."

Hannah jumped at the sound of Susan's voice behind her.

"You scared me," Hannah breathed, her heart kicking in her chest. "Are you okay?"

Susan made a choked sound that was probably supposed to be a laugh. "No, I'm nowhere near okay, but I heard you. I tried not to listen, but I heard you. I'm done hiding, done running, done with everything but trying to put an end to this."

Hannah wore a grim smile, relieved she wouldn't have to do this alone. "I'm going to get Ashley. I think I know where they have her. I have to get her before the ceremony."

Susan nodded. "Let's go, before I lose my nerve."

They stepped out into the twilight. Hannah glanced back and her heart ached at the sight of Scout watching her through the screen door.

You might never see him again.

The thought came unbidden and threatened to break Hannah's resolve. She whispered a choked goodbye and turned off into the night.

She led the way across the yard and into the woods. Beneath the trees, the darkness was complete. The faint glow left in the sky was taunting them, offering no resistance to the shadows. Hannah moved cautiously, stealthily, in case any of Mama Bayole's people were out looking for her or simply heading to the clearing.

She had considered asking Susan to help her find the clearing so they could try to save Ashley there, but it was too risky. They would be vastly outnumbered and in the middle of nowhere.

Getting Ashley out of the cellar before Mama Bayole realized she was gone was their best bet.

Hannah had never taken the woods to Mama Bayole's but thought she would find it easy enough. The forest seemed thicker, more threatening the closer they got to the farmhouse. Mosquitoes feasted on them, making the trip feel endless. Finally, Hannah spied lights through the trees well before they were in any danger of being spotted by anyone at the farm.

They stopped behind a thicket of bushes to make a plan.

"I'm pretty sure she's in the cellar. The bulkhead is blocked up and I don't know where the entrance is from inside the house, which means we have to go in through the window. Or rather, *I* have to go in through the window. You stay outside and run like hell if anything happens."

"I'm not leaving you there, Hannah."

Hannah smiled in the darkness. Susan's talked tough but her trembling voice betrayed her. Hannah didn't think, after what the woman had already lived through, that she had it in her to back her words up.

"No, you're not leaving me. You're going to get help."

"Hannah—" Susan started.

"Never mind." Hannah cut her off. They could stand here arguing about it until it was too late, or just get on with it. "Nobody's going to catch me. I'll go in with the rope in case I need help getting her out, like if she's already been drugged. As soon as you have her, you get her to the woods. I'll be right behind you. Got it?"

"Okay, yeah. Got it." Susan's voice was stronger.

"Good. Once we start toward the house, no talking. Ready?"

"No … Yes … Okay, let's just go."

They made their way closer to the farmhouse, staying in the cover of the trees. Lights shone in several of the windows, but Hannah saw no movement inside. There were a few cars parked in front of the house, but it was too dark to see if the car that had followed her the other day was among them. The tree line ended about thirty yards from the house, but the mangy grass was high enough that if they crawled, they would be able to get to the side of the farmhouse unseen. The darkness was their friend now.

Hannah got down on all fours and began crawling toward the target: the small cellar window on the side of the house. She felt vulnerable even though the grass made her harder to see. She knew the extra time it would take to get to her feet and run might be the difference between getting caught or not. Between living or dying.

Thirty yards seemed like thirty miles. The combination of crawling, trying to stay quiet, and the constant fear of being discovered were all weights. It was like one of those dreams in which you're trying to run but you're moving in slow motion. A nervous breakdown was a strong possibility.

The sound of an engine silenced the crickets, growing louder as it approached. Headlights cut through the night like twin laser beams. Hannah dropped flat to the ground and heard an "oomph" behind her as Susan did the same.

Despite Hannah's silent prayers, the car pulled up in front of Mama Bayole's and the engine ceased. A single car door slammed, followed by footsteps on the porch, and eventually the screech of the screen door opening and closing. Hannah didn't dare look up until it banged shut.

She scrambled to her hands and knees and continued toward the house. She kept her head up, watching for movement in the windows. Even if someone looked out, they would be unlikely to see anything, but Hannah couldn't pull her gaze away.

Finally, she reached the side of the house. She spun into a sitting position with her back to the stone foundation and watched Susan cover the last few feet. It dawned on Hannah that short of breaking the glass, they had no way to get in the window.

Out of sheer frustration, she grabbed the molding and pushed. When the window swung in with a rusty squeal, she froze. Her eyes bugged in shock and surprise. She held the window up, as still as a human mannequin, afraid to move and make more noise. She listened for sounds in the house or the front door opening, but all was quiet. Her arm began to tire, then Susan was there with a stick to prop the window open. Hannah took the rope from her backpack, handed one end to Susan, and then slid feet-first into the abyss.

She landed hard, the drop longer than she'd expected, and rolled to the floor. The moist dirt beneath her hands made her cringe and she quickly scrambled to her feet. Wispy filaments clung to her and she imagined giant hanging spiders as she swatted madly to be free. She stood, making sure there weren't any footsteps approaching upstairs. Satisfied she'd made it inside undetected, she pulled out the flashlight and snapped it on. Dust motes clouded the beam, which barely made a dent in the blackness.

The cellar was a hoarder's paradise, far worse than the jumbled clutter of the barn. Stacks of rotting newspapers and magazines stood taller than Hannah. Cardboard boxes with their contents spilling out like the guts of rotting carcasses littered the floor. Old toys and broken pieces of furniture completed the obstacle course.

Hannah picked her way through the debris, not daring to even brush any of the objects for fear she would send them crashing down around her, and alert Mama Bayole and whoever was with her that she was down here. At first, based on the wide array of clothes and different age-level toys and games, Hannah thought the junk might be from former owners. Then another possibility hit her, one that left her breathless.

What if these were the leftovers—trophies—from all the previous sacrifices?

Hannah shook the thought off. Mama Bayole was old—this was probably family stuff. Then she moved the flashlight again and froze. Her chest tightened, like a boa constrictor was squeezing the breath out of her, not letting her take in any air.

Her bike stood upright on its kickstand like it belonged there. Hannah's stomach inched up her throat. She closed her eyes and drew in a slow breath, willing herself not to puke in this unspeakable place. When the nausea subsided, she opened her eyes.

Ashley is here.

It took a moment to gather her composure before she moved on. She passed a final teetering stack of moldy newspapers and saw the stairs leading up to the main house. She made her way around them to the opposite side of the cellar. Instead of more piles of trash, Hannah stood in front of a crudely constructed wall. The two-by-fours and rough plywood looked much newer than anything she had seen in the house. She followed the wall until she came to a homemade door held shut by an oversized slide bolt.

Hannah knew what was on the other side of the door—*who* was on the other side. She glanced up the stairs, barely able to tamper down the irrational urge to run up and throttle the old woman. Instead, she reached out and grasped the handle of the slide bolt. As gently as possible, she pulled it. Hannah expected a metallic screech to rip through the room, but the bolt slid easily and quietly as if it had just been oiled.

She flashed the light to the far side of the door, noting the heavy hinges mounted there. That meant the door would swing out. Holding her breath, she pulled the handle, praying that the hinges were as well-oiled as the slide bolt. The door swung open effortlessly. She took another long, angry look at the stairs, then turned toward the room.

The inside of the door was covered with thick, foamy squares. It took her a moment to realize they were soundproofing tiles. A kid she went to school with had lined his garage with them so he could practice playing the drums without driving his parents crazy.

Hannah hesitated. Her legs refused to obey the command her brain was sending. Going into that room would put her in the victim's shoes—make her feel like the ones that had come before Ashley. Alone, scared, and isolated. Doomed. It would be so easy for someone to run down the stairs, slam the door, and slide the bolt home.

Summoning every ounce of courage she had, Hannah forced a step forward, then another. The flashlight shook in her hand, creating a dizzying strobe-like effect. The walls and ceiling were also soundproofed, making the space seem like a rubber room in a crazy-house movie.

She inched her way farther inside, the beam finally reaching the far end of the room, where a rusty steel bedframe stood. Hannah moved the beam up, now desperate to see Ashley, to know that she was safe.

The bed was empty.

There were no tiles behind the bed, only the stone foundation, soundproof in its own way. Bolted into the stones were two sets of chains. They snaked down the wall and onto the rancid, stained mattress, ending in wide manacles.

Cold panic rose in Hannah. *It was all real, not just some silly Nancy Drew mystery.* She struggled to maintain her composure, but the terror was overwhelming. Her breath came in short gasps and the room began to shift. She moved to the nearest wall and leaned against it, trying to breathe deeper to feed her oxygen-starved brain. Tiny black spots began to dance in her peripheral vision. She closed her eyes and again willed her breathing to slow.

Ashley needs me, time is running out.

Never mind that if she passed out, she'd likely be caught.

These thoughts did nothing to calm her down. *Focus on something else, anything.* She began singing an earworm pop song in her head. She pushed away from the wall and took a closer look around the bed. There might be something, a clue to let her know Ashley had been here, but Hannah saw nothing. It was like Ashley had never existed.

Hannah retraced her steps back to the window. It was an endless journey through a sea of castoff objects that she didn't want to look at. The stench of rotting paper was heavy in the air. *How did I not notice it on the way in?* She reached the window and gasped at the pale face staring through. It was Susan, wide-eyed and frantic. She was gesturing wildly for Hannah to hurry.

She moved toward the window, her hip bumping a cardboard box. What happened next reminded her of the game Mouse Trap. The stack of boxes leaned over against a pile of newspapers. The newspapers pushed against an old coatrack that held a bunch of out-of-style, moth-eaten overcoats. The coatrack crashed into an ancient television that was sitting on an old end table, smashing through the screen.

The clamor shattered the eerie quiet of the cellar. Hannah bolted toward the window and grabbed Susan's outstretched hands, finding footholds in the rough stone wall until she was high enough to wiggle through the window.

"It's all right, they're gone. They went into the woods a few minutes ago. I heard the golf cart."

Hannah stared at her uncomprehendingly. The commotion she'd made was harmless, other than the years it had probably taken off her life from sheer terror. Then the implication of Susan's words hit her. It was time for the ceremony.

They would have to go to the clearing.

"We have to follow them."

Hannah was starting to panic again. She didn't know how much of a head start Mama Bayole had and no clue if they would even be able to find the clearing.

"I watched them go. I think there's still time. That golf cart of hers doesn't go much faster than a walk anyway," Susan replied.

She started toward the back of the property, but Hannah hesitated. She closed her eyes, trying to picture the inside of Mama Bayole's house. *Was there a phone?* She couldn't remember seeing one, but it was worth a try.

"Wait, Susan. I'm going in the house. If she has a phone, I can call my dad. It will only take a minute."

Susan nodded, then glanced warily at the old farmhouse. Her face was lined with a horrible expression of fear, making her look ancient. Hannah recognized the look. It said *we don't have a minute.* Then her eyes softened, and she knew Susan was thinking the same thing she was—it might be the last time Hannah would talk to her father.

"You don't have to go in. Wait here," Hannah said.

She darted around to the front of the house. If anyone was still inside, they would have come running when she knocked over all the stuff in the cellar. Now was the time for speed, not stealth. She ran up the rickety front steps and yanked the screen, cringing at the cat-like screech of its hinges. She turned the knob and the door opened. It didn't really matter. She'd been prepared to smash the glass if she had to.

She entered the house, her mind traveling back to the first day when Mama Bayole had tried to screw with her mind. Not tried, she corrected, *succeeded.* She heard the buzzing of the flies, felt the lethargic pull of sleep. She dismissed the thoughts as bad memories and flipped on the lights, then ran to the kitchen where she spotted the old wall phone.

She grabbed the receiver and stared at the rotary dial phone. Hannah had only seen them in the movies, except for her old toy phone with a rotary dial she'd had when she was a child. She began dialing Dad's cell phone number. The return trip of the dial after each digit was excruciating. She waited, afraid the call wasn't going to go through. After a few staticky clicks, it began to ring.

"Hello?"

Hannah sobbed at the sound of Dad's voice and her knees buckled. She broke down completely, unable to utter an intelligible word.

"Hannah? Honey, is that you? Are you all right?" Dad

sounded hysterical.

"It's me. I'm okay, Dad," she finally managed to say, her voice somehow thick and squeaky at the same time.

"Hannah, thank god. Where are you? I've been trying to call you."

"No time. I'm at Mama Bayole's. She took Ashley, Dad. She ..."

Hannah heard Dad talking to someone. She assumed it was Officer Benson.

"Hannah, listen. Get out of there, go to the house, we're on our way. We'll be there in less than an hour."

Hannah's stomach dropped, like she'd just gone down that first big hill of a roller coaster. An hour was too long. An hour meant she would never see Ashley again.

"Dad, no. They're going to kill her. Tonight. In the woods, the clearing ... Dad ..."

Hannah's last word trailed off to an anguished whine. She had to try to save Ashley without him. "I'm going after them. Please, hurry."

She hung up the phone without waiting for his response. The shrill ringing brought fresh tears, knowing Dad had hit call back on his cell. Hannah's heart ached when she realized she hadn't told him she loved him. She reached for the phone, then let her hand drop. She ran out the back door and called to Susan. The woman came from the side of the house and they jogged toward the back woods. When they reached the tree line, Susan moved into the lead. Hannah handed her the flashlight.

"I saw them go in here." Susan pointed the light at an opening in the brush, barely discernible as a path. "Let's go."

Hannah was surprised at Susan's fearlessness. She really had no skin in the game. She could turn around, go back to her life. She didn't owe Ashley or Hannah anything. At the same time, Hannah knew that wasn't true. Susan had *plenty* of skin in the game. All the regret, remorse and fear she'd endured since escaping. She was here for redemption, or maybe retribution.

"Susan, what are we going to do if we—*when* we get to the clearing?"

Susan was breathing hard, but she was keeping a steady pace.

"We're going to save your friend and put an end to that voodoo witch or whatever she is."

"How?"

The sound that came from in front of her might have been a laugh. "Haven't figured that out yet."

Hannah shook her head as she ran, unsure who was crazier— Susan for charging head-on into this or her for following.

A lunatic slideshow of scenarios played in Hannah's head. In one, they found the clearing and heroically saved Ashley, defeating Mama Bayole. In all the others, they arrived to find Mama Bayole standing over Ashley's pale, lifeless body. Or they were captured themselves and sacrificed to whatever pagan god or demon Mama Bayole worshipped.

For the next half hour, they clambered over rocks and shoved their way through branches. Hannah's face and arms were covered in myriad scratches. Several times, Susan stopped to get her bearings, once having to backtrack when she realized they were off the path.

Hannah didn't know what kept Susan on the right trail, some instinct from her experience years before, a latent memory etched in her subconscious, or something else. When the flashlight's beam reflected a metallic glint, Hannah knew Susan had done it. Mama Bayole's golf cart was just ahead.

Susan stopped and turned. Her expression was hard to read in the darkness, but her eyes held a look of dread and resignation. And something else. Courage? Conviction? It didn't matter. They would enter the clearing and whatever happened after that was probably out of their hands. She prayed to whoever or whatever might be up there.

"We go in here. When we get near the clearing, I think we should split up. At the very least, we'll be harder to catch that way. Before the ..."

Hannah knew the next word was supposed to be *sacrifice* but Susan didn't say it, either out of respect for Ashley or out of fear.

"There's a prayer that Mama Bayole leads. Last time, we were all facing her with our backs to the altar. That might be the only chance we get. I'll go to the far side of the clearing where I think Mama Bayole will be. You go the other way and wait behind the altar for the prayer. I'll create a diversion. The altar has ropes, not chains, so you should be able to cut her loose pretty quickly."

"What do you mean a diversion? They'll catch you, Susan, I can't."

Susan grabbed her by the shoulders. Her grip was fierce. She leaned in close. "It's the only way, Hannah. Trust me. I let them end one life while I stood by and did nothing. I can't let it happen again."

She let go of Hannah and turned toward the thicket, then she was gone, swallowed whole by the darkness.

CHAPTER TWENTY

Hannah paused for a second, then followed, feeling her way through the thick underbrush. There was nothing in front of her but darkness. The only sound was the rustling of the branches they made. She paused again, making sure she *could* still hear Susan up ahead. She imagined being lost in the pitch-black maze and shivered, forcing herself to keep moving.

When the tangled brush became too impenetrable to walk, Hannah got down on all fours and crawled, squeezing between branches and small tree trunks to keep going. The air was redolent with the combination of old pine needles and an earthy scent, and somehow comforting in spite of the circumstances.

She stopped when she saw Susan's sneakers in front of her. The flickering firelight through the bushes provided the illumination. The clearing was just ahead. Susan signaled which way she was going and pointed for Hannah to go in the opposite direction. Hannah gave a thumbs-up and they parted, a golf ball-sized lump forming in Hannah's throat. As with Jacob, Hannah felt like she'd known Susan for longer than just a few hours. They'd already been through so much.

Hannah resumed crawling around the perimeter of the clearing, careful to be quiet and to keep a safe buffer of undergrowth between her and the red-robed figures she could now make out in the firelight. It was slow going, the fear of being heard magnified now that she was that much closer. And now that she was alone.

Hannah's gaze moved from one figure to the next. Then she spotted the stone altar. Cold talons gripped her when she saw the white sheet, knowing Ashley was under it. Burning acid bubbled up her throat, and she fought to choke it down. She began dry heaving, her stomach convulsing. She scurried deeper into the scrub pines, desperate to put some distance between her and the people in the clearing. She slid behind the trunk of the largest pine in the vicinity just as her body rejected the contents of her stomach.

She collapsed to the ground, choking back gasps and sobs, her throat on fire. She felt gutted, all the fight gone. Her mind flashed back to the reaction she'd had when she'd first realized what Scout had carried out of the trees.

It struck Hannah that closing her eyes and drifting off was a fine idea. Then she thought of that white sheet, of Ashley. She sat up, wiped her mouth on the bottom of her shirt, and began crawling again.

Scratched and dirty, minus a layer or two of skin on her palms and knees, Hannah reached her destination. She found a spot as close to the altar as she could get without being seen, the stone slab acting as a shield from the gathering on the other side. Just as she got situated, a murmuring rose from the group.

Hannah craned her neck to see what was causing the stir, but all she managed to get a look at was the shape under the sheet on the altar. Logic told her to look away, but she couldn't. She watched for movement, something to let her know Ashley was alive, but the sheet remained still. A wave of desperate sorrow crashed over her. The urge to burst from hiding and yank the sheet away was overwhelming. She remembered what she'd said to Ashley.

"You might end up on that stone altar with Mama Bayole or the crazy librarian or someone worse standing over you with a knife."

She had to know Ashley was still alive.

A voice rose from the clearing, strong and loud, and Hannah recognized it as Mama Bayole's. It sounded like some kind of prayer or chant, but it wasn't in English. The robed people had grouped together just on the other side of the altar. Hannah counted at least ten of them, probably more.

Are there thirteen in a coven? Is that what this is?

Mama Bayole stopped speaking and the group responded as one, but Hannah couldn't make out the word.

Then they all dropped to their knees and there was Mama Bayole. She wore a black robe and some sort of headdress with antlers, but her face was uncovered. Her eyes blazed a demonic red from the torches' reflection. Hannah watched the old woman's lips move but heard nothing. The old woman was whispering now, her followers silent on the ground.

Then her voice boomed. "Who shall bring me the gifts?"

Hannah watched, mesmerized by the scene playing out in front of her. Two members of the group stood and walked toward Mama Bayole, each with their arms outstretched in front of them. One held a long, deadly looking knife. Mama Bayole took it and raised it above her head, chanting another prayer in the same unrecognizable language as before. It was all proceeding just as Susan had described.

The second person held what looked like an ornate cup, maybe a chalice. Again, Mama Bayole raised it over her head and recited another prayer. Hannah was reminded of the traditional Catholic ritual of bringing up the gifts at church. The two people turned to rejoin the group, when movement behind Mama Bayole caught Hannah's eye.

One of the torches on the far side of the clearing was leaning, tipping over. The group was still kneeling, heads bowed, as Mama Bayole continued to chant. Mama Bayole and the followers were in the throes of the ritual and didn't notice the torch.

The torch bobbed up and down and Hannah realized it wasn't tipping over on its own—somebody was moving it. *Susan.*

Mama Bayole's voice exploded above the dark quiet. "Show me the offering!"

Her voice held the strength of a woman half her age. One person stood and walked to the altar. Hannah stared, suddenly realizing how close she was to them. Something about the way the person walked struck her as familiar. *The librarian?* The thought disappeared when the sheet was pulled away with a flourish. A pervasive dread stopped Hannah's breath.

A mewling sound escaped Hannah's lips, but it was drowned out by Mama Bayole's prayers. Ashley was indeed on the slab, tied down. *Knowing* it was her, and *seeing* her there, vulnerable and utterly helpless, were worlds apart. Hannah trembled, and she was suddenly sure she would sit there, paralyzed with fear while they murdered Ashley. *Tharn,* she thought, like the rabbits in *Watership Down*. Then the clearing became more illuminated, brightening with some unholy light.

The person that removed the sheet froze, stumbled, then turned to go back to the group. The source of the light wasn't anything supernatural. The woods behind Mama Bayole were burning. Hannah watched as the flames crept across the clearing, fueled by the layers of dead leaves and pine needles that blanketed the ground.

She remembered one January when Dad had burned the Christmas tree after it had turned brown. It had gone up like it had been soaked in gasoline. She wondered how quickly the woods might burn.

"Fire!" the voice from one of the robed figures echoed in the clearing.

The congregation, or whatever they were, rose as one and looked in the direction of the flames. A cacophony of voices and screams rose as people began to mill about, unsure of what to do. Hannah waited as their fear and confusion turned the clearing into chaos. Some people were running toward the flames trying to put them out, others were running toward the small gap in the trees where the path was.

Mama Bayole, though, just stood staring at the origin of the fire. Then her voice rose above the confusion, silencing the people.

"Intruder, get her!"

Some of her followers obeyed and ran toward the tree line where the fire was the worst.

This is my chance, Hannah thought. She jumped to her feet, the tremors of fear gone, and scrambled through the last of the tangled bushes toward the altar.

She stayed low to the ground, using the altar to shield her. By the time she reached it, she had the knife out and quickly began slashing through the ropes that bound Ashley. Ashley's head lolled toward her, revealing the glassy-eyed stare of a heavily drugged person.

Hannah cut through the final bond and tried to pull Ashley toward her. She was deadweight. Hannah leaned close to her and hissed in her ear. "Ashley, we have to go. Please."

Ashley squinted and Hannah thought she saw her eyes clear for just a second. "Hannah?"

"It's me, Ashley. Can you get up?"

The crackling roar of the blaze drowned out the cries of the followers. A blanket of heat hit Hannah's face, carried on the slight breeze. She tried to push Ashley up but was afraid she would just roll her off the altar.

I'm running out of time.

Hannah grabbed the sheet from the ground and tossed it over Ashley. She was going to have to carry her and wanted to protect her from the bushes and tree branches as best she could. With strength she didn't know she had, Hannah scooped her friend up in her arms and turned toward the woods. She felt Ashley's arms loosely loop around her neck as she half-ran, half-staggered toward the safety of the forest.

"Stop them!" a voice commanded from behind her. *Mama Bayole!*

Hannah paused, compelled to turn around, not knowing why. Her eyes found Mama Bayole's across the clearing and goosebumps sprouted on her arms despite the heat from the blaze. Mama Bayole glared at her and even at this distance and through the thickening smoke, the look of hatred was something

Hannah would never forget. The growing flames behind the old woman made her seem more formidable, bigger than life.

A few of the hooded figures turned in Hannah's direction. Hannah pulled her gaze away and ran.

She reached the edge of the clearing and crashed through the bushes, ignoring the scratches, scrapes, and gouges the underbrush inflicted. If only she'd been able to get into the woods before being seen, maybe she could have hidden until Ashley was able to move on her own. Now, she was at an impossible disadvantage.

She ran, the branches grabbing and clawing at her, doing their best to slow her down. The bloody scrapes and torn clothes would be a small price to pay for Ashley's safety. A sharp branch raked Hannah's face just below her right eye and she felt a gush of warmth spill down her cheek, but she didn't stop.

It was impossible to tell if anyone was in pursuit. The sound of her own perilous journey—her harsh breathing and the branches ripping and scraping—echoed in her ears, drowning out the rest of the world. Hannah took the path of least resistance, darting left or right when she encountered anything she couldn't get through with brute force or sheer will. Even when the ache in her arms became unbearable, somehow, she continued.

It wasn't Ashley's deadweight or the branches that finally stopped her—it was her own teenage clumsiness. Hannah tripped. Over rock or root, she didn't know, but she went down hard, landing on top of Ashley. The fall knocked the wind out of her, and in her oxygen-deprived state from running it made sucking in air impossible. Hannah rolled onto her back, futilely scratching at her throat as if she could somehow help the air get through. Her head throbbed, pulse pounding in her ears.

She managed to catch her breath before passing out. She sat up, staring back the way she'd come, looking and listening for any hint of a red-robed figure crashing toward her. Or worse, Mama Bayole.

The forest was silent. The growing orangey brightness of the flames through the trees almost made her smile. It would bring help, she knew. But even more satisfying was the chaos it had caused.

How far had I run?

Hannah wondered if Mama Bayole's people had all scattered to the wind, unable to do anything about the fire, unwilling to do anything about her and Ashley. She remembered Mama Bayole's cold stare. It was all she needed to get moving. There was no way the old woman would stop pursuing her. Maybe ever. Hannah remembered Jacob's words all too well.

"I ran until I found my way back to the rest of the crew, the old witch's laughter in my head the whole way. I still hear it sometimes, when I'm feeling low."

Hannah knew she was right. Mama Bayole would never stop.

A new thought, arriving with the suddenness of a summer thunderclap, threatened to paralyze her. *Did they get Susan?* She forced it away, burying it behind the need to save Ashley.

Hannah stood, and with a sigh, bent to pick up Ashley. She felt her friend's body tighten at her touch. Ashley's eyelids fluttered open.

"Mom?"

Hannah barked out a laugh, more relief than humor. "Ash, it's me, Hannah."

"Hannah. I dreamed you came …"

Ashley's eyes shut again, and her body went limp. Hannah

slid one arm in the crook of her knees and the other under her back and lifted. Her muscles screamed, trembling with fatigue, but she lumbered onward. Hannah was essentially walking blind, the darkness ahead of her absolute. Branches grazed her face and arms, and mosquitoes swarmed around them, but she kept moving. The sheet that she'd wrapped around Ash kept getting caught on branches and she'd heard it rip over and over. Hannah imagined there was nothing left but shredded strips of white.

Like hanging flesh.

At some point, Hannah had exited the thicket without realizing it, the going now much easier without the constant pulling of the branches.

She could no longer feel her arms and her shoulders howled with pain. Her legs wobbled with every step and she knew she'd have to stop soon. She wondered again if Susan was safe. Had Mama Bayole's people caught her? Was Mama Bayole sacrificing Susan in place of Ashley? She tried to push the thought away again but couldn't. Her exhaustion was making it hard to think. Her thoughts ran together until they were like a constant drone. Or buzz. Like flies.

She worked on pure muscle memory—one foot in front of the other. Then she was singing that song from an old Christmas cartoon. From there, a memory surfaced from when she was seven or eight. All she'd wanted from Santa that year was a new bike. She had outgrown the one she had been riding since it had training wheels.

I wake up early, well before sunrise, and pounce on Mom and Dad. Together, we go to the living room and I search for my new bike, but it isn't there. Tears run down my face. Nobody should cry on Christmas.

Dad hands me a card and kisses me on the head. I open it with no enthusiasm, too disappointed to care about a stupid card. A piece of paper, more like parchment, falls out. I unfold it carefully and stare at the crudely drawn treasure map.

I look at Mom and Dad and they both shrug, both smiling. I follow the clues on the map, eagerly moving from one room to the next with my parents following. The map leads me to the kitchen, then to the back door. There is a big red 'X' on the map just beyond the door. There it is, on the porch. The pink paint glittering in the porch light's glow, the pink and purple streamers flapping in the icy breeze. I turn and hug my parents, shedding tears of joy. Maybe it's okay to cry on Christmas after all.

Hannah blinked and looked around, idly wondering where that bike was now. The thought of another bike, standing proudly on its kickstand in the hell of Mama Bayole's dungeon, brought her fully alert. It dawned on her that she had sort of fallen asleep on her feet, or at least been close to it.

Fresh tears tickled her cheeks from the memory. She saw something ahead, looming—a rock formation. There was a small cave where she could rest and be well hidden from anyone looking for them.

She managed to wrangle Ashley inside the cave first without banging her around too badly on the rocks. Hannah climbed in next to her friend and adjusted Ash, so she at least looked comfortable. Every muscle ached and Hannah's hands were all pins and needles as normal blood flow resumed. She felt the distant pain of scrapes and gashes all over her body, but for the moment they were both alive, and that was all that mattered.

Her thoughts became jumbled again, exhaustion and stress combining to force her mind to shut down.

She took a deep breath and the aroma of pine sent her back once again to that Christmas morning. When the sun had come up, the temperature had risen with it. After breakfast, Dad had let her take the bike for its inaugural spin up and down the road. Hannah couldn't remember being that happy in her life. She had been a blur of pink, her winter jacket, hat, mittens and boots all the same color as the bike.

Back in the present, something dug into Hannah's back as she drifted off. She reached under her aching body in a sleepy daze and grabbed it. The object felt funny, not like the stick or rock she'd expected. Her hand closed on it but before she could identify it by shape, sleep took her.

I'm walking through a long tunnel. I see a light at the far end, but it seems so distant. That's where the voice is coming from.

"Hannah? Hannah Green?"

I turn to look behind me and see an army of red-robed people advancing. Dogs bark somewhere in the distance, but I can't tell which end of the tunnel the sound comes from. I run toward the light but it's like running in quicksand. I turn and one of the robed figures is right behind me, reaching ...

The hand on Hannah's shoulder shook her gently and she screamed. She sat up, bumping her head on the rocks.

A man peered in at her. "Are you Hannah Green?"

Hannah looked around, completely disoriented. It was light out and she saw a body next to her, covered by a dirty and tattered once-white sheet. The sheet was pulled up over the face, conjuring images of death in Hannah's mind. She yanked the sheet and Ashley's pale face lolled toward her, eyes closed.

"Ashley, wake up … please …"

Hannah leaned over and patted her friend's cheeks, another lesson learned from television and movies. She breathed a ragged sigh of relief and mild surprise when Ashley's eyes squeezed shut tighter, then blinked open. Hannah burst into tears and hugged her friend. Ashley returned the hug weakly.

"Let me help you out of there."

Hannah pulled away and turned to the man, noticing his police uniform for the first time. Panic bubbled up in her gut. *Is he one of them?* No, she couldn't jump at every shadow. The officer extended a meaty hand toward Hannah. She nodded slightly and reached out with her own, letting him pull her from the crevice. Pain ripped through Hannah's arms, shoulders and legs. She grimaced, biting back a moan and wanting to collapse to the ground, but she reached in and helped the officer pull Ashley out. Ashley *did* collapse but the officer still had a grip on her and eased her to the ground.

He turned toward Hannah with a wistful, faraway smile. "Your dad is going to be happy to see you, young lady."

At the mention of her father, fresh tears slid down Hannah's cheeks. *Was it possible to run out of tears?* There had been dark moments since she and Susan had seen the car pull up to the house, moments where Hannah had wondered if she would ever see Dad again.

The thought of Susan sent another wave of despair over her, but Hannah held it at bay, needing to see Dad.

"I'm Officer Wilding of the New Hampshire State Police, by the way. We've got transportation en route. Your dad will be with them."

"Thank you, Officer," Hannah replied, marveling at how

steady her voice was. "Did you get them?"

A keening sound rose, and Ashley started shaking. Hannah knelt beside Ashley. "What is it? Are you hurt?" Ashley shook her head and Hannah wondered if the mention of *them* brought it all back to her friend.

"Did you get them?" Ashley cried.

Wilding darted a glance at Hannah before answering. "We're still trying to clear things up," he said.

Ashley began to sob, as if knowing what that meant.

She's still out there, Hannah thought.

The buzz of engines approaching caught Hannah's attention. The sound quickly grew louder, and three ATVs crested a small rise, zigzagging through the trees to reach them.

Dad leaped off one of the vehicles before it even stopped. Despite her protesting muscles, Hannah sprinted to meet him. They held each other tightly, Dad whispering he loved her over and over. Hannah opened her eyes and noticed Officer Benson watching, smiling.

Someone cleared their throat and Hannah saw a young EMT standing next to her. Another helped Ashley to one of the ATVs and began working on her. Officer Wilding was talking to one of several other State Police officers on the scene.

"I'm sorry, miss, but we need to make sure you're doing okay."

The paramedic motioned to one of the other vehicles.

Hannah gave her father's arm a final squeeze and followed the man.

"My name is Ian. You're Hannah, right?"

She nodded and climbed onto the back of the ATV. Ian listened to her heart and took her blood pressure. He gave her a bottle of water and watched while she drank it down, then gave her another.

"You're dehydrated, not too bad, but better safe than sorry. Drink this one slowly. Are you hungry?"

As soon as the words were out of his mouth, Hannah's stomach responded with a growling rumble. She couldn't remember the last time she'd eaten. She nodded and Ian reached into a pack and pulled out some crackers and a banana. Ashley was already digging into an orange. Hannah peeled the banana and ate it slowly, watching Dad converse with the police. Benson stood next to him, a hand on Dad's shoulder.

The horror of the night before exploded in Hannah's mind in a flash of red-hooded figures and flames. Ashley looked at her just as she turned to her, fear in her eyes.

Mind meld.

Ash grinned and held up her water bottle as if to toast them. Her smile somehow made it better. Hannah lifted her water bottle and returned the grin.

They eventually piled into the ATVs and headed out of the woods. Hannah sat with Ashley but could feel Dad's eyes on her. She wondered if he would ever let her out of his sight again.

The ride was bumpy, but the motion had a calming effect on her. She felt her eyelids fluttering. The smell of burned wood and leaves mixed with the normal scent of the pine forest. Hannah was drained, running on empty both physically and mentally. Ian had given her ibuprofen, but the pain was still there. Weird, distorted memories teased her from the fringes of her mind but refused to come into the light. Hannah didn't know if they were real or fading dreams.

The ATV bounced to a stop, jarring her from a half-sleep.

Hannah expected to be in her backyard but realized with a start that she had no idea where they were. For a panicky second she wondered if escaping and being rescued was just a dream and she was in the back of Mama Bayole's golf cart. Hannah's fear was allayed when she saw Dad, not to mention the collection of emergency vehicles.

Just thinking of Mama Bayole conjured up disturbing thoughts, patchwork memories of her cellar and the clearing. Hannah had so many questions for Ashley and Dad.

She hopped off the ATV and helped Ashley down. There were police cars, fire trucks, and an ambulance and Hannah saw Dad's car as well. It struck her that they must be on Route 33. The cascade of questions grew longer when she connected Route 33 to Jacob Mather, but they would have to wait.

Darkness descended on Hannah's backyard, and she wondered if it would always bring fear with it now. They had spent the day giving statements at New Hampshire State Police Headquarters in Manchester, answering the same questions over and over. It was infuriating and exhausting. Hannah watched each police officer with suspicion. What if one of them had a red robe in the trunk?

The people she did trust: Dad, Ashley, and Officer Benson were all with her. Hannah put Jacob and Susan in that category. Jacob was still recovering in County Memorial and Susan …

"Come sit, Hannah, there's nothing out there."

Dad was patting the couch next to him. Benson sat next to him, absently stroking Scout's back. Scout had taken a liking to the cop and was curled at his feet. Ashley was on the recliner, struggling to keep her eyes open.

Hannah joined them, plopping down next to Dad, but her eyes wandered toward the window again and the gathering darkness beyond.

Was Susan out there somewhere? Was Mama Bayole?

"Dad, Officer Benson, what do we do now?"

Dad dropped an arm around her shoulder and pulled her in for a hug.

"We let the police do their job." Dad sighed.

Officer Benson's face held the same doubt that Hannah felt. This had been going on for decades and the police had done nothing. Why would anything be different now?

"It's all out in the open, Hannah. Those people have nowhere to hide anymore." Her father's voice was calm, soothing.

"Nobody even knows who they are, Dad."

Officer Benson had told them earlier that Mama Bayole's house had burned to the ground last night. There was nothing left.

"They don't have to hide, that's the problem," Hannah replied.

Her face flushed with anger and frustration. Officer Benson was watching her. She could tell he had something to say. Finally, he turned his gaze to Dad.

"I hate to say it, Brian, but Hannah's right. All we have are suspicions that the librarian and Dietrich are involved. The Staties haven't found anything connecting them to Bayole. It doesn't look like there's going to be anything salvageable from her place. From what Hannah told us, the contents of the basement might have at least helped us identify some of the other victims, but ..."

His voice trailed off. Hannah finished the thought in her head. *It's gone. All of it.* Not only had the farmhouse been destroyed, but the fire in the clearing had consumed any possible evidence there. Nothing remained but the stone altar. They would find bone fragments, sure, but nothing to connect those remains to Mama Bayole. Crews would continue to sift through the rubble at her farmhouse, but Hannah doubted they'd find anything useful. She wondered absently if they'd find the remains of her bike.

"What about getting search warrants for that librarian and Dietrich? Maybe they could find something to connect them to Bayole?"

Benson shook his head. He took a deep breath and let it out slowly, like he was trying to calm himself down.

"No judge is going to issue a warrant based on hearsay. We need something definitive to connect them to Bayole, and we just don't have it."

He slammed his fist on the arm of the couch, sending Scout scurrying toward Ashley. Hannah slid to the floor to pat him. He immediately rolled onto his back, waiting for a belly rub.

"The guy at the library that pretended to be the blogger. I took pictures, recorded his voice." Ashley's voice was triumphant.

Hannah glanced around the room, seeing the disappointment mirrored on each face. She turned back at Ashley and saw her lips quiver. Ashley had recognized the look the others had shared and already knew that piece of evidence was gone, too. Benson broke it to her.

"When we went out to look for you in the woods, we left the phone behind. Jacob got scared. He still wasn't convinced I wasn't part of it. He grabbed the phone and took it with him. A car forced him off the road and his tire blew. Another car came by shortly after and offered to help. Jacob doesn't remember anything after. He woke up later in the hospital. There were traces of chloroform in his system."

Hannah knew the rest. Jacob had had what the doctors called "a minor cardiac event." It could have been the stress, the chloroform, or just old age. He was expected to make a full recovery. The phone was gone.

He had gained consciousness long enough to tell Dad and Officer Benson where on Route 33 they'd have the best chance of finding the clearing. Benson had called in a favor with a friend in the State Police to get the search party going. Hannah had heard Benson talking in hushed tones to Dad earlier. His captain at the Hopeland Police Department had suspended him while they investigated his breach of protocol.

"So that's it?"

Ashley sounded so small, so defeated. Benson jerked his head in her direction. Hannah couldn't quite read his expression, but it looked somewhere between anger and resolve.

"No, Ashley. That is most definitely *not* it. I was born and raised in Hopeland. This is my town, too. I won't rest until we find them all and put them behind bars. I'll do it with or without a badge."

Hannah admired Officer Benson's determination—*can I still call him Officer?*—but all the determination in the world didn't mean any of them were safe.

That old witch marked me with her glare. She'll never stop coming for me. For us.

Hannah knew the librarian and Dietrich were part of the cult or coven or whatever it was. There was also the guy who had posed as the blogger and whoever drove the dark-colored car that kept showing up.

"That could be a long time. Or never. They could be anywhere. Any*one*." Hannah hated how scared she sounded.

Benson tried to put her fears to rest. "Hannah, I've already discussed this with your dad. I'm going to stay here for a while until we get a handle on the situation. You have nothing to worry about."

Hannah felt the stress leave her body. Ashley relaxed as well; Hannah could see it in her body language. They both trusted Benson and would certainly sleep better knowing he was here. The fact that he carried a gun didn't hurt either.

Dad stood, touching Brian's shoulder as he got to his feet, "I'll grab you a pillow and blanket."

Hannah glanced at Dad, wide-eyed. She felt Officer Benson's gaze on her and glanced at him. He had a faint smile on his face. She knew what her dad had been lying about and why her mom left.

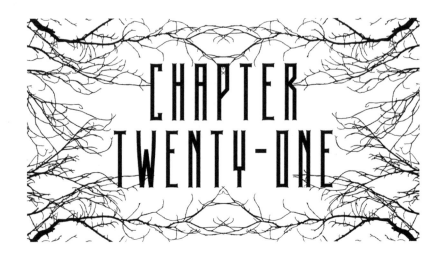

CHAPTER TWENTY-ONE

ater, while Dad and Benson conversed in the living room, Hannah and Ashley finally had a chance to talk. They sat cross-legged on her bedroom floor while Scout sprawled out on the bed. At first Ashley was quiet. Hannah insisted she didn't have to talk about everything this soon, but Ashley was determined to get Hannah up to speed. She thought she might be missing something that Hannah would pick up on. Before she could begin, Hannah blurted out, "I think my dad is gay."

Ashley stared at her, as if trying to figure out if Hannah was joking. Then Ashley's expression changed. She looked pensive. After a moment, she began nodding. "Benson?" she whispered.

"I think so," Hannah said, feeling her face redden. "It was just the way he touched Benson's shoulder when he got up. It was so … intimate." She leaned forward. "It explains why Mom left. And why Dad was lying."

Ashley smiled. "It does explain a lot. But you're okay with it, right?"

Hannah paused. She hadn't even had time to think about that part of it, she was so busy putting the pieces together. She took a minute before answering. "Yeah, I am. I mean, I'm sure when it gets out I'll get picked on, but—" She thought about it for another minute, "I'm really happy for him."

Ashley grimaced. "Yeah. Hopeland isn't exactly known for its progressive views." She straightened up, squaring her shoulders. "But if I hear anyone bad-mouthing Mr. G, you know I've got his back. And yours."

Hannah smiled, "I know, thanks Ash." She blinked back tears. "Now, about this blogger?"

"He seemed nice at first. I was so excited to get information out of him that I think I was blabbering," she began.

Hannah smiled. Ashley talked a lot in most situations, but when she was nervous or excited, look out.

"After a few minutes, I realized something was off. Nothing specific—he was just acting a little weird. Like he didn't know some of the things he should know. I asked him where he came up with his email name and I could tell it took him by surprise. He gave some half-assed answer, and I knew he wasn't the real blogger. I also knew I was in trouble. As soon as I had the chance, I snapped a few pictures and turned on the voice recorder. By then he was getting agitated.

"I agreed to leave when he threatened you. I guess you heard that part. We got out to the parking lot, and he wrapped his arm around my neck and shoved a rag over my face. When I woke up, I was …"

Hannah remembered the terror she'd felt in Mama Bayole's basement, and she hadn't been chained to that disgusting mattress in the pitch black. Her jaw tightened, the thought of

Ashley's suffering brought a toxic anger. That fury turned into a dangerous thirst for revenge.

"I didn't know where I was. It was so dark and the smell … I had such a headache that at first, I just cried. Finally, I tried to get up and felt the chains." Ashley crossed her arms across her chest. She glanced toward the window, her expression haunted.

"Ashley, please, we can finish this later. Whenever you feel up to it."

Ashley stared toward the window for a long moment, then turned to Hannah. Her eyes were blazing with ferocity, not fear. Hannah looked away.

"I was so scared, Hannah. You've heard people say they were paralyzed with fear? That's a real thing. I couldn't move. I wondered if I was dead. It was so dark and quiet. I forced myself to calm down and remembered being half-dragged through the woods to where the foot was. It was so vague, like the remnants of a bad dream …" Ashley took a moment to gather her thoughts. "Eventually, I broke down. I screamed and screamed until I couldn't anymore. Nobody came."

Outside, the sounds of cicadas and crickets paused. Both girls turned toward the window. Scout picked his head up off the bed, sniffing. Something, a coyote probably, howled in the distance. Scout let loose a low growl and his head flopped back down on the bed. The insects resumed their night music and the girls exhaled in unison.

"The room was soundproofed," Hannah said quietly.

Ashley looked at her, confused. Hannah quickly recounted her own time in Mama Bayole's cellar. Ashley's eyes filled with tears.

"You … you went down there? What if …?" She bit her

lower lip.

Hannah just shrugged. "You would have done the same for me."

The truth was Hannah didn't know where the courage to do it had come from. Just thinking about it now sent trails of goosebumps up her arms and made her heart beat crazily.

Ashley was looking at her with an expression Hannah couldn't identify.

"Eventually someone came. I didn't know until the flashlight clicked on. I couldn't see anything, could barely keep my eyes open against the brightness. I felt a jab in my shoulder. Next thing I knew I was on the stone slab."

Benson had told them the doctors had done an emergency tox-screen and found evidence of Propofol, a powerful sedative, in Ashley's blood.

Was one of the cult members a nurse or a doctor?

"It was like a dream, or a nightmare, I guess. It was still daylight, barely. Dusk. The torches were already lit. People drifted around in those robes like blood-colored ghosts. I started screaming. Two of them came over to me. It ... it was like one of those alien abduction movies. They stared at me while I screamed my throat raw. All I saw were their eyes shining behind the hoods. They looked at each other, one pulled out a needle, and I was out again."

Hannah said a silent prayer of thanks. Ashley being drugged through most of the night was probably a blessing. She couldn't imagine being tied down, having to watch that crazy ceremony from the cold stone slab. It was too much to even think about. She wondered if Ashley would ever be Ashley again.

"Do you think the real blogger, Susan, got away?" Ashley's

voice cracked and she wiped her eye with the heel of her hand.

Would either of us get through a day without tears?

"I'm sure they spotted her when she set the fire, but it all happened so fast."

Hannah thought about it again, closing her eyes and trying to picture the scene.

"Intruder. Get her!"

Then chaos.

"I think she probably got away. People were kind of just running around, nobody seemed to know what to do. Then Mama Bayole saw me. I think maybe they all focused on us. By then, the fire was really spreading, and Susan would have been on the other side of it. Maybe they all just panicked and ran."

Hannah wanted to believe Susan had gotten away but wondered if she was just trying to convince herself. Susan's car had still been at the house when they'd arrived home from giving their statements. The police had sent a tow truck to bring it in as evidence.

Ashley was looking at Hannah, head cocked. Hannah smiled and raised her eyebrows in question.

"You saved my life," she whispered.

Hannah barely heard the words. A warm flush spread up from her neck to her hairline; she didn't know why. She looked down at the rug, unsure of what to say. When she looked up, Ashley was still staring at her, smiling now. Hannah finally realized the look on Ashley's face was gratitude, so profound it made Hannah look away again.

"Like I said, you'd have done the same for me, Ash."

Ashley's expression turned thoughtful, then she smirked. "Yeah, but I would have done it different. I would have crashed that clearing and laid those suckers out with seven kinds of pain."

Hannah's jaw dropped in mock horror and they burst into laughter. *And I was worried about her?*

When they stopped laughing, she told Ashley about meeting up with Marcus at the park and him walking her home. Ashley teased her to no end, but Hannah knew she was happy for her. Their laughter continued until Dad came and told them to wrap it up.

They drifted off, still giggling, the sounds of the woods drifting in on the cool night breeze.

Hannah woke the next morning feeling like she'd been hit by a bus. Every muscle in her body resisted her attempts to move by sending shockwaves of pain to her brain. She climbed out of bed like an old lady, thinking about that commercial where the woman yelled, "I've fallen and I can't get up!"

She was surprised to see the bed empty. A ripple of fear shot through her. *What if they came and took her?* The fear dissolved when she heard Ashley's laughter from the other room. Hannah shuffled out to the kitchen where Ashley sat with Dad and Officer Benson. They all turned when she stepped into the room.

Dad smiled. "Good morning." He glanced up at the clock. "Barely."

Hannah gave him her best "you're not funny, Dad" look and joined them at the table. She crossed her arms on the table, and rested her head on them, closing her eyes. "Anything new?"

"No rest for the weary, Hannah. We're going to the hospital to pick up Jacob. He's being released."

Hannah straightened. "He's okay? So soon?" The events of

the past few days had programmed her to expect the worst.

"He's going to be fine. He's a tough old bird, that one," Dad said with a laugh.

Hannah smiled. Mom's old expression sounded strange coming out of Dad's mouth.

She rose dramatically to her feet. "I'll get dressed. Can we drive by Mama Bayole's? I just need to see it …" The words were out before she had even thought about them. She noticed Dad and Benson exchange a look.

"Sure, but we're not stopping." Dad spoke carefully, measuring each word.

Hannah nodded and went to her room. She dressed quickly and threw on her Sea Dogs cap, wondering what compelled her to want to see the burned ruins of Mama Bayole's farmhouse.

Yesterday's clothes had been tossed on the floor in a messy pile. Hannah grabbed them to put them in the laundry before Dad gave her a hard time about it, when something fell and bounced onto the rug. She looked down, confused, not recognizing the object. The clothes fell back to the floor and she bent down, picking up the small gold locket as if it were a fragile relic. A foggy memory surfaced of trying to get comfortable in the rocky crevice, something digging into her back.

She held the locket close to her face, staring in disbelief. *Could it really be?*

She flipped it open. A grainy, faded picture of a woman holding a small child, both smiling, both dressed in what Ashley would call "olden days" clothes. Hannah closed the locket, slipped it into her pocket and went to join the others.

Hannah and Ashley huddled in the backseat as Dad drove toward Mama Bayole's. It was clear he wasn't thrilled about going there, based on his old-man-slow speed and the million times his eyes flicked to the rearview mirror to look at her. Hannah kept her eyes forward and pretended not to notice, waiting for the scorched remains of the farm to come into view. All the windows were down, and she smelled charred wood in the air long before she saw the ruins. As they neared the house, Hannah's heart pounded, hard and fast. Ashley clamped a hand on her knee. Ash's fear and anxiety had to be a hundred times worse than her own.

The car rounded the corner and there it was. Yellow tape cordoned off the area and there was a fire inspector's car parked in front of the ruins. Hannah's heart settled and Ashley's grip loosened. Under the crystal blue sky, with the summer sun bathing everything in its brilliant yellow light, it was just a pile of burnt wood. Where the tall grass had surrounded the house was nothing but blackened earth. The outbuildings had also been torched. Clearly this was arson; the fire inspector's job would be an easy one.

Dad turned the car around and headed back. This time, his gaze lingered in the rearview mirror and Hannah gave him a nod. He nodded back, almost imperceptibly, and drove toward the hospital.

The ride was somber, each of them preoccupied with their own thoughts. Hannah was surprised when Dad pulled into the hospital parking lot. She had been thinking about last night, the events in the clearing, and kind of zoned out. She turned to Ashley and saw her friend was sound asleep.

When they got to Jacob's room, he was sitting on the edge of the bed, already dressed in street clothes. He looked smaller to Hannah, his face older, less radiant. She hoped it was just the result of the hospital stay, not the aftereffects of dealing with Mama Bayole's minions.

They exchanged greetings, then stood in awkward silence. Hannah felt Jacob's gaze on her and looked at him. His expression was hard to read.

Dad finally broke the silence. "Well, I guess we should get going."

They shuffled toward the door, but Hannah noticed Jacob wasn't moving.

"Mr. Green, Brian? Do you mind if I have a word with Hannah in private?"

Hannah looked at her dad, a hint of unease settling in. He nodded and gave a tight-lipped smile, motioning for the others to leave the room with him. When they were gone, Jacob stood unsteadily and closed the door. He returned to his perch on the side of the bed and patted the spot next to him. Hannah joined him, more and more afraid of what was coming.

"I've got to get right to it here, Hannah. This isn't over. I know most of what happened in the clearing and that she had her house burned down. She ain't gone. I can still *feel* her. That old witch … No way she's gone that easy. Her people, well, you know."

"What are you trying to tell me?" Hannah asked shakily.

"The other people, you called them followers and that's exactly what they are. Sheep. Weak and lost and without a leader, they're nothing. You cut the head off a snake, the snake dies. The whole thing. You get me?"

Hannah had heard the expression before but had never really thought about it. It clicked into place now and brought all her fear back.

"You mean we have to find her? Kill her?"

Jacob took a wheezing breath and shifted on the bed, so he

was looking at Hannah. Up close, his face looked ancient. His eyes were clear, though, and shone with wisdom.

"One step at a time. First, we got to find her. What happens after that is up to her."

The ride to Jacob's house was uncomfortable, to say the least. Hannah felt everyone's eyes on her, felt the questions hanging in the air.

"What did Jacob want to talk to you about? Does he know something about Mama Bayole?"

Twenty minutes later, they pulled up to Jacob's house and got out of the car. Hannah hadn't realized how claustrophobic it had been until she stepped out into the fresh air.

Jacob's house was a tidy one-story ranch on a quiet street full of not-so-tidy one-story ranches. Well-trimmed rhododendrons and lilac bushes grew next to the house, and the small front lawn was a lush green despite the hot weather.

Jacob invited them in, and Hannah admired the coziness of the small home. Pictures lined the walls, covering almost every square inch of space. She walked the perimeter of the living room, stopping to look at each one. There appeared to be generations of families pictured. Hannah stared at an old black-and-white photograph.

In it, Jacob towered over a man she recognized from the newspaper picture that Dad had shown her—her great-grandfather. The two men were standing side-by-side, Jacob's arm slung across the smaller man's shoulders. Jacob was wearing an enormous gown and a too-small graduation cap.

"Graduation day," Jacob said, startling her. Hannah hadn't

noticed him come up behind her. "Proudest day of my folks' lives, seeing me graduate high school."

Hannah continued circling the room, amazed at the stories captured in the photos. It was like a scrapbook on his walls, a family history.

I have to take more pictures, she thought. *Memories are too important.*

Her thoughts were disturbed when Dad called from the kitchen. Hannah blinked, surprised to find she was alone in the room.

She joined the others in the kitchen where Jacob was stirring a giant glass pitcher of iced tea and freshly sliced lemon.

"My mother, God rest her soul, always said there's no better way to greet summer guests than with a fresh glass of iced tea. It's one of her many lessons I abide by."

Jacob filled the glasses, and they all had a drink. The iced tea was delicious, quenching a thirst Hannah didn't realize was there.

"Now, I got a nice picnic table out the back, How about we set out there for a chat?"

Everyone murmured in agreement and followed Jacob outside. The backyard was spectacular. Giant dogwoods and more rhododendrons lined the perimeter, giving the small yard privacy from the neighbors. Rosebushes and beds of flowers surrounded the cozy brick patio and a sprawling willow shaded most of the space. A picnic table took up a good part of the patio. Beside it was a compact gas grill.

They all sat at the table while Jacob remained standing. The same unease Hannah had felt at the hospital crept over her again.

Is he going to give everyone the same spiel? Or does he have something else to say?

"First, I want to say I'm sorry that you all got dragged into this. This world can be a strange, sometimes ugly place. I found that out at a very young age, thanks to the old witch. I made it my mission to do as much good for people as I could. I found the love of a good woman, maybe the *best* woman. We had two beautiful children. We were all very faithful, devout. We went to church. We volunteered at the shelters together. We made a lovely home." He gestured to the surrounding beauty.

"Mother always said that God works in mysterious ways. Well, I'll be damned if I know what He was up to when he took Marcy and the kids from me." Jacob paused; pain etched on his face. "The driver of the other car was drunk. Crossed over the center line into their lane, hit them head on. The three of them died in the wreck."

Jacob paused to wipe his eyes and blow his nose on an old hankie he pulled from his pocket.

"The guy driving the other car ... Seems like it happens this way a lot ... He made it. I went to see him in the hospital. He didn't escape unharmed—he was all hooked up to tubes and wires, his head and face all bandaged up. I think he knew who I was when I walked into the room. The heart machine started beeping like an old metal detector that hit on a tin can."

He seemed to be growing older as he spoke. "I held up my hands and told him I didn't mean him no harm. I just wanted to ask him one question. He looked at me, still scared, and told me to ask away. I asked him how it felt. He looked at me like he didn't know what I meant. Right then I reconsidered my stance on not meaning him any harm."

Jacob let out a strangled laugh and leaned heavily on the picnic table, causing the ice in each of their drinks to rattle against the glass.

"I clarified my question. I asked him how it felt to kill someone. He got real mad, can you imagine? He took my sweet family from me and he was mad at me? He started shouting and grabbed for the call button. But I was faster, still a young man."

Hannah's stomach tightened into a hard ball and began to creep up her throat. She grabbed her iced tea, then put it back down on the table without drinking any. She didn't like where the story was going and liked the look in Jacob's eyes even less.

"Well, younger than I am now, at least. I held the call button away so he couldn't reach it. I asked him again how it felt to kill someone. How it felt to kill children. He started breathing real heavy, panting. I thought he was going to break down. I reached out for his hand, but he yanked it away.

"Then I asked him again, said I was going to keep asking until he gave me an answer. He looked up at me and there was no remorse in those eyes. I saw something there, something like I hadn't seen since the clearing. It was beyond hatred, it was evil. He told me it felt good knowing there were three less black folks in the world. Only he used an uglier word."

Hannah gasped and heard the others muttering in disbelief. Her nausea had turned into a fist, one that was squeezing and twisting her guts. Jacob straightened and walked to the edge of the patio. Without turning, he finished the story.

"I leaned in real close and told him I could not forgive him. Then I put my hand over his face and held it there until the light in his eyes went out."

Hannah watched the shocked reactions of the others. Her stomach roiled. She knew this story was meant for her, a continuation of his "head of the snake" talk.

"Jacob, you realize I'm still a police officer?"

Benson's voice was low and steady, but Hannah heard a touch of mirth in it. Jacob's expression showed his amusement.

"Go ahead, Officer Benson, arrest me. Only thing to come of that is someone else will have to put soup in the bowls of homeless people every weekend. If it's something you need to do, I understand."

Benson shook his head. "My point is you might want to keep that story to yourself."

Jacob nodded. "*My* point is, sometimes things have to be done. Bad things. Ugly things. I wish I could tell you that it was the old witch that made me do it, but it wasn't. It was all my doing, my *will*. I couldn't forgive him for what he'd done, but I have asked the Lord to forgive me. The thing is, I don't think He can, because I'd do the same thing again."

Hannah watched a pair of small red birds flutter in and out of one of the dogwoods. She didn't know why Jacob didn't just come out and say what he meant. That he was willing to kill Mama Bayole.

"Jacob, are you sure you're going to be all right here?"

Hannah realized Dad's question might have two meanings. Did he mean was Jacob going to feel safe from Mama Bayole's people, or was he questioning Jacob's mental stability based on his admission?

"I made it this far, Brian. I'll be right as rain. Those people have no need to bother an old man. If they thought they had cause, I guess I wouldn't be standing here. They would have killed me out on Route 33. 'Course it would have looked like an accident." Jacob looked out over his gardens, his face haggard and sad. "No, they'll leave me be. I'll just tend to my plants and mind my own business."

Hannah watched Benson and Dad for a reaction, but they seemed satisfied. Ashley had been quiet the entire time but now she was squirming. Hannah knew Ashley had something to say, maybe a question to ask. She caught her friend's eyes and raised her eyebrows. Ashley tightened her lips, then she spoke.

"How are any of us really supposed to go back to our old lives? We know the librarian is one of them. We think at least one cop is. I ..."

Ashley buried her head in her arms on the table, like a kindergartner at nap time, except she was weeping. As much as Jacob and Hannah had been through, Ashley had it the worst. How could she ever feel safe? Hannah put a hand on her back and looked up at Benson and Dad.

"The librarian is gone. The name she used and all her background information was false. Her apartment was under a different name, also fake. It's empty. Our tech guys found keystroke loggers on all the computers at the library." He looked at Ashley, then at me. "That's how they intercepted the emails. Then they hacked into Susan's email account to contact you. You'd both better change your passwords."

Ashley's head snapped up, her face smeared with tears. "What about Mrs. Cheevers?"

Hannah looked at Benson, eyes wide. She had forgotten about Mrs. Cheevers and felt like a horrible person for it.

"Mrs. Cheevers is fine. She caught a touch of a summer cold is all. She's back to work already."

Jacob snorted a laugh. "Summer cold, eh? What a coincidence." His voice dripped with sarcasm.

Dad stared at him incredulously. "Jacob, you can't possibly

think—"

Jacob cut him off with a look. "You think these are just crazy people. Zealots. They're more than that. At least *she* is."

There was ice in Jacob's words and it chilled Hannah. She folded her arms, waiting for Dad or Benson to respond. It occurred to her that she hadn't told them what Susan had said about the ritual. How Mama Bayole somehow fed on the youth of her sacrifices. Did Dad and Benson even believe that Mama Bayole was the same woman Jacob saw in the clearing?

Then Hannah saw the looks on their faces and understood what Jacob already knew—they wouldn't believe *any* of it. It was easier for them to see Mama Bayole as a religious fanatic than some kind of real witch or voodoo priestess or whatever she was. To them, she'd kidnapped Ashley for a sacrifice, sure, but there was nothing supernatural about it.

Jacob was looking at Hannah. He gave a slight nod, as if reading her thoughts. Everything fell into place. This was *all* for her. Her and Ashley. She tried to smile but knew it fell short. She gave Jacob a nod in return.

"Well, I guess we should probably get going. Let Jacob get some rest." Dad stood, looking a little confused.

Hannah wondered if he thought Jacob was the crazy one.

They exchanged goodbyes and Hannah felt a deep sadness, a finality. Before she left, she ran to Jacob and gave him a hug. He closed his arms around her, and Hannah felt him sigh before they separated. "It's all going to be okay, Hannah. I promise."

He smiled, a real Jacob smile, and she believed him.

They stopped for lunch in town on the way home. Hannah saw a sign in the diner advertising the next concert at Champlain Park. It was the next night. She thought about Marcus and wondered if they would still go. It seemed so unreal. Somehow, in just a matter of days, the normal and the unusual switched places. Weird was the new normal.

Dad and Benson had a hushed conversation about Jacob's confession. Benson said he had no intention of doing anything other than satisfying his own curiosity by checking out the report on the guy Jacob said he killed.

Hannah still hadn't told Ashley that Marcus had asked her to the concert. It didn't seem like the right time now, not with Dad so close. Instead, they talked of inconsequential things like the upcoming school year and clothes and stuff that used to be casual but now seemed alien.

During the ride home, Hannah kept catching herself looking out the windows for a late-model, dark-colored car. The new normal.

At home, they retreated to the backyard with Scout for some privacy.

"Ash, are you doing okay? I know it's a stupid question, but after what you went through?"

Ashley didn't answer for a minute. When she turned to Hannah, her eyes were free of tears, her expression thoughtful. Closer to the old Ashley.

"I think I'm going to be fine. Stuff like this, people adapt. But I won't start being fine until she's dead or locked up. You know that, right?"

"I know," Hannah answered, "Jacob knows, too. That's why he pulled me aside at the hospital." Hannah filled her in about the snake conversation. "That story he told at his house, I think it was meant for me. For us. I think he wants us to find Mama Bayole so he can kill her."

CHAPTER TWENTY-TWO

The rest of the afternoon was uneventful, but Hannah's anxiety rose as evening approached. There was still no news about any of Mama Bayole's people and no sign of Susan. Hannah feared the worst—the cult had caught her and killed her. It led her to wonder if the ritual really kept Mama Bayole alive. If so, what happened if she didn't perform it on schedule? Would she age in fast-forward and shrivel up and die? It seemed too Hollywood.

Those types of thoughts were going to make for a long night.

"I think I'm going to the concert at Champlain Park with Marcus tomorrow night."

The words came in a rush, like she had to get them out quick or they'd turn around and run back. Ashley stared, her mouth hanging open. A familiar heat crept up Hannah's face. Before Ashley started teasing her—there would plenty of time for that, Hannah knew—she blurted out that he'd asked her the day they had walked home together from Champlain Park.

"Well, well, well, I get kidnapped and you're out getting

dates instead of trying to rescue me. You ought to be ashamed of yourself, Hannah Green."

Ashley's eyes were bright with humor. Hannah knew her friend was happy for her, but it didn't stop the flush from reaching her ears.

"I figured I'd need a new best friend if you were going to be a zombie or something, so why not somebody cute?"

Ashley giggled and began to sing, "Hannah and Marcus sitting in a tree. K-I-S-S-I—"

She punched Ashley's shoulder to shut her up, blushing profusely.

"Ow!" Ashley rubbed her shoulder. "Hello? I just went through a traumatic event and may be scarred for life, in case you forgot."

"Well, you deserve it."

"'Well, you deserve it,'" Ashley mimicked. "Are you going to call him? I mean, I'm happy for you, really. I just wish it didn't take a near human sacrifice for you to get off your butt to find a boyfriend, but whatever."

"I'm going to call him tonight. After everything we've been through, calling a boy is about the least scary thing I can think of."

Ashley insisted that Hannah call him right then—she had to know this was for real. Hannah let Ashley lead her into the house and over to the phone.

What am I doing?

Dad and Benson were in the kitchen stacking a plate with burgers and dogs, about to head out to the grill. As soon as they did, Ash grabbed the phone and handed it to her.

Hannah looked up the number and dialed before she lost her nerve. As soon as Ashley was sure she was going through with it, she left the kitchen, though Hannah was positive she was going to listen from around the corner.

Hannah listened to the ringing, her body tensing up. She considered hanging up but knew caller ID would give her away even on a missed call.

"Hello?"

It was Marcus. At least she didn't have to blunder her way through asking a parent or sibling to talk to him. She wiped her sweaty palms on her shorts one at a time.

"Hi, uh, Marcus? It's Hannah. Hannah Green."

"Oh, hi Hannah. I was going to call you but I heard ..."

Hannah cringed. She hadn't bothered to pay any attention to what the news reports were saying happened. *What* had *he heard?* Hannah wasn't sure what to say.

"I heard some pretty weird stuff. Are you okay? And Ashley?"

"Yeah, I guess so. I mean, it's been a rough few days."

Hannah waited, desperate for something to say to fill the awkward silence.

Marcus spoke first. "Oh crap, the concert is tomorrow night. We ... I ... Do you still want to go?"

Hannah almost dropped the phone. This was going to be an actual date. Hannah started thinking about what to wear when she realized she hadn't answered.

"Oh, I mean, yes. I do want to go."

Dummy, way to sound overanxious.

"Oh, that's great. So, do you want me to pick you up? I mean, not me. Well, I'll be there but I won't be driving ..."

Hannah smiled and suppressed a giggle. Knowing Marcus was this nervous had a calming effect on her.

"I can have my dad drive me. We can meet there, if that's okay?"

"Sure. Hey, I know Ashley is staying with you, so, if you

want, I could see if Ken wants to come so Ashley won't feel like a third wheel."

Hannah felt like she was in one of those cartoons where hearts floated out of a character's head. Marcus's shyness was endearing. She was glad he wasn't some super-slick smooth talker.

"That's really sweet of you to think of Ashley. It would be cool if she came with us, if Ken wants to go too."

Ashley popped her head around the corner and gave her a thumbs-up, then made kissy faces at her. Hannah flipped her the bird, then turned around and talked to Marcus about where and when to meet. They chatted for a few minutes longer, just small talk, then hung up.

Ashley ran around the corner and practically tackled her. She was bouncing up and down with her hands-on Hannah's shoulders, chanting, "Hannah's got a boyfriend!" when Dad and Benson walked in.

Benson looked amused while Dad looked somewhere between "about to throw up" and "having a heart attack." Ashley wasted no time in taking control.

"Mr. Green, your daughter, Hannah, will need a ride to Champlain Park on the morrow evening to meet a Mr. Marcus Diaz for a concert and some potential lip-to-lip contact." Her British accent was passable.

Hannah gasped and swatted her while Benson burst out laughing. Dad looked a lot closer to "about to throw up."

"Never fear, Mr. Green, for I, Ashley Wallace, shall be there to chaperone and make sure the proper etiquette and decorum is upheld."

Benson almost dropped the plate of food he was holding, he was laughing so hard. Hannah wasn't sure if it was Ashley's antics or Dad's expression. Despite her embarrassment, Hannah was laughing right along.

Dinner was a mixture of laughter and cross-examination from Dad about *this Marcus character.* They stayed at the kitchen table long after they had finished eating. The girls drank lemonade, the men beers, while they talked.

Dad was the one to break it up, saying he wanted to watch the ballgame. He and Benson moved to the living room while Hannah and Ashley went to her bedroom for what Dad called girl talk.

Hannah drifted off to sleep that night feeling the tide of normal and unusual beginning to revert. She was safe and content. More than content, she was happy. The shadow of Mama Bayole still hung over her, but it was less ominous, at least for the night.

Other than the fact that a suspended police officer was having sleepovers, Hannah was happy for Dad to have some adult time.

Is that what it is? She'd been watching Dad and Benson and wasn't sure. Another mystery.

Her dreams were of summer nights and concerts and Marcus's hand in hers.

The sound of raindrops woke Hannah and she rolled over to stare out the window. The sky was gray and so turned Hannah's mood. She watched the raindrops zigzag down the window, willing the rain to stop so the concert wouldn't be canceled.

"Let's go grab breakfast, I'm hungry."

She turned to face Ashley, unable to hide her glum mood.

"Even if the concert gets rained out, he still likes you, Hannah. Cheer up. Let's go get cereal. I need my sugar fix."

Hannah crawled out of bed, finally able to move like a teenager instead of an old lady. She raised her arms over her head, then bent down to touch her toes, checking if anything still hurt. A few twinges but pretty much back to normal.

"Going for a run?" Ashley asked, one eyebrow raised.

"No, still recovering from dragging your sorry ass out of the New Hampshire woods the other night."

Ashley punched her shoulder and pushed past her, headed toward the kitchen. She went to the cabinet and grabbed a box of Cinnamon Toast Crunch and a bowl.

"You know that crap has like ten cups of sugar in it?" Benson said, getting up off the couch.

Ashley didn't even turn around. "Of course, I know. That's the reason I'm going to eat the rest of the box, to save you from working on your spare tire."

Hannah snorted a laugh. *Ashley's back, all right.* She mused at how comfortable they all were together, especially with Benson, who had been a complete stranger just a few days earlier.

The thought sent a pang of unease through her. *What do we really know about him?*

"What's all the commotion?" Dad shuffled out of his room, hair askew and face puffy with sleep.

Hannah wondered how late they'd stayed up watching the game. She glanced at the clock and was surprised to see it was only seven-thirty. Ashley and Hannah never got up this early, except for school.

"Well, Ashley was just calling me fat," Benson said in a mock pouty voice.

"Sounds about right," Dad muttered, and went for the coffeemaker. "Hey, it's raining."

Dad was looking out the window over the sink.

"Thanks for the news flash, Dad." Hannah couldn't stop thinking about the concert.

"Oh, don't mind her, Mr. Green. She's just upset that her date might get rained out."

Hannah pivoted and glared at Ashley. She sometimes pushed things too far. She turned to read Dad's expression. He seemed surprised for a second, like he had forgotten last night's conversation. Then he just looked sad.

"I guess staying up all night doing the rain dance paid off," he said it without a smile, without any humor.

Hannah felt bad. She knew Dad was thinking she was growing up too fast. The parents' lament, Ashley called it. The thought of him living here alone one day, after she went off to college did nothing to lift Hannah's already damp spirits.

Dad was still at the sink, filling the coffeepot with water to pour into the coffeemaker. "What the—"

He dropped the pot in the sink and ran toward the back door. Benson leaped to his feet, pulling a gun from nowhere and yelling at her and Ash to stay put, before following Dad out the back door.

Ashley and Hannah almost collided trying to get to the window. It took her a minute to register what she was seeing. It took another minute for Hannah to believe it.

"We're gonna need a bigger boat." She felt Ashley staring and turned to her, the first smile of the day crossing Hannah's face. "Ash, meet Susan."

They watched as Dad and Benson approached the woman.

Susan threw her head back, opened her mouth wide, and screamed. It was a real horror-movie job, shrill and piercing and filled with panic. Dad and Benson stopped, hands in front of them in the classic "we mean you no harm" position. Susan took a step back, shaking her head from side to side. Her clothes were a mess, torn and muddy, and her hair hung in greasy clumps, but it was her face that scared Hannah. She was terrified, probably in shock.

Dad and Benson kept talking to her, slowly approaching. Finally, Susan nodded, and they went to her side. They each put one of her arms over their shoulders.

Hannah filled the coffeemaker and started the brew cycle, then went to Dad's room to get one of his sweatshirts and a couple of blankets. As soon as they made it to the porch, Hannah ran to them and gave Susan a hug, ignoring her soaking, mud-covered clothes. The woman's skin was like a cold slab of meat.

"Susan, here, put this on." Hannah helped her with the sweatshirt, then wrapped the blanket around her. Ashley was by her side, and together they guided Susan to the couch. Scout was running under their feet, sniffing like crazy.

Hannah started to get up to fetch her a cup of coffee, but Susan gripped her arm. Hannah looked at Ashley and motioned toward the kitchen. Ash went to grab the coffee.

"Susan, it's all right. You're safe now. Thank God."

Susan didn't respond, just sat there clinging to Hannah's arm. She looked like an extra from *The Walking Dead*. Her hair hung in strings, wet and dirty. Her clothes were torn and her face emaciated. Her eyes were haunted, worse than before.

Ashley returned holding a steaming mug of coffee. "I put cream and sugar in it … I wasn't sure …"

She held the mug out, nodding at Susan to take it. Susan

looked at Ashley, looked at the coffee, then looked back at Hannah.

"Is she dead?" Susan's voice was flat, monotone. A voice reserved for narrators in the history documentaries Hannah had suffered through in junior high.

Dad and Benson were nowhere in sight, giving Susan some space.

Hannah tried to smile. She shook her head, unable to meet Susan's eyes.

Susan made a noise that sounded like an animal whimpering, then began to shake. She bumped Ashley's hand and hot coffee splashed on the three of them. Susan shrank into the corner of the couch, shaking and whining, not even crying.

Hannah looked down at her arms and saw the bleeding scratches where Susan had held her. Dad and Benson appeared, and Benson took charge. He knelt in front of Susan and tried to take her hand, but she pulled away with another strange animal-like sound.

"Listen, Susan. You've been through a lot, but I promise you, you're safe now. I think we need to get you to the hospital."

Susan let out a long keening sound and her shaking got worse. She began to swing her head back and forth, slowly at first, then faster and faster with more and more force.

"Okay, no hospital. What if we brought a doctor here, just to make sure you're not injured?" Benson countered.

Mercifully, Susan stopped the head thing, but she was still trembling uncontrollably, and she was making a low moaning noise.

"Susan, please, we're here to help. We are not going to let anything happen to you. We just want to make sure you're not dehydrated or anything like that. Do you have a doctor that you trust? We could call them and get them to make a special visit."

Hannah watched Susan's lack of response and felt her own anxiety growing. At some point, Ashley had taken Hannah's hand and was squeezing it too hard. It occurred to Hannah that if Ashley wasn't the person she was, she could have ended up like this. By the feel of Ashley's grip, she was thinking the same thing.

Benson was still talking softly, telling Susan over and over that it was going to be okay, she was safe. Susan was non-responsive.

A sudden thought, an idea, hit Hannah. She pulled away from Ashley and bent down to face Susan.

"Wait here. Don't move." As soon as the words were out of her mouth, she realized how dumb they sounded. Hannah bolted for her room and dug through the pockets of the shorts she had worn the day before. With a grunt of satisfaction, she ran back to the living room and practically pushed Benson out of the way.

Without a word, she knelt in front of Susan and opened her hand, letting the locket dangle in front of her face.

Susan's eyes widened and the shaking started to subside. She looked at Hannah, her expression unreadable. Then she reached tentatively for the locket, as if she was afraid it was a mirage.

Susan took the locket and raised it to her face. She clicked it open and gasped, the hint of a smile touching the corners of her mouth.

"Thank you," she whispered, hugging Hannah.

Benson convinced Susan to let a doctor come to the house. It was someone who Benson had helped out of a jam once. The doctor owed him a favor, and Benson trusted him completely.

Right after lunch, the living room became a makeshift exam room. It didn't take long, and the diagnosis was fluids and rest. She also had a burn on her leg that the doctor recommended some ointment for. He wrote a prescription for Ativan in case she continued to experience anxiety. He also advised therapy despite not knowing the real story. Benson told the doctor that Susan had gotten lost hiking in the woods. The doc looked skeptical but didn't question Benson on it.

Once the doctor left, Dad drove to town to get the prescription filled. The rain had slowed to a drizzle and Hannah still had hopes that the concert would go on. She couldn't help looking out the window every few minutes, waiting for the clouds to part and the blue sky to appear.

Benson grabbed a kitchen chair and set it close to the couch, where Susan was stretched out.

"Susan, are you able to tell us anything that happened that night in the clearing? Anything, no matter how small or unimportant it seems might give us a clue to where Mama Bayole is or who her other followers are."

Susan didn't respond. Other than blinking, she didn't move. Benson continued.

"We know from what Hannah told us, the two of you split up. She saw Mama Bayole turn in your direction just as the fire started. We know you set the fire as a diversion to help save Ashley. That was a great idea, and it worked."

Hannah watched their interaction carefully, her gaze bouncing between Susan and Benson. She thought she saw a shadow of a frown cross Susan's face. Hannah wondered if it was because of the tone he was using, like she was a child, or stupid.

Ashley must have picked up on it as well because she spoke next.

"I never got a chance to thank you, Susan. What you did was amazing. I mean, I was out of it for the whole thing, but Hannah told me. You saved my life. You're a hero."

Again, Hannah watched Susan for a reaction and thought her face hardened when Ashley said *hero*. It was Hannah's turn to try.

"Susan, I know this is hard, but when you were part of it, were you ever allowed to see the others outside of the clearing, without the robes and hoods?"

At this, Susan slid her eyes shut. She looked for a moment like she was dozing off, then her eyes squeezed tighter, as if she was trying to block out something. Finally, she shook her head and then turned to face them.

"No. Mama Bayole was the only one whose face I ever saw. The other night in the clearing, when she saw me, she *knew* me." Susan closed her eyes again before continuing. "I never felt like I did at that moment. It was like she was looking through me or examining me somehow, violating me with just a look." Susan shivered under the blanket. "I don't know if I was just too scared to move, or if she did something to me."

Hannah again remembered the day at Mama Bayole's house and how powerless and out of it she'd felt. If Scout hadn't barked and snapped her out of it …

"The flames were already getting hot around me. The fire spread so quickly. I saw some of the followers start to move in my direction but all I could focus on were her eyes …"

Susan's head snapped at the sound of an approaching car. Benson jumped to his feet, hand moving automatically to his gun.

"It's okay. It's Brian." Benson said.

Dad walked in a minute later to find everyone staring at him. "Sorry, I didn't mean to startle anyone. Susan, I have the pills the doctor prescribed. Do you want to take one now, or are you doing okay?"

Susan looked scared again. Hannah surmised she was afraid to be drugged, to not be in control. If she thought that way she'd never sleep again.

"It's okay, Susan," Hannah said. "We're not leaving you alone and you do need to get some rest. We can talk later."

Susan forced a nervous smile. "Thanks, Hannah. Maybe just a half, Brian?"

Dad smiled. "Sure, I'll go cut one in half and get you some juice." He hustled back a moment later with a glass of orange juice and the pill. "Here you go. Let me know if you need anything else."

Susan continued. "Anyway, I was saying, I couldn't pull myself away even though I saw them coming toward me. I mean, I knew I was in danger, but I couldn't move. Then the flames got closer, singeing my leg, and I … kind of woke up, I guess. I turned and ran, and just kept running."

Hannah wanted to ask if Susan thought Mama Bayole had some kind of powers, but she was too afraid. Not to ask, but to hear the answer.

"Is there anything else you can think of that might help? The sound of a voice, the mannerisms or movements of one of the followers?" Benson kept his voice low, soothing, but Hannah detected an underlying sense of urgency. They needed something to go on.

The question jarred Hannah. She recalled thinking that something about one of the robed figures was familiar, but it had already faded like a bad dream. She turned her attention back to Susan and saw the fierce concentration on the woman's face. Then Susan sighed, shrugged, and shook her head.

"A couple of the voices sounded familiar. What I mean is, they sounded like people who were followers when I was involved. I know that doesn't help."

Benson continued questioning Susan, gently probing her, trying to help bring more memories to the surface. After thirty minutes, he'd gotten nothing useful out of her.

Susan's words were starting to sound thick, and Hannah realized the pill was taking effect. Susan's eyes were a little glassy and when she blinked, they stayed closed longer than they should. Hannah shivered, remembering Ash's eyes looking that way when she pulled her off the altar.

"I do remember one thing. I was looking for somewhere to rest and I thought I found the same rock formation that I did before." A sleepy smile touched her face. "I crawled in and tried to get comfortable. I dreamed that I wasn't alone, that there were two other people there with me. When I woke up, I was alone and just sleeping up against a tree trunk. Isn't that strange?"

Her voice trailed off and her eyes remained closed. Hannah glanced at Ashley and knew they were thinking the same thing—they had slept in that rock formation. Hannah knew it because that's where she had found the locket.

They moved into the kitchen to let Susan sleep. Hannah was shaken about the weird coincidence of Susan's dream. She glanced outside and her spirits buoyed at the swath of blue cutting through the gray sky.

"Benson, we need a plan. Our little commune here is not really sustainable, you know?"

Benson smiled at Dad. "I know. I'm just not quite sure what to do. Until I can establish if anyone on the force besides Dietrich is part of this, I can't involve them. I mean, it was the captain that pulled me off the case. Did he do that because he's one of the followers? What if there's someone at the hospital involved?"

Hannah studied them both. Benson was starting to look a little frazzled. Dad was watching him, his expression one of concern, and something else. She filed the thought away for later consideration. She had a growing list of thoughts about Dad filed away. A whole filing cabinet's worth.

"Well, we can't hole up here for the rest of our lives. Quite frankly, I'm not planning on looking over my shoulder, seeing followers that aren't there, everywhere I go."

Benson narrowed his eyes, and his lips formed a tight line. Hannah knew he was frustrated. Before she spoke up to try to diffuse things, Ashley stood. She'd been quiet, listening intently but not offering her usual wisecracks.

"What is it about adults that make you like this?" Her eyes moved back and forth between Dad and Benson, her expression fierce. "Think about what Susan, Hannah and I have been through for a minute." She spun to face Dad. "You're worried about, what, a couple of extra houseguests when your own daughter was put in harm's way?" She wheeled on Benson. "You! You don't know what to do. You're supposed to be a cop, but it's been Hannah and I that have done all the work in figuring this thing out. I think you both need to get your sh—act together."

She stalked over to the back door and stood there looking out. Hannah wanted to go to her but was curious to see how the men would react to Ashley's outburst. They both remained silent for a long moment. Benson still looked mad; Dad looked sheepish. It was a word Hannah had read in books all the time but never really experienced. She almost laughed.

"Well, Rick, I guess we've been put in our place."

Dad walked over to Hannah and gave her a hug.

"I'm sorry. Ashley is right—you've all been through the wringer while Brian and I weren't much more than spectators. We'll get through this and our house can be home base for as long as we need it. One thing, though, we're not getting robes and hoods."

"Too soon, Mr. G," Ashley said quietly. She faced Benson. As if feeling her gaze on him, he turned to her, then put his hands up defensively. The anger had seeped from his face and he just looked tired.

"Wow. Ashley, Hannah ..." He glanced toward Susan to include her, but she was sound asleep on the living room couch. "I'm sorry. You have been through a lot and you're still willing to fight. I haven't been doing my job." He laughed humorlessly. "If I even *have* a job."

Benson stood and paced between the kitchen and living room, pausing to look at Susan. Hannah saw his lips moving and he occasionally rubbed his buzz cut. Dad got up and fixed a cup of coffee, apparently not as intrigued with Benson's animated style of thinking. Or his *getting his act together*, as Ashley had put it.

The phone rang, startling everyone. Benson reached for his gun and Dad splashed his coffee all over the place. Hannah laughed and ran to grab it.

"Hello?" Her voice was tentative; the thought that it could

be *one of them* crossed her mind just as she put the phone to my ear.

It was Marcus, calling to make sure they were still on for the concert. He told Hannah he'd been watching the Weather Channel all day to see if it was going to clear, and it was. He started to drop some meteorological lingo, but Hannah cut him off with a laugh, asking him to hold on.

"Dad, it's Marcus." Out of the corner of her eye, she saw Ashley making kissy faces at her. "He wants to know if I can still go to the concert tonight."

Dad looked torn. There was really no way he could say no after his "I'm not looking over my shoulder speech." He ran his hand through his hair and sighed.

"I'll drive you there and pick you up. You all stay together the entire time. Got it?"

Hannah blew him a kiss and mouthed "thank you" before getting back to Marcus. She told him she would meet him at the basketball courts at seven. They chatted for a few minutes before saying goodbye. Hannah hung up and turned to find everyone staring at her.

Dad and Benson wore twin masks of concern while Ashley looked kind of smug.

"What?" Hannah asked innocently.

"Your dad is right, Hannah," Benson finally said. "I don't want to scare you, but you will be vulnerable there. Sure, you'll be out in the open in a crowded place, but we don't know who in that crowd is a follower. You *have* to stay together. There's no way they can make a move if you do that."

"So, your plan to sneak off with Marcus is off the table."

Hannah gave Ashley her best withering look while Benson

cracked up. Dad had that "my baby is growing up way too fast" look again. It made Hannah sad a little, like she was trading her time with him to spend it with Marcus.

"Don't worry, Dad, I'm not really interested in another night in the woods trying to save Ashley's sorry butt. Mama Bayole's little house of horrors is just a pile of ashes, so I think we're good."

She did her best to sound nonchalant, but she was afraid. Even in a crowd, there were ways Mama Bayole's followers could get to them. Hannah pushed the thought away, musing about when *followers* had become the word to describe Mama Bayole's people. They had all, at some point, just fallen into the habit of using it.

"Okay, girlfriend, let's go find you a sexy outfit for the concert." Ashley grabbed her arm and pulled her toward the bedroom, leaving Dad and Benson shaking their heads.

CHAPTER TWENTY-THREE

The blue sky had been a cruel tease. The clouds moved back in with a vengeance as the afternoon wore on. Getting out of the house for the concert was an absolute disaster. Dad nixed the first outfit Hannah put on, complaining that she "was going to Champlain Park, not Bourbon Street." Hannah wasn't even sure what that meant, other than she had to put on more clothes. She ended up in white shorts that highlighted what little tan she had but made her legs look long and coltish. Her top was a simple blue off-the-shoulder blouse that almost made her look like she had a figure. It definitely brought out her eyes—she and Ashley agreed on that.

Benson and Dad debated on what to do with Susan, who was still sleeping. Benson thought *he* should take the girls to Champlain and keep an eye on them because it was the more likely place for Mama Bayole to try something. Dad, of course, wouldn't let that happen.

Then the phone rang, and Ashley's parents were freaking out about all the urgent messages they'd received. A storm on the island had taken the phones down for almost twenty-four hours. Dad talked for a long time—between loud, panicked interruptions from the Wallaces—bringing them up to date on everything that had transpired since they left. Finally, Ashley got on the phone and told them she was fine. The Wallaces insisted on cutting their vacation short in spite of Ashley's insistence not to. More fallout from her bad decisions, Hannah thought glumly.

Susan woke up just as they were ready to go. Benson suggested they *all* attend the concert. Strength in numbers, he said, and Hannah agreed, as long as they didn't hover. She would have agreed to just about anything, the excitement for the date had taken hold of her.

Hannah and Ashley met up with Marcus and Ken as planned, after promising Dad for the hundredth time they wouldn't sneak off anywhere or split up.

The four of them sat together on a big blanket listening to a local band massacre a Beatles song. Hannah felt the watchful eyes of Dad and Benson at all times, and found herself scanning the crowd for them. Ashley nudged her and made a face, and Hannah tried to focus on the bad music.

The rain held off, but the evening remained cloudy and humid. The band continued its assault on songs Hannah loved, and as hard as she tried not to, her attention kept drifting to the other concertgoers. It was getting difficult to make out people's features in the dimming light. Dusk came early with the sun nonexistent, buried behind thick clouds. The park lights were already on, a light fog or mist drifting by them. The band mercifully took a break and the crowd stirred, stretching and beginning to mill about.

Hannah stood, cramped from sitting, and began alternately bending her knees. She turned her head from side to side to relieve a crick in her neck and glimpsed a figure in the distance staring at them. She froze and squinted, trying to get a better look. The person was tall and wore a windbreaker and jeans, with a baseball cap pulled low. Hannah couldn't distinguish if it was a male or female.

The person must have noticed Hannah staring back, because they lowered their head and ducked into the crowd, disappearing. Hannah's breath came in short gasps and beads of sweat formed on her face. Ashley and the boys were engaged in a conversation about how bad the band was and not paying her any attention. She scanned the crowd again, now wishing Dad and Benson *were* hovering, but couldn't spot them.

The darkness was thicker, nearly complete. Lights lined the perimeter of the park, closer to the basketball courts and playgrounds. They didn't illuminate the middle of the field—in fact, they caused so much glare they did more harm than good. The way the light filtered through the mist gave everything a dreamy, surreal quality. Soon Hannah wouldn't be able to see the person standing a few feet away from her. The thought terrified her.

"Hannah, are you okay?" Ashley had noticed something was off.

"Uh, yeah, I think so. Do you think we have time to go to the restroom?"

"I'll walk you over. Ashley and Ken can save our spot," Marcus volunteered. "It's not like we'll miss anything if they do come back while we're gone," he added with a grin.

Ashley grabbed her arm as she turned to go.

"We're supposed to stay together," she hissed. "Your dad will flip if you go off alone."

Hannah blinked at her friend. Ash was usually the one to ignore rules, even ignore common sense at times.

"It's okay, Ash, Marcus will be with me. Besides, if we all go, we'll lose our spot."

Ashley looked over to the restrooms, then back at Hannah, and grudgingly agreed.

Hannah half-smiled and nodded to Marcus, and they weaved their way through the crowd toward the brick building that housed the snack bar and the restrooms. Off in the distance, thunder rumbled like a faraway freight train. Part of Hannah hoped for the rain to come and send everyone home.

Am I really any safer there?

Anger bubbled up, pushing back her fear. She should be enjoying this night, enjoying her first date, not looking for witches or cult members or whatever they were. *Followers.*

A hand touched Hannah's shoulder and she jumped. "Hey, are you okay?"

She looked over at Marcus and he pulled his hand away. She wondered what her expression was to give him that reaction.

"I'm sorry. I'm still jumpy from … everything that's been going on."

For the first time, she realized she might be putting Marcus in danger, too, and the thought both sickened and depressed her.

"Do you want to talk about it?"

His voice was low, almost shy, but the tenderness in it touched Hannah. They were almost through the crowd to the concession stand that housed the restrooms. Marcus was a nice kid, and the truth was she *did* want to tell him what was going on. Partially so he wouldn't think she was a total nut job based on her behavior, but also because she thought she'd feel better talking with someone that wasn't right in the middle of the whole mess.

Both of those reasons seemed selfish, and she might be putting him at more risk by telling him. *Why does this have to be so hard?*

"I'd like that, Marcus. Just not tonight, okay?" Hannah hoped it didn't sound harsh but by his expression she guessed it did. She reached out and put a hand on his arm. "I mean it. I just want tonight to be special."

His face lit up and Hannah immediately felt better. Then he started leaning toward her.

Oh, my. He's going to kiss me. She'd imagined her first kiss a million times in a million different places. At that moment, under the misty sky at Champlain Park with Marcus, made all those fantasies seem bland. This was going to be perfect. She couldn't move, had no idea what she was supposed to do.

Then the lights went out.

People screamed but mostly out of surprise or just to be funny. To them, the lights going out was nothing more than a power glitch. A reason to be silly and playful. To Hannah, it meant Mama Bayole. Her hand was still on Marcus's arm and she clung to it like a lifeline. She reached for her cell phone, but she'd left it back at the blanket.

"Marcus, we have to go back. We have to find my dad." Her throat was closing, an ugly panic rising inside her.

"Um, okay. I'm sure the lights will be back in a minute."

Hannah's eyes began to adjust, but it wasn't much of a help. That part of the park was surrounded by trees on all sides and the night was cloudy. The darkness was eternal. Suffocating.

"You don't understand." Hannah choked, barely resisting the urge to bolt.

A commotion in the crown nearby caught her attention. People were yelling at someone about pushing or something. Every instinct in Hannah screamed at her to run but she didn't know where. The angry shouts were getting closer. She knew whoever was being shouted at was coming for her.

She yanked on Marcus's arm, pulling him toward where she thought they'd find Ashley and Ken. Staying mixed up in the crowd was a better way to hide than running out in the open.

Marcus grabbed her hand, and they ran together. *You wanted to know what it would feel like, right?* Not the romantic handholding she'd fantasized about.

She mumbled "excuse me" and "sorry" as she bumped into people. The two kept moving forward through the sea of bodies, though it was too dark to tell if they were going the right way. Hannah had no idea how she'd even spot Ken and Ash and the blanket, unless they tripped over them, but moving felt safer than standing still.

"Hey, watch it."

"What the …?"

The angry shouts were not directed at them but someone— *one of them*—was getting closer. Someone was chasing her. *Maybe it's Dad or Officer Benson.* Hannah dismissed the thought; they would be calling out her name.

Hannah saw a light waving up ahead and she realized it was someone holding their phone over their head as a signal.

Ashley. She knew it was Ashley. *Mind meld.*

"Marcus, I see Ashley, this way." She pulled him in the direction of the light.

When his hand slipped from hers, Hannah thought somebody in the crowd had bumped him and he'd lost his grip. She didn't stop but did turned to make sure he was keeping up. He was gone. Lost in the churning bodies.

Hannah had to get to Ashley to call Dad, then they would all find Marcus. She began pushing through the crowd in the direction she'd seen Ashley waving the light. She bumped into someone and mumbled an apology as she tried to sidestep him. He moved to the same side she did. In another situation, Hannah might have laughed. It was one of those awkward *let's dance* moments that sometimes happened. She tried again to slide by but this time a strong hand grabbed her arm. The rat-tat-tat explosion of firecrackers from the far side of the field got everyone screaming in mock horror and turning in that direction.

Hannah tried to pull away from her assailant, but the grip was unrelenting. About to let out a scream, she looked up and saw nothing but a flash of white cloth. She gasped and inhaled the sickly-sweet odor of whatever the cloth had been soaked in. Her hands and feet went numb. The sound of the crowd began to dim, then darkness.

Ashley and I are huddled under a blanket, giggling. It's a reaction to the movie we're watching. It's not a silly giggle, it's a defense mechanism. We're scared out of our wits and trying to cover it up. On the television, a diminutive old woman with a weird voice is saying to go to the light. There is peace and serenity in the light.

"She's coming around."

"Good, we don't have much time."

"Is everything ready?"

"Of course."

Pain exploded in Hannah's skull when she opened her eyes. *There is no peace and serenity in this light.* She was chilly and reached for the blanket, Ashley must be hogging again. But there was no blanket. No Ashley.

As her head cleared, she saw the shadowed faces staring at her. She blinked. Then she recognized them, and her heart rate doubled, tripled, each beat sending fresh throbbing pain to her head. Her muscles went limp. Before her stood Mama Bayole, flanked by Officer Dietrich and the librarian.

"There you are, child. Mama's been waiting."

The old woman's face was lust and hunger and menace. Something else, too. She looked older, frailer than before, if that was possible.

The clearing.

It couldn't be—there was no smell of fire and no charred branches. Hannah couldn't see beyond the small circle of light cast by Mama Bayole's lantern.

"It ain't the sacred place but it'll have to do."

How did she know what I was thinking? Whatever had been used to drug Hannah was wearing off and left just the headache in its wake. She was in a sitting position, hands and feet bound. She struggled to move but discovered she was also lashed to the tree behind her.

The librarian bent and unzipped a backpack at her feet. She pulled out the chalice and knife that Hannah had seen that night in the clearing. Up close, the knife looked huge. Deadly. Despite the terror that threatened to paralyze her, a red-hot fury surged in her gut. She'd been scared enough. She was done.

"Aren't you going to dress up in your Halloween costumes

and prance around?" Hannah spat.

Mama Bayole was unfazed. "No time for that, child, but don't you worry. Your sacrifice'll be no less 'preciated."

The librarian snorted a laugh. Hannah glared at her but being tied up and helpless ruined her attempt at being intimidating. The woman just smirked and shook her head. It was the smug look of someone that knows they've already won.

Mama Bayole's matter-of-fact tone and the librarian's knowing sneer popped the balloon of Hannah's anger. Hot tears spilled from her eyes and her body began to tremble almost convulsively.

The old witch was chanting softly in the same language Hannah remembered from the night in the clearing. Dietrich and the librarian stood on either side of her, heads bowed. The librarian held the chalice, Dietrich held the knife. Mama Bayole's words were making Hannah's head hurt worse. They took on an insectile buzz. *Like the flies.* She struggled against the ropes, but it was futile—she only succeeded in scraping up her back on the rough bark of the tree, sending warm rivulets of blood snaking down her back.

Thunder rumbled, closer than before. Hannah wondered how long she'd been unconscious. Maybe someone had seen what happened and had gone to get help. Fat raindrops splattered around her, as if to drown out any remaining spark of hope she might have. Lightning flashed, followed by thunder, closer still. The wind picked up, whooshing through the lush trees.

There was another flash in the distance, but it wasn't lightning. Hannah squinted. There *was* light visible through the trees.

Flashlights. It's a search party.

She was about to start screaming her head off when she realized it wasn't flashlights after all. She was seeing the lights at Champlain Park flickering to life, the power restored. A gnawing pain swelled in her gut, knowing help was so close. She struggled harder against the ropes, frantic to escape. Blood dripped down her back mixing with the summer rain.

More lightning followed immediately by the crack of thunder. The downpour intensified. Mama Bayole's voice rose above the sound of the rain hitting the leaves around them. She finished her chant and Dietrich handed her the knife. She stepped closer. Hannah squirmed futilely against the ropes, a helpless moan escaping her lips.

Another brilliant blaze of lightning, the brightest yet, and in its fading glow Hannah saw a hulking figure looming behind Mama Bayole.

"Ain't gonna be no more killing, witch!"

Jacob stepped into the light holding a pistol. From where Hannah sat, the gun looked ridiculously huge, like something a gunslinger would wield in an old western movie.

Dietrich reached for his holstered weapon, but Jacob stopped him with just the shake of his head.

"You want to die like that, underling?" Jacob boomed.

Dietrich held his hands out by his sides.

"Well, well, look who's come home to roost?" Mama Bayole eyed Jacob with amusement. "Couldn't resist my call, could ya?"

Jacob's expression remained firm but in the flickering glow of the lantern Hannah saw a hint of something. Doubt? Fear?

"That's right, son. Mama don't forget," she cooed.

Jacob squeezed his eyes shut for a second and shook his head. "You can't have her, witch. Just like you never had me."

Mama Bayole's laugh was a lunatic shriek. "I've *always* had you."

Rain poured down around them as Hannah watched the standoff, helpless. The thunder and lightning were almost simultaneous. A deafening crack followed the last flash and Hannah knew a tree had been struck close by. Jacob motioned toward Dietrich.

"I'm gonna need you to unbuckle that holster, real slow. Let it drop to the ground, then kick it over to me. I see anything that looks like you want to make a play, you're gonna feel the wrath of a Ruger Blackhawk. Understand, minion?"

Dietrich stared at Jacob, but he complied.

"Now the knife, witch. Same thing." Jacob's voice was even, almost calm. His gaze steely.

Hannah thought about their first meeting. Aces and eights. Wild Bill Hickok.

Mama Bayole stared at him, eyes bright with fury. "You think I need this knife?" She let out a cackle. "Here, take it."

She moved quicker than Hannah would have believed possible, throwing the knife at Jacob with a snap of her wrist. Hannah watched in horror as the blade found its mark, settling deep in Jacob's shoulder. Jacob screamed in pain and the gun dipped as he struggled to stay on his feet.

Dietrich lunged, but despite his injury, Jacob was ready. He leveled the gun and fired. The explosion muffled the thunder. Dietrich stumbled backward, his head crashing into the librarian's with an audible crack, and they both fell to the ground. Jacob then turned the gun on Mama Bayole and chambered another round.

"Go ahead, witch. Make your move." Despite the knife

sticking out of his shoulder, his voice remained steady. Formidable.

Mama Bayole was laughing, her head thrown back in the rain. The thunder and lightning were almost constant, and all Hannah heard was that unholy laughter. "I don't need to make no move. I'll just wait for you to bleed out."

Jacob switched the gun to his bad hand, the one attached to the knifed shoulder, then reached up with his good hand and pulled the knife out. He winced and gritted his teeth, but the gun never wavered.

Hannah watched with detached amazement. If she'd seen it happen in a movie, she would have scoffed, but here she was, watching it in real life.

"You're right, witch, I'm gonna need some help," Jacob said, almost amiably. He moved slowly, deliberately, over to where Hannah was tied. He cut through the rope that held her to the tree, then through the ones binding her wrists. He handed her the knife and motioned for her to cut the bonds that held her feet.

When he did, Hannah saw just how weak he was. His eyelids fluttered, like he was about to take a nap, and his hand was not nearly as steady as she'd thought from a distance.

"That's right, you sho' gonna need some help," Bayole said in a singsong voice.

The old woman inched closer as Hannah cut the ropes on her ankles.

"Jacob, watch out!" she screamed.

Hannah leaped to her feet as Mama Bayole lunged at Jacob. Thunder and lightning exploded around them. Jacob's knees buckled and the gun fell from his hand. Mama Bayole staggered the other way, dropping to her knees.

Hannah ran to Jacob, slipping on the muddy ground and practically falling to his side. His eyes were open, glassy, and she thought for a second he was dead. Then he turned to her.

"Did I get her?" he asked, blinking, trying to see around Hannah.

Hannah turned to make sure Mama Bayole wasn't coming, then helped Jacob to his feet, picking up the gun as well. Jacob's shirt was soaked in blood, and she realized he might be dying. She wondered how he could even stand.

A nearby tree had been cleaved in half by the last lightning strike and was burning despite the torrential rain. Smoke billowed around her as she approached the tangle of bodies on the ground.

The librarian was still motionless beneath the dead weight of Dietrich's body, but Mama Bayole was nowhere to be seen. Another bolt of lightning lit the woods and Hannah spotted a figure stumble from behind a tree and head for the woods.

"Hannah, there she goes!" Jacob yelled.

Mama Bayole stopped when she heard Jacob's voice. She turned toward them. The smoke was getting thicker, and Hannah could have sworn that the old woman changed. For a split-second, she saw the beautiful young version of Mama Bayole that Jacob spoke of. The old woman grinned and turned to flee into the woods.

Without thinking, Hannah raised Jacob's gun in both hands, suddenly aware of its weight. She cocked the gun's hammer. Everything around her disappeared. It was just her, the oversized gun, and Mama Bayole. She took aim. Mama Bayole turned to escape into the cover of the trees, but to Hannah, she was moving in slow motion. Despite the weight of the gun, Hannah's hand did not waver. She tracked the old witch, one eye shut tight, squeezing the trigger slowly as Mama Bayole disappeared into the smoke-filled trees.

The recoil nearly knocked her off her feet. Through ringing ears, she heard a shriek in the distance. Then silence.

"You got her, Hannah, you got that old witch," Jacob said reverently.

Hannah huddled under a blanket between Dad and Ashley in the waiting room of County General Hospital. Susan sat across from her, watching Hannah with a curious expression. The bizarre memory of waking up in the woods and thinking she was watching some old horror movie with Ashley flashed into Hannah's head. Jacob was in surgery to repair the deep knife wound, and the doctors were concerned that his age and the amount of blood loss were against him.

After she'd taken the shot at Mama Bayole, she'd helped Jacob walk toward Champlain Park while keeping the gun on the librarian. By that time, there had been a full-fledged search going on and they were quickly whisked up by paramedics.

Marcus hadn't seen what happened to her—he'd just known something was wrong. He'd found Ashley and called Dad. Benson had called in the cavalry immediately, but they had no idea if Hannah had been taken in a car or not. Units had been sent to the clearing while others searched the park and got the lights back on.

The librarian was in custody. Dietrich was dead. They were still searching the woods for Mama Bayole.

The *whoosh* of automatic doors caused Hannah to look up. A

266

doctor walked toward them. He moved slowly, each step an effort. His face was pale, and he had bags under his eyes. They all stood, and Hannah braced for the worst. Then the doctor's grave expression broke into a tired smile.

"That guy might outlive us all," he said in quiet amazement.

Tears spilled from Hannah's eyes and she fell into a group hug with Ashley, Susan, and Dad. Even though she'd only known him for a few days, Jacob meant a lot to her. Hard times forged strong bonds.

"He'll be out for a while, but he made me promise I wouldn't let him wake up alone. It's completely against the rules, but what the hell?" The doctor smiled again. "You can wait for him to come around once we get him settled in recovery."

A short time later, the four of them sat around Jacob's bed, waiting. He looked withered to Hannah, nothing like the hero that had showed up in the woods in a flash of lightning. Susan and Dad were talking in hushed whispers, while Hannah told Ashley what had happened.

"That's all very exciting, Hannah, but you should have seen Marcus's face when he couldn't find you. That boy *really* likes you."

Hannah thought about the moment just before the lights went out. *He was going to kiss me.*

"Hey, what's that face?" Ashley asked, one eyebrow cocked.

She looked at Ashley and felt her cheeks flush. "Oh, nothing."

A raspy voice interrupted them. "I must still be alive. I don't see no angels."

"Jacob!" they shouted in unison.

Hannah jumped up and went to his side, tears springing to

her eyes. She'd cried more in the past few weeks than she had in her entire life, but these were tears of joy.

Dad stood on the other side of the bed. "Jacob, take it easy. The doc said you wanted us here, but I think you need your rest."

A smile spread across Jacob's face, transforming him from haggard into something magical. "I'll get plenty of sleep when I'm dead." His Sam Elliott impersonation was passable.

"Roadhouse!" Dad, Ashley and Hannah exclaimed, then they all laughed.

Susan was confused, but also something else. A slight grin snuck across her face. She looked different, the haunted look in her eyes fading. Not gone but going.

The doctor came in and checked Jacob's vitals and bandages. Then, with an attempt at a stern look, he turned to the visitors. "Just a few more minutes, okay?" He winked and slipped out of the room.

Jacob locked on Hannah's eyes and she knew what was coming. He didn't have to say it out loud, but he did anyway.

"Is she dead? Is that old witch gone?" His voice was flat, lacking any curiosity.

Hannah looked around the room, not wanting to be the one to answer.

Dad spoke, "They haven't found her body yet, but they're still out there with the bloodhounds."

He didn't sound any more confident than Hannah felt.

The doctor came back a few minutes later with Officer Benson. He was still in his street clothes, but Hannah noticed he wore his gun belt and a badge.

"The units have all been called back. They found Bayole's

clothes but no body, no trace of her. Dogs can't hold the scent because of all the rain."

Jacob looked thoughtful, as if considering Benson's comment. Hannah expected him to be upset but his face remained bright. "She's gone, all right. They might not find her body, but she's gone." He raised a hand and pointed to his head. "I can't feel her anymore."

Hannah took Jacob's hand and squeezed it. Ashley put an arm across her shoulder.

"Okay, folks, party's over."

A nurse had stepped through the door and she did not look pleased to find a crowd in the recovery room.

Benson took her cue. "Brian, girls, go on home. Get some rest. I'll stay with Jacob and make sure he doesn't try to bust out or ask any of the nurses to marry him."

The nurse shook her head but couldn't hide her grin. They all said their goodbyes and started leaving. Like he'd done the last time he was in the hospital, Jacob called Hannah back. Dad nodded his approval, and she went to Jacob's side and took his hand.

"You okay, Hannah?" he asked, his concern evident.

"I guess I am," she whispered after a pause.

He looked at her for a long time before saying anything. His gaze was powerful. She couldn't look away.

"She's really gone, Hannah. She's been in my head, haunting me, almost my whole life. Think of a mosquito buzzing in your ear when you're trying to sleep, that's what it was like. Sometimes she was so loud, so strong, I thought I'd go crazy. Now there's nothing but quiet. For the first time in as long as I can remember, it's quiet."

Hannah held his gaze, looking for a sign that he was just trying to placate her, but all she saw in his eyes was truth. "Cut the head off the snake, right?"

Jacob smiled and gave a tired nod.

Hannah leaned over, kissed his forehead and gave his hand a final squeeze, then went to join the others.

EPILOGUE

The weeks following the events at Champlain Park were a frenzy of interviews and statements at the police station and visits to the hospital to see Jacob. Hannah and Ashley were minor celebrities, a role Ash took with enthusiasm while Hannah felt constant embarrassment.

The police never found a trace of Mama Bayole, dead or alive, beyond the pile of clothes. Hannah imagined her hit by the bullet, aging, and turning to dust, just like in the movies. The librarian had spilled her guts once she was in custody, but she only named a handful of the followers. The police had apprehended the ones she identified, and they were being charged with conspiracy to commit murder and a bunch of other lesser crimes.

Jacob was on his way to a full recovery. He came over for dinner once a week and his presence was helping Dad get back to his old self. Benson was spending a lot time at the house as well, and she was happy for her father. She thought Benson was probably going to be around a lot.

Hannah was happy for Dad. She knew he'd loved Mom in his own way, but this was different. How must Mom have felt when she'd realized Dad couldn't love her the same way she loved him? It was why she'd left, and while Hannah was glad she had a reason that didn't involve drugs or another guy, she still had mixed feelings. Hannah missed her but was angry at the same time. In time, she would have a long tearful talk with Dad, she was sure.

Labor Day weekend arrived, signaling the unofficial end of summer. That Sunday, they had a big cookout to say goodbye to summer. Benson, Jacob, Susan, Ashley, and Ashley's parents all came. Dad bought enough food to keep every belly in Hopeland full for a week.

The afternoon was a spectacular New England late-summer day—blue skies, sunshine, and no humidity. Everyone milled around, talking and laughing, but Hannah hung back, watching the festivities from the edge of the woods with Scout. He whined, looking at her like he knew something was wrong.

Dad was grilling on the deck, talking with Ashley and her parents. They'd come back from vacation smack in the middle of the circus following the adventure at Champlain Park. Despite trying to get home early, they got stranded at the airport. St. Barth's airport was home to one of the world's deadliest runways and flights were not allowed during bad weather. Hurricane season had arrived, and they were stuck in a series of storms that kept the planes grounded.

The good news was they were still together. Ashley said

they'd been getting along better since the trip. Time would tell, Hannah figured.

Ashley's folks wandered off the deck to talk with Susan, Benson, and Jacob, who were seated on lawn chairs in the yard. Ashley hung back with Dad, and Hannah watched them talk for a few minutes before Ash bolted into the house. Even from where Hannah was, she saw the excitement on her best friend's face.

She imagined Ashley and Dad had been teasing each other about something and Ash thought she got the better of him. When she came out of the house, she said something to Dad, then headed in Hannah's direction.

"What's up, party-pooper?" she said, plopping down on the grass next to Hannah.

Hannah shrugged. The truth was she didn't *know* what was up. She always got a little sad at the end of summer. Not because she had to go back to school, just because it was the *end*. There would be other summers, but this one was gone and would never be back. She didn't bother trying to explain it to Ash.

"Not in a partying mood, I guess." Hannah shrugged again, signaling she didn't really want to talk about it.

Ashley was grinning like a lunatic. That grin always made Hannah nervous.

"What, exactly, are you up to?" she asked suspiciously.

She feigned shock and batted her eyelashes at Hannah.

"I don't know what you're suggesting, Hannah Green, but I feel insulted."

Hannah laughed. "You've never felt insulted a day in your life, Ashley Wallace."

Dad called from the deck that all former barnyard creatures were ready to be eaten. Hannah would have to wait and see what

Ashley had up her sleeve.

They all sat at the picnic table while a ridiculous amount of food was set out on a folding table, buffet style. Hannah was just about to sit down when she heard the doorbell.

"Hannah, would you mind getting that?" Dad called.

He was already folded into his seat and stuffing his face with chicken wings. Hannah gave an exaggerated sigh and headed through the house. *Who would be ringing the doorbell on the Sunday of Labor Day?*

A sudden unease came over her. *What if they hadn't rounded up all the followers?* Her mind had been working that way since the night at the concert. She figured it was some form of post-traumatic stress. Or maybe she was just a wimp.

She pulled the door open and felt a hot flush rise in her cheeks.

"Hi, Hannah. Ashley called and said I should come over."

Marcus's face was beet red too, but that was because he'd ridden his bike over. Based on how short a time it had been since Ashley had gone into the house, presumably to make the call, he'd ridden pretty damn fast. Behind him, Ken skidded to a stop and hopped off his bike, gasping for breath.

Hannah grinned. "I hope you guys are hungry."

Ashley was staring at her with that grin again. "So …?"

"So, what?" Hannah asked innocently.

Ashley tossed a pillow at her. It was just the two of them in Hannah's room. Everyone but Benson had left around eleven. He was out on the deck with Dad.

"So, did he kiss you?" she asked, eyes wide.

Hannah tried not to react, but her face grew warm. "A lady doesn't kiss and tell, Ashley."

Ashley's jaw dropped. "He did!" she squealed.

Hannah imagined her entire head was a deep shade of scarlet, but she couldn't help the smile that spread across her face. Ashley leaned over and gave her a hug. She pulled away, her hands on Hannah's shoulders and an expression of extreme seriousness on her face, then she burst out laughing and gave her another hug.

She was back in the clearing, behind the altar, waiting for her chance to free Ashley. The hooded figures were milling around. Mama Bayole hadn't started chanting yet. Hannah stared at one in particular, something drawing her gaze. The person looked her way and Hannah slouched lower, desperate to stay out of sight.

The figure walked slowly toward her. Hannah was frozen in place, helpless to do anything but watch. The person was directly in front of her, holding an old-fashioned tape recorder. A finger reached out from the sleeve of the robe and hit play.

The fake blogger's voice from the library that she'd heard on Ashley's phone rang out: "Hannah will be as gone as her mother."

Then the person was reaching for the hood, pulling it off. Hannah screamed ...

She sat up in bed, gasping for air, unsure if she had screamed in real life or just in the dream. Sweat dripped from her hair and her T-shirt clung to her. It was as if a terrible fever had broken. Ashley put a hand on her back.

"Hannah, you're okay. It was just a nightmare." Ashley's voice sounded groggy but steeped with concern. "Do you ... do you remember what you dreamed of?"

Confused and scared, Hannah nodded, still catching her breath.

"You screamed, 'Mom,'" Ashley said quietly.

Tears sprung from her eyes and convulsive sobs ripped through her. Ashley held her until she was able to get control of herself. She'd been having nightmares off and on since the night of the concert, but nothing like this.

Should I tell her?

It's Ashley. Of course, she would tell her.

"That night … the night in the clearing … one of the people …"

Hannah's entire body, her entire *being* trembled and Ashley held her tighter, telling her it was all right. Hannah took a deep breath and let it out slowly.

"This one person came over to take the sheet off you when you were tied to the altar. There was something familiar, I remember thinking it that night, but when she pulled the sheet off all I could think of was saving you."

Ashley stared at her with wide eyes. It was a rare moment that she didn't have something to say.

"I think it was Mom. I need to find her."

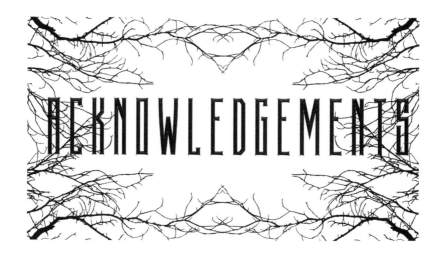

ACKNOWLEDGEMENTS

I think I've started out my acknowledgements page for every book I've written the same way, by saying that writing a book is hard. Until that changes, which I doubt it ever will, I'll continue to preach it. The Clearing was certainly no exception. Like every other book, you wouldn't be holding it in your hands without the love and help of a lot of people.

First, many thanks to my agent, Italia Gandolfo. Her patience in answering my countless questions and still managing to get this book into the wild deserves a major award. The same goes for LK Griffie and the whole Vesuvian Media team. Thanks for putting up with me.

I owe Monica S. Kuebler a debt of gratitude for editing an early draft of the manuscript and helping me get over some big hurdles.

Special thanks to Monique Snyman for giving me the courage to make a dramatic change in one of the characters that made this book a thousand times better and more meaningful.

The support system goes much deeper than the editors, agents, and publishers. I appreciate the enthusiastic encouragement from Kevin Lewis, who also read an early draft of The Clearing. There are so many people that have had my back and kept me going over the years ... Chris Golden, Bracken MacLeod, Ben Eads, Tony Tremblay, Dave Jeffery, Jonathan Maberry, Josh Malerman ... I love you all. Same goes for everyone in the HWA and the NEHW, I am blessed to be part of the horror community.

Finally, as always, it comes down to family. The book is dedicated to my daughters, Shannon and Alyssa, who continue to believe in me. My brother, Mike, who has been my beta reader from the beginning. My wife, Sheila, who has been my number one fan – but not in the creepy, cut my feet off way – I love you.

So many more people that I haven't named, but you all know who you are and how much you mean to me.

ABOUT THE AUTHOR

Tom Deady's first novel, *Haven*, was published by Cemetery Dance in 2016 and won the Bram Stoker Award® for Superior Achievement in a First Novel. He has since published a novel entitled, *Eternal Darkness*, as well as several short stories and novellas, his most recent being *Coleridge*.

His novel, *The Clearing*, is book one in a horror trilogy and inspired by true events. (Vesuvian Books, 2021) Tom holds a master's degree in English and Creative Writing from Southern New Hampshire University, is an Active member of the Horror Writers Association, and a member of the New England Horror Writers. He resides in Massachusetts where he is working on his next novel.

www.TomDeady.com